D0291368

THE DARK CITY:
AN ELIOT NESS MYSTERY

MAX ALLAN COLLINS

WOLFPACK
PUBLISHING
EST 2010

WOLFPACK PUBLISHING
— EST 2013 —

The Dark City: An Eliot Ness Mystery

Paperback Edition
Copyright © 2020 (as revised) Max Allan Collins

Wolfpack Publishing
6032 Wheat Penny Avenue
Las Vegas, NV 89122

wolfpackpublishing.com

All rights reserved. No part of this book may be reproduced by any means without the prior written consent of the publisher, other than brief quotes for reviews.

This book is a work of fiction. Any references to historical events, real people or real places are used fictitiously. Other names, characters, places and events are products of the author's imagination, and any resemblance to actual events, places or persons, living or dead, is entirely coincidental.

Paperback ISBN 978-1-64734-106-0
Library of Congress Control Number: 2020944472

THE DARK CITY:
AN ELIOT NESS MYSTERY

For my friend
Dominick Abel
The Eliot Ness of literary agents

O N E

DECEMBER 11-17, 1935

CHAPTER 1

A smoky, cloudy haze hung over the city, turning the afternoon into night. Crane your neck back as far as you liked, you still couldn't make out the top of Terminal Tower, the Van Sweringen brothers' fifty-two-story tribute to the city and themselves. The Vans were broke now, or claimed to be, and their tower complex—with its department store, office building, bank, hotel, and restaurants—loomed over the city like a joke, an ironic middle-finger reminder of more prosperous times, when the Depression wasn't hanging over the city like the smoke and clouds that for almost a month now had made every day a night.

Traditionalists continued to call it "the Forest City," and the Chamber of Commerce flacks were insisting it was "the Vacation City"; but the papers were calling Cleveland "the Dark City," and not only because of these sunless days. Times were hard. On Public Square, amid statues of the city's founder, Moses Cleaveland and legendary mayor Tom L. Johnson and various Civil War heroes, near the foot of a lavishly decorated, gaily lit giant Christmas tree, panhandlers and prostitutes prowled, often seeming to outnumber pedestrians. Those pedestrians seemed weary, cloaked in cynicism, as gray as the afternoon night around them, seldom speaking to one another, the cold wind from Lake Erie chilling their bones.

Not that everyone in Cleveland, on the afternoon of Wednesday, December 11, 1935, had given in to depression, either emotional or financial. At least one man was feeling good. He was one of the lucky ones: he was employed.

More than that, he liked the line of work he was in, even if in recent months his job had begun—he would have to admit, if pressed—to bore him.

But not this afternoon. This afternoon, this bleak gray afternoon, he was smiling with anticipation. It was a tight smile, a poker player's barely-there smile, though the laugh lines around his gray-blue eyes gave him away. He was eager. He could smell the kill. He was handsome, in a boyish, almost baby-face manner, with a trail of freckles across his nose, and his Norwegian stock was apparent, despite the dark brown hair. He was a young man of thirty-two who stood six feet but seemed taller, possibly because he was so slim. This slimness belied his powerful arms and shoulders, the legacy of a stint in one of Chicago's South Side auto plants dipping radiators in his youth. His tan camel-hair topcoat seemed a bit big for him, but the snap-brim fedora gave him the proper air of authority for the Chief Agent of the U.S. Treasury Department's Alcohol Tax Unit.

He was sitting on the rider's side of a ten-ton flatbed truck, the back of which was loaded with scaling ladders, the front of which was a specially constructed metal prow, an ugly sideways v whose point was aimed forward. The truck was moving in low gear down Sweeney Avenue, just outside Cleveland's industrial flats along the winding Cuyahoga River, through an area of ware-houses and working class housing, rumbling over miles of railroad tracks. Two carloads of agents were already at the large red brick building on Sweeney Avenue, having preceded the truck by a minute or so. Agents from these cars would unload the ladders, once the steel bumper had burst open the door of the suspected distillery.

Eliot Ness had done his homework on this one. But the agent behind the wheel of the truck—a heavyset, grizzled veteran named Bob Hedges, who didn't much like his college-boy boss—had done most of the legwork. A week ago Hedges had walked Ness around the building at Sweeney and Fifty-third, on an afternoon as gray as this one.

"Take a look," Hedges had said, pointing to the back of the brick building where yellow-stained icicles hung like frozen urine.

Ness had nodded. The staining was characteristic of an illicit distillery.

Steam and fumes seeped through the walls and discolored the ice.

"Bob, we've had this place under surveillance for months," Ness said, shaking his head, digging his hands in his topcoat pockets. "We've never seen any molasses or sugar go in, and nothing ever seems to come out."

Hedges lifted a thick finger and lectured his chief. "But they got a guard on the front door. A regular gorilla. *Something's* the fuck up."

Ness sighed. He didn't much like Hedges and his rough manner, but he did respect the hard little man's instincts. Hedges was a good, honest cop. Ness didn't ask for anything else from his men.

And there indeed was a guard posted at the big brick building, except for occasional lunch and supper breaks like the one the guard was on now, giving Ness and Hedges the opportunity to case the joint.

Also, the location was perfect for a mob distillery. It was roughly halfway between the Woodland Avenue neighborhood, home of many Italian-Americans, some honest and some not so, and Newburgh Heights, where just beyond the city limits wide-open gambling joints like "Shimmy" Patton's Harvard Club and "Gameboy" Miller's Thomas Club flourished. As a cost-cutting measure, the Mayfield Road mob had been supplying their clubs with tax-free bootleg hooch, often filling and refilling bottles that had once contained legal liquor and retained the proper labels.

Ness found a broken window to peer in. He could see nothing, except what appeared to be a cinder floor.

"Looks empty in there," Ness said.

"It's a still, I tell you," Hedges said. "The mother of all stills."

Ness nodded noncommittally. "Let's get out of here before the gorilla gets back."

Hedges shook his head in frustration, but he brightened in the car, when Ness told him, "I think you're right about that place. And I think I know what's going on back there ..."

He had directed Hedges to check the records in the city engineer's office at City Hall. "Look for any abandoned sewer line that might be near the Sweeney Avenue building."

"Bingo," Hedges had said, entering Ness' small office in the Standard Building without knocking. He had blueprints in his arms; he spread them out on Ness' battered rolltop desk, on top of the other papers there. "Abandoned sewer—brick construction, with an interior diameter of five feet.

Runs right by the place."

Ness looked over the blueprints. "The same sewer runs past Molaska Products, I see."

"I noticed that too," Hedges said and grinned. "That's Mo Horvitz's molasses company."

"It sure as hell is," Ness said, sitting up. "And we know what they're up to, don't we. They're pumping molasses through the old sewer line from their storage tanks to the basement of the Sweeney Avenue building."

"Agreed. But how the hell are they getting the alcohol out?"

Ness reexamined the blueprints. "I don't know. Is there a gas station in the area?"

"It don't show on there," Hedges said, waving at the blueprints, "but yeah, there's a couple. You think they're pumping the booze out of the basement through these old sewer pipes, to a gas station?"

Ness nodded. "Old Chicago trick. Big tank truck comes into the station, supposedly to fill the station's storage tanks. Only the tank trucks come in empty . . . and go out full."

"But not of gasoline."

"Not hardly," Ness said.

Now they were nearing the padlocked double front doors of the brick warehouse, the truck in second gear. The burly but sleepy guard bundled in an overcoat and sitting on a barrel reading the Police Gazette, suddenly sprang to, his eyes round as poker chips, and yelled, "Hey!", and headed for the hills.

Ness braced himself on the dashboard as the wooden doors grew larger before him, and then with a splintering crunch the steel prow and the truck behind it flattened the doors and rolled right over them, into the big, open—and very empty—warehouse.

Ness hopped out of the truck, yanked his .38 from under his arm, and called back to his agents. They were pulling the ladders off the back of the flatbed, to cover the roof, where most distillery escapes were made. Several agents were already posted in back and around the building.

Hedges climbed down from the cab of the truck and his feet scuffed at the cinders on the floor.

"Let's find the basement," Ness said, and Hedges tagged along, an axe in his hands.

The axe carved open the basement door, and the two men headed downstairs, into another massive open area.

"Shit," Hedges said. "They've cleaned it out."

It was cold down there; their breath was smoking.

"Not quite," Ness said.

The stills had been dismantled and moved out, but their shadows remained in the cement; there had been six of them, each around four feet in diameter. A major setup. Doing some quick math, Ness figured that when they were up and rolling, they were turning out two thousand gallons daily, minimum.

A massive operation like this one could only have been pulled off with the collusion of Cleveland's celebratedly corrupt police force. Those sons of bitches made Chicago's bent cops look straight.

"Look at this," he said to Hedges. The smaller man came over as Ness pointed up to a galvanized iron pipe, a flume containing several electric blower fans. "We need to find out where this leads."

"There's a metal company next door," Hedges said. "Probably there."

"Makes sense," Ness said. "Smoke from the boilers and fumes from this distilling room could be passed off as coming from the metal works."

Ness prowled the basement further, discovered five workmen in the boiler room, all of them cowering near one of three massive boilers, several with tools in hand.

"What is this?" one of them said, shrinking back.

Ness laughed shortly, put his .38 away. "A federal raid, but I wouldn't worry about it. You boys are dismantling these boilers, I take it?"

"Yeah," the spokesman said. He was a beefy guy with five o'clock shadow and close-set dark eyes. "We're with Acme Boiler and Welding. We been working all week, dismantling these three steam-boilers."

"Well, go on with your work," Ness said.

Hedges bristled. "Christ on a crutch! Are you kidding? Let's take 'em in for questioning."

"Dismantling a steam boiler is not a federal offense," Ness said. "Let's see what's going on upstairs."

Hedges shook his head in disgust as the men resumed their work, and the sound of clanging metal followed the pair upstairs, where the other raiders had found nothing to speak of. No suspects, no alcohol, no nothing.

A few minutes later, one of Ness' men did discover a six-inch water line that had been run across Sweeney Avenue to a railroad roundhouse, and connected with the city's water mains. Water for the operation of the distillery, then, had been heisted off the city of Cleveland. Probably with the complicity of city officials, Ness thought. Well, at least that goddamn Davis administration was past history now. Unfortunately, the city's tarnished coppers seemed to thrive no matter whose administration was in power.

"I scratched my initials on one of those boilers," Hedges told Ness. The heavy set little agent had ducked back downstairs for a while,

"Why did you do that?"

"It'll turn up again, when they set this big still back up someplace else in town, and I'll be able to identify it."

Ness shrugged. "Maybe."

"What do you mean, 'maybe'?"

"I think this operation may simply be shut down."

"Bullshit! We didn't move fast enough on this, and they got wind of our raid, and they're moving it!"

"Or maybe they're just out of business. Maybe they figure the risk isn't worth it."

"Don't talk stupid."

"It's over, Agent Hedges. Show's over. It's getting too late in the day to be a Prohibition agent—considering Prohibition's been over for, how many years now?"

"The Mayfield Road boys ain't gettin' out of the alcohol business," Hedges insisted. "There's still dough in it."

"You may be right," Ness said. He didn't want to argue the point.

And to a degree, Ness knew, Hedges probably was right. The illegal product was cheaper than legal, what with federal and state taxes added on. Bootlegging would continue.

But not like before. Not like Chicago. In both Chicago and more recently, in Cleveland, where the flow of liquor from Canada was the primary concern, there had been enough activity to keep the life of a "revenooer" lively. It had taken a long time after the advent of Repeal for a steady supply of good, legitimate liquor to reach the market, for the American liquor industry to gear back up and serve its public. The mob had been taking care of that public for a long time, and a transition period was to be expected.

That transition period was over. These days the Cleveland boys—the Mayfield Road mob—were moving into gambling and numbers and union racketeering. Just like the Capone outfit back home. To Ness, the huge, empty warehouse on Sweeney Avenue, and the remnants of the mammoth distillery that haunted it, were symbols of an era's end. And proof that the job that had once done him proud was now a farce. It just wasn't about anything anymore.

He checked his watch. It was nearly four; he would have to get one of his raiders to give him a lift. He had a four-thirty meeting at City Hall with newly elected Mayor Burton, but he had no idea what it was about. Coordination between federal and local law enforcement perhaps.

That would be a joke, considering the state of Cleveland's infamous police force. The boys in blue, not to mention the plainclothes dicks, had helped make Ness' job as a fed damn near impossible whenever he worked within Cleveland city limits. How he'd like a crack at those venal sons of bitches.

Eliot Ness walked out into an afternoon that was turning into evening, though the difference was indiscernible. He tugged at his fedora, keeping his face out of the chill wind, not realizing that he had just raided his last still.

CHAPTER 2

On the northern edge of downtown Cleveland, a whisper away from Lake Erie, two buildings faced each other like granite reflections: the Courthouse and the City Hall. Between them was an expansive park, a continuation of the Mall, that 104-acre tract of land around which various public buildings gathered like pompous old men. The greenery was brown at the moment, except for the occasional fir, with patches of snow littering the expanse of lawn. On this afternoon, the imposing structures were lost in the fog like everything and everybody else in the city; they were ghosts of the boom that had followed the Great War, fading stone memories of a Cleveland with a future.

Harold Burton, mayor of Cleveland for just over a month, stood at a tall, wide window in an office that struck him as damn near decadent, and looked out at his gloomy city. He was not a naive man, and the gloom did get to him. But he felt nonetheless that the town could be turned around.

Many years ago as a Harvard law student, he'd been inspired by what he'd read of Tom L. Johnson, the Mayor of Cleveland just after the turn of the century. Johnson was a man of money who waged war against the privileged class, a mayor whose four terms became the embodiment of progressive government in America. Young Harold Burton had decided Cleveland would be a fine place to establish a law practice, and besides, it was where his girlfriend Selma came from. A picture of Selma and their four children was on his desk nearby.

He went to that desk but did not sit. From a plain wooden box amid many papers and between two telephones, Burton withdrew a big black Havana cigar. He lit it and puffed at it with some gusto. He never felt more the mayor than when he was puffing one of his big black cigars.

Burton was just short of tall, a wedge-shaped, broad-browed man with short, prematurely white hair, a strong jaw and placid gray eyes above dark circles. He was forty-eight years old and looked every year of it. His brown suit was rumpled and the only natty thing about his apparel was the yellow-and-gold tie with the ruby stickpin (Selma's work).

He felt ill at ease in the sprawling, lavish office with its high, ornately sculptured plaster ceiling. It was known as the Tapestry Room, after the five massive tapestries depicting the Indians of the Western Reserve in the wilderness days, draped here and there above the room's fancy oak paneling. His desk was nestled in the corner between a tall, wide, beige-draped window and a fire-place, its mantel covered with more pictures of Selma and the kids. One hundred thousand on relief, Burton thought, and I sit here like Nero fiddling. Only he wasn't sitting, nor was he fiddling. He was pacing, waiting for the man who could enable His Honor to carry out his top-priority campaign promise, if that man said yes to the job Burton planned to offer.

Unfortunately, Burton felt the odds of this man's taking the job were slim. But goddammit, he had to try....

Burton had been elected as a reform mayor—a Republican who had run as an independent, steamrolling over both parties' machines. Elected by the largest majority ever won by a mayoral candidate in Cleveland's one hundred years, Burton had a clear mandate. But the political waters where he had to swim remained muddy.

The Republican mayor he replaced, Harry L. Davis, had used his two years to turn Cleveland into a wide-open town, with the loosest of standards at City Hall. Not only had crime increased, particularly gambling and vice, but the business of government had, through Davis' patronage tactics, gone all but bankrupt. Scrip was issued to meet city payrolls. Deficiency taxes were levied in order to have some cash on hand. Meanwhile, Davis spent much of his time out of town, and the newspapers, with which he'd feuded from the beginning, gleefully, and correctly, labeled him an absentee mayor.

Burton had promised a return to efficiency in government; he had promised to bring a businesslike approach to City Hall.

But he had promised more than that.

He stalked the office, puffing the cigar, checking his watch. At four-thirty, he checked with his secretary.

"When Ness arrives," he told her over the intercom, "send him right in."

"Mr. Ness has been here for ten minutes, Your Honor."

He didn't snap at the girl; he hadn't been in office long enough for his staff to learn to read his mind. He'd give them another week to do that.

"Send him in," he said, and clicked off the intercom and put out his cigar.

He smoothed his suit as best he could, and walked to the door to greet Ness as he came in. The slim man in the tan camel-hair topcoat, open to reveal a rather natty gray-striped double-breasted suit and maroon tie, slipped in, hat in hand, from among a horde of waiting politicos and job-seekers, the likes of which had thronged Burton's office doorstep for weeks.

Burton hoped his disappointment didn't show. From all he'd heard about Eliot Ness in the past two weeks, he had expected someone more physically impressive. In his mind's eye, he'd been picturing, foolishly, he knew, the movie actor Chester Morris. But this was no movie tough guy.

This was a man who looked even younger than his thirty-two years. This was a man who looked like he should be wearing a college graduation mortarboard, not a headful of pomaded, parted-in-the-middle hair, a dark disobedient comma of which made its way down his forehead.

"Your Honor," Ness said, his voice soft, husky, "allow me to be the last to congratulate you on your election." With a smile, he extended a hand.

Burton took the hand, shook it, relieved that the grip was as strong as it was.

He said, "I'm glad to finally get around to meeting you, Mr. Ness. I've heard so much about you, I feel I already know you."

Again Ness smiled, almost shyly Burton thought, and stood and waited until the Mayor rather awkwardly moved across the spacious office, gesturing toward a chair waiting opposite the desk in the corner.

"Sit, please, sit," Burton urged, taking his place behind the desk.

Ness sat, keeping his topcoat on, in apparent anticipation of a brief meeting. He crossed his legs, ankle on knee. Good, Burton thought, he wasn't nervous. He might look like a collegian, but he didn't intimidate easily.

"Smoke, if you like," Burton said, trying a smile out on the young Treasury agent.

"No, thanks. I don't smoke cigarettes."

Burton opened the cigar box on his desk. "Perhaps you'd like one of these Havanas?"

"No. Thanks. Go ahead, though."

Burton smiled tightly and shook his head no and shut the box. Then he said, "I do hope you have some vices. I don't trust a man who's too goddamn pure."

"I'm known to take a drink now and then."

"Ah. That's reassuring somehow. The most famous Prohibition agent of them all is a drinking man."

Ness lifted an eyebrow. "I've never had anything against drinking. The Prohibition law was a lousy piece of legislation."

Burton smiled again, not tightly this time. "That's interesting, coming from a man in your line."

Ness leaned forward a little, turning his hat in his hands restlessly. "The trouble with Prohibition was that so many people didn't believe in it. They were either against it or figured it was for the other guy. A law like that breeds contempt for the law in general. That helps make the underworld very strong, very wealthy. It gives them plenty of money to corrupt the law."

"So it's the . . . 'underworld' you've been after."

"I've never put John Q. Public in jail, Your Honor. I did put some gangsters out of business though."

"Al Capone, for instance."

Ness smiled, shrugged.

"And you're proud of that."

"It's going to be a hard one to top."

Ambitious. Burton liked that, too. That would help.

Feeling more at ease, Burton reached for the cigar box

and withdrew and lit a Havana. He puffed it regally. "Do you know," he said, "that I've had you under investigation for two weeks, now?"

"No," Ness said, with mild surprise. "But where in hell did you find a Cleveland cop up to the job? No offense meant—to you."

Burton smiled and shook his head. "None taken. But truer words were never spoken. I had to rely on myself and some handpicked staff members. We've been checking around. Dwight Green speaks highly of you."

Dwight H. Green was Federal Prosecutor in Chicago.

"I'll speak highly of Dwight," Ness said, "if given half a chance."

"Frank Cullitan is another booster," Burton said.

Frank T. Cullitan was Cuyahoga County Prosecutor.

"Cullitan's a Democrat," Ness said.

"Does that matter?"

"Not to me."

Burton blew out a dark cloud of cigar smoke. "Every phone call I've made—Joe Keenan with the FBI, for instance—has resulted in high praise for Eliot Ness."

Ness smiled faintly, a hint of cockiness in his expression. Burton didn't mind that, either. That trait, too, would be necessary if this man were to take this job.

Actually, Burton would have been greatly surprised if Ness hadn't been at least a touch arrogant. The young man's record was impressive, to understate the case. Ness had been just twenty-six when he was recruited by the Justice Department to head up a special independent Prohibition Unit in Chicago that was designed as part of a two-pronged federal effort, born in the White House, to put public enemy/public embarrassment Al Capone away. While the other prong, a crack IRS team, worked to build a tax case, Ness and his raiders hit Capone's breweries, confiscated trucks and equipment, and made numerous arrests. This distracted Capone, dented his bank account, and disrupted his business practices by limiting the amount of payoff money available, without which countless crooked cops—both local and federal—had gone off the take.

The ten men in Ness' unit, handpicked by himself after poring over hundreds of government records, were widely respected as that rarity among big-city cops in this damn Depression: they couldn't be bribed.

These "untouchables," as the Chicago papers had dubbed them in the aftermath of Capone's fall, routinely turned down bribes, at times being offered weekly payoffs damn near as large as their yearly salaries.

After Capone's conviction, Ness was appointed Chief Investigator of Prohibition Forces in Chicago, a post he held down till mid—1933, when he transferred from the Justice Department to the Treasury and became a "revenooer," closing down hundreds of hillbilly stills in the moonshine mountains of Kentucky, Tennessee, and Ohio. In August 1934 he became Chief Investigator of the Treasury Department's Alcohol Tax Unit in the northern district of Ohio, working out of Cleveland.

He'd attracted some publicity in Cleveland, though Burton had only been vaguely aware of Ness until two weeks before, when several newspaper reporters, including Sam Wild of the *Plain Dealer* and his city editor Phil Porter, began touting Ness. They knew Burton was shopping around for the right man to clean up the police department, and Ness—who was relatively new in Cleveland, and had no political ties or interests—seemed ideal for the job.

"The people will eat it up," Wild had said. A tall wiry guy right out of The Front Page, Wild had worked in Chicago and knew Ness from there. "He's the perfect P.R. move, and he can probably come as close to getting the job done as anybody."

Now Eliot Ness was sitting across from Burton's desk, and the question was whether or not Burton could convince the young G-man to take one hell of a gamble.

"Do you know why I've called you here?" Burton asked.

"Coordination between your people and mine?"

"No. I want to offer you a job."

Ness uncrossed his legs, then crossed them the other way. "Go on," he said.

"My top priority right now," Burton said, "is law and order. Do you know what I mean by that?"

Ness lifted an eyebrow slightly, set it back down. "Frankly, it's usually just a political catch phrase."

"Granted. But what I mean is, I want this city to have a real police department again. Let me put it another way. I figure I can't clean up Cleveland until the police department itself is clean."

Ness sat forward. "That makes sense to me."

"I need a strong man to reorganize—to transform—that pitiful excuse for a police department into a modern, honest law enforcement agency. You've shown yourself to be a tough cop who doesn't flinch in a dangerous situation. And wading into our corrupt force will be dangerous as hell. The corruption is firmly entrenched. You won't just be stepping on toes, you'll be stepping on livelihoods."

"And lively hoods," Ness said, wryly.

Burton smiled momentarily, then soberly said, "It isn't just the Eliot Ness who drives trucks through locked doors that I'm interested in. It's the Eliot Ness who is a scientifically trained criminologist. The Ness who was an honor student at the University of Chicago, the site of some of the most advanced thinking in America, as regards social concerns. Your major fields of study, my investigation has revealed, were commerce, law, and political science."

"What job are we talking about, Mayor? Chief of Police?"

Burton shook his head no. "We have an honest chief. He happens to be rather ineffectual, but never mind. He is well-liked, and I would have some difficulty pulling him out without stirring up a political fuss that would just get in our way. No, I'm talking about the Director of Public Safety. The top slot."

Ness smiled, just barely. "That's a job I'd be interested in."

Burton pressed on. It was too early for such an acceptance. Ness didn't know the facts yet. "You'd be the youngest Director of Public Safety in the city's history. I consider you the ideal candidate to direct the investigation into, and purging of, our corrupt police department . . . but your role would be much more wide-ranging than that. You'd be in charge of twenty-four hundred men in the city's police and fire departments. It's a big job for a young man. Are you up to it?"

"Yes," Ness said.

"I think you are, too. I don't think there's a better man for this job."

"Do I sense a 'but' in all this?"

Burton sighed, nodding gravely. "You do. In all honesty, this job is not a plum. In effect, I'll be tossing you a hand grenade and you'll be smothering it with your body."

"Frankly, Your Honor, I'm not exactly following you."

Burton stood. Almost absently, he said, "You realize, I'm sure, that I may well owe my election to the previous Director of Public Safety ..."

Safety Director Martin J. Lavelle, a former police captain who had driven a Rolls Royce, had been present last summer at a wild, drunken party on a boat on Lake Erie, where a young woman had fallen overboard and drowned. The safety director had failed to report the death, and when the papers got hold of it, several days later, there was hell to pay for the Davis administration.

"I think," Ness said, smiling with wry self-confidence, "I can get you just as much publicity, but with a slightly different slant."

"That's what I'd be counting on. Frankly, your publicity value is as important to me as your credentials, impressive as they are. I'm not unlike a theatrical producer in this, Mr. Ness. That is, I'm looking for a star. And you're it."

Ness shrugged. "The headlines'll happen. I'm not worried."

"But you should be. You'll be under the gun. The clock will be ticking'."

Ness frowned, in confusion, not displeasure. "What clock will be ticking?"

Burton went to the window. He brushed back a beige curtain and looked out at his dark city. "You'll be up against possibly the most corrupt police force in the nation. And they're a well-established part of the city's landscape. The Detective Bureau and the precinct commanders in particular have strong political ties."

"Excuse me, but what do you care? This is your administration now."

Burton looked at the young G-man and smiled. "You really aren't political, are you, Mr. Ness? The city council is going to be up for grabs. The reform Republicans, with whom I'm shakily aligned, will go toe-to-toe with the old-line Republicans, while a couple varieties of Democrats sow dissent and pursue their own vested interests. All the while former mayor Davis will be working behind the scenes to make me as unsuccessful as possible, largely but not exclusively through his friend Councilman Fink."

"Could make for merry hell."

"Could make for merry hell indeed. For me to accomplish anything as mayor, I'm going to have to hold onto this office for several terms. And to survive this term, I have campaign promises to keep."

Ness nodded. "Chief among them, cleaning up the cops."

"Exactly. But corruption isn't our only police problem. We've got a badly out-of-date, poorly equipped police force whose very squad cars are falling apart. The fire department's in similarly sad shape."

"So it comes down to money."

"Money. Budget. Take the job, and you'll have to submit budgets on both the police and fire departments within two weeks." Burton sat back down.

"Budget hearings will begin shortly after the first of the year. By early March, the council will vote. And if we don't get our budget you'll be hamstrung from the outset. You won't be able to get a damn thing done. You'll be an automatic lame duck."

Ness breathed out slowly. "By that you mean you'd have to let me go at the end of your term, and try again with a new safety director."

"I'd most likely let you go before that. And I think you know what it would do for your career in law enforcement. Having come in with great fanfare in the press and then accomplishing nothing, you'd look a fool. I won't pretend otherwise. I won't sugarcoat it. Meanwhile, I'd most likely bring in a new safety director about this time next year and, I would hope, find someone else with impressive credentials who might help me land the budget I need next time around."

"I see what you meant about that hand grenade."

"I'm not sure you do. What this comes down to is that you would have to get results in the police corruption investigation—spectacular results—before March. That's your ticking clock. You'd have barely more than two months to produce. You'd have to fill the headlines with such derring-do and miraculous modern police work that even a politically divided and quite possibly corrupt city council cannot ignore your budget demands."

Ness shifted in the chair. "Specifically, what sort of results would you expect?"

"There are, obviously, some high-ranking police officers in this city who are up to their brass buttons in graft. Rumor has it that a sort of 'department within the department' exists, ruled over by men such as these. You'll have to identify, and suspend, and then arrest, at least one of them."

"Before March."

"Before March," the mayor said.

"That won't be easy. There's a code of silence among cops. Even the honest ones tend not to 'rat' on the bent ones."

"That would be your problem."

"Yes, it would."

"And you'd have to make some inroads on other fronts . . . lead some raids on these wide-open gambling joints around town and these so-called 'policy' banks ..."

Ness was nodding. "Those day-to-day illegal lotteries are what get cops on the 'pad' in the first place. There's a direct relationship between gambling and police corruption."

Burton narrowed his eyes. "Do you have any objection to leading raids yourself? We need your publicity value. We can't get that if you stay behind a desk."

Ness stood. He walked to the window, tan topcoat flapping, and looked out, smiling to himself.

"Before you leveled with me about the career risk entailed in this thing," Ness said, glancing back at him, "I was about to tell you my conditions for taking this job."

"Which are?"

Ness walked around to the front of the desk and leaned one hand on its top, the other clutching his fedora, as he looked Burton square in the eyes.

"I was ready to say I would take the position on two conditions: one, that I not be deskbound, that I can be as active in investigative work as I choose, turning over the administrative duties to an assistant; and two, that I be given a free hand, without political interference. No whitewash jobs. Chips fall where they may."

"I see no problem with that."

"We talked about stepping on toes before. What if I have to step on the toes of some city council members? Councilman Fink, for example? Won't that defeat your purpose?"

Burton laughed. "If you pull this thing off, the city council will have to vote us our money, sore toes or not."

Ness smiled on one side of his face.

"What do you say, Mr. Ness? Do you still want the job, after what you've just heard?"

Still smiling, Ness again shrugged. "How's the pay?"

"Not great, but it's a few thousand more a year than you're currently getting. There are some fringe benefits. We'll provide you with a city car. What are you driving now?"

"A black Ford coupe that belongs to the federal government."

"Well, in the future you'll be driving a black Ford sedan that belongs to the city. How's that for a step up?"

"My predecessor got a Rolls Royce, but what the hell. I live in Bay Village. Is that a problem?"

"You'll need a residence within the Cleveland city limits. I believe that can be provided for you. We could work out all these details—if you're interested in the job."

"Your Honor," Ness said, grinning like a kid, "I wouldn't miss this party for the world."

"Then let's get you sworn in," the mayor said, reaching for his phone. "The party starts tomorrow morning."

CHAPTER 3

It was almost nine that night when Eliot Ness, behind the wheel of the government Ford he would be turning in tomorrow morning, pulled into the drive of his Bay Village home. Several lights were on in the downstairs of the gray stucco, blue-shuttered two-story house. He hoped Eva hadn't waited dinner for him. He'd called to tell her not to, but she did have a considerable streak of martyr in her, God love her.

He left the Ford in the garage, a separate building with a rentable loft—they just hadn't gotten around to renting it yet—between the main house and the lakefront. A friend in Chicago, with the old Retail Credit Company he'd worked for in his early private detective days, had put him in touch with a friend who'd helped him land this nice house for a song. A very nice investment it was, even if such Bay Village homes as this were bungalows compared to the near-mansions of Lakewood and Rocky River. On his long drive home well over an hour from downtown, he drove by those lavish homes each night and smiled and shook his head and promised himself, *one day. . .*

Tonight it occurred to him that his evening daydreams might soon come true, if he could pull off this new job. Of course if he failed, he might never achieve his career goals and the material comforts his success would bring.

But, what the hell—not trying was in itself failure.

And he felt good about Burton. Burton had laid it on the line and hadn't hedged about the risk involved. Ness had met a lot of public officials in his years as a federal agent, but he couldn't recall one that had impressed him the way Burton did. If he could trust his instincts, and he always did, Ness saw this mayor as a man with brains and guts and even integrity. Ness wondered if such a man could last in the political arena.

He held in his hand a bouquet of flowers. His cute red-headed secretary Doris had had them waiting for him at his office in the Standard Building when he returned from his conference with Burton at City Hall, a block away. Doris had claimed they were from "the staff," but he knew they were her idea. He was a detective, after all.

Under his arm was a bound copy of the city charter, and a copy of the crime and law enforcement survey of Cleveland made a few years back by Felix Frankfurter and several others. Both were "gifts" from the Mayor. The job began tomorrow, officially, but he would begin his homework tonight.

The night was cold and the wind whistled in off Lake Erie. It would be good to be in his warm house, with his warm wife, who was waiting for him in the doorway. Eva was a shapely, handsome woman of twenty-nine, a dark blonde with a heart-shaped face and light blue eyes, her Scandinavian heritage stamped on her every feature. She wore a simple dark blue dress with a patterned lace V-neck collar, and a light blue apron.

"I was beginning to worry," she said. Eva had a rather musical voice, though the notes she hit of late were too often melancholy.

"I told you not to," he said, leaning in to peck her cheek.

"Oh, Eliot, you shouldn't have . . ."

She had noticed the flowers.

"Uh, well, they are rather pretty, aren't they?"

She beamed as he handed her the flowers, red, white, and yellow with ferns. "You didn't have to do this. It isn't exactly the first night you've been a little late."

"I'm glad you like them," he said, and stepped inside. She placed the flowers in a vase on a small table nearby. She helped him out of his topcoat and took his hat, hanging them both in the closet by the door.

"I waited dinner," she said.

"You needn't have. You should've eaten."

"I wanted to wait. I want to hear about this big surprise of yours."

The vestibule opened onto the large living room, with stair to the second floor rising on the right. Through an archway on the left was the dining room, but they ate in the kitchen, at the rear of the house. There was a breakfast nook where they took many of their meals.

"I hope the roast beef isn't dried out," she said, bending to open the stove and look in. She had a nice rear end, Eva did. She had a nice shape in general, just this side of plump.

The roast beef did prove a little dry, but gravy took care of that. He was hungry and wolfed down several servings of both the beef and the boiled potatoes. Eva was a good cook, and in fact he had to restrain her a bit. He liked simple meat and potatoes. Her special Swedish meatballs, which drew raves from family and friends, made him sick to his stomach.

"Please tell me," she said, picking at her food, studying

him. "I'm not like you, Eliot. I don't like suspense."

He wiped his mouth with a napkin and smiled at her. "I guess you don't realize you're dining with one of the most powerful figures in city government."

"Powerful? City government?"

"Your husband is Cleveland's new Director of Public Safety."

Her face lit up the room as she clasped her hands together. She rose, and came over and sat in his lap. She was soft and warm and smelled very good, like the flowers he'd (sort of) brought her, and her face was glowing.

"I'm so proud of you," Eva said. "This is the day, the day we've been waiting for."

He squeezed her. "Yes, it is. We've been working toward this for a long time."

"You deserve a big kiss."

"I think I do."

She kissed him—a long, soft, sweet kiss that nearly ended dinner.

"Eliot," she said, blue eyes flashing as she fell into a private joke of theirs, "is that your gun?"

"Maybe I'm just glad to see you."

She slid off his lap. "Maybe you should finish your roast beef. I have apple strudel for dessert."

"We may have dessert all evening."

"We may," she conceded, and she sat across from him and began eating with more enthusiasm now.

He had met Eva Jonsen in elementary school so perhaps it could be said they were childhood sweethearts. But they had gone to different high schools and, in truth, barely knew each other in those days. Both had grown up on Chicago's South Side, in Roseland, a working-class residential area outside the Pullman industrial district.

Her father had worked at the Pullman plant, in fact, while Eliot's had owned a small but successful bakery. They hadn't gotten to know each other until years later, when she'd been Alexander Jamie's secretary.

Jamie, who was married to one of Eliot's older sisters, had left the Justice Department to become Chief Investigator for the Secret Six, a group of Chicago businessmen who were trying to break the Capone stranglehold on their city. The Secret Six had worked hand-in-hand with Ness and his squad of "untouchables," and Eva had eventually become as much Eliot's secretary as Jamie's.

With the kind of hours he was putting in, in those early Chicago days, he didn't have much contact with females— at least not decent females—and Eva had always been interested in his work and in him. She seemed to look up to him. She'd made it through high school and was a well-trained secretary, but the idea of a "college man" made her swoon. They spent a lot of time together at the office, and elsewhere, with her swooning and him catching. Now their sixth wedding anniversary was approaching.

By a little after ten o'clock they were cuddled on the brown mohair couch in the living room, their shoeless feet up on the coffee table being warmed by the considerable blaze that he'd got going in the fireplace. The only other light in the room came from the electric bubbling liquid decorations on the small Christmas tree on a table in one corner.

He looked at her radiant face, the glow of the fire making it even more so, and felt very much in love with her. He knew they'd been drifting apart—his long hours, separation from her family back in Chicago, their failure to have a child, all of that and more, had been working against them. They were both quiet and tended to hold things in, and that didn't help, either.

But right now, he loved her. He loved her very much. He promised himself to do something about their situation. It did not occur to him, however, simply to tell her how much he loved her.

"I'm happy for you," she said.

"Be happy for *us,* " he said. "This means more money. A real standing in the community. A real chance to try out my theories, my ideas about law enforcement."

"You learned so much at the university, and you've had so little chance to use it."

He knew she meant that in a positive way, but it rubbed him a little wrong.

"What do you mean?"

"Oh, you know, dear. All these years of chasing boot-leggers. Kicking down doors and swinging an axe."

He laughed. "Sometimes I do feel like Carrie Nation in trousers."

"No longer. You've busted your last still, Eliot Ness."

He laughed shortly. "I hadn't thought of that. I suppose I have."

"That's behind you, all of that awful, dangerous work. And I'm so glad."

Eva reached her face up to his and kissed him. That was unusual for her.

She rarely initiated a kiss, or anything else. But her lips were warm on his, and she was eager, and he began to help her out of her dress. Then he undressed, and in the flickering light of the fire, on the mohair couch, they made love, with a desperation and enthusiasm that outdistanced any coupling of theirs in recent memory.

Soon—well, not too soon—they were a naked married couple clinging to each other, watching the fire slowly die. The lovemaking done, Ness was thinking about work again, his other marriage. Reviewing his day.

Just to keep things kosher, while still in Burton's office Ness had phoned his secretary at the Standard Building and dictated his resignation from the Treasury Department. He told her he'd be right over to sign it, and relished the disappointment in her voice as she said, "Yes, sir." Then he broke the news: "Your old boss is the city's new safety director." And he relished the girlish squeal that followed as well.

As he stepped from the mayor's office, with His Honor at his side, he'd been greeted by a small mob consisting largely of curious city employees, but in the front row were half a dozen reporters. This was no surprise as there was a press room just down the hall—right across from the safety director's office, actually—and, as it turned out, one of the reporters had seen Ness going into the Tapestry Room, and put two and two together.

The group included Clayton Fritchey from the Press, and Wes Lawrence and Sam Wild of the Plain Dealer. They were in shirtsleeves and suspenders and had pencils and pads at the ready.

Burton gave them a brief statement. "I consider the appointment of the Director of Public Safety to be of the greatest importance ..." and so on, and then the news-hounds started in.

"Does the appointment of Mr. Ness presage the naming of a new police chief?" Lawrence asked.

"I have no statement on that subject at this time," the Mayor said. "But I should point out that removal of a police chief requires a Common Pleas Court trial."

"No new police chief," Sam Wild said, scribbling. Wild was tall and lanky and pale, with dark blond curly hair. He had rather pointed features, like a pleasant Satan. He wore a red bow tie and a smirk. Ness knew the shrewd, cynical reporter from Chicago and liked him, within reason.

Fritchey, a man who talked the way he wrote, asked: "What instructions have you given your new safety director about dealing with the staggering problem of reviving such a demoralized and corrupt department?"

"Yeah," Wild added, looking up from his pad skeptically. "It's no secret our police force is undermanned and stuck with ridiculously substandard equipment. It's also no secret the department's been drained of energy and ambition by two years of self-serving, dirty politicking."

Ness had to admit Wild had balls, and Fritchey, too. Balls were what it took to ask the Mayor those questions, even if it was the previous administration they were skewering, even if it was silently understood by all parties that Burton's future depended upon his press.

Burton's smile was a thin, unreadable line. He said, "Mr. Ness will have a completely free hand to develop the law enforcement policies of this city, as he sees fit. He will in fact be his own chief investigator."

The reporters exchanged wide-eyed glances of a sort jaded newsmen rarely shared.

"That's unheard-of," Fritchey said.

"Well, you heard it now," the Mayor said. "Mr. Ness is a former G-man, who wouldn't have it any other way. Now, if you'll excuse me, gentlemen."

"Excuse me, Your Honor," Wild said, standing so that he blocked the mayor's way back to his office. Borderline rude but ballsy, Ness thought.

"Are you sure this G-man stuff isn't just a ploy to squeeze some budget dough out of your upside-down cake of a city council?"

"As I recall, Mr. Wild," Burton shot back with a nasty little smile, "you yourself were one of those who suggested Mr. Ness as a possible candidate for this job."

And Burton brushed past Wild and ducked into his office.

That, of course, hadn't really been an answer to Wild's question, but Burton—brains, guts, integrity or not—was still a politician. He knew all about answering questions without answering them.

Ness quickly exited the mayor's outer office, and was soon out on the balcony beyond which the City Hall atrium rose. Quick footsteps on the marble floor and overlapping voices echoed.

Finally Ness stopped in his tracks, turned to the gentlemen of the press who followed him in a pack, and said, "I'm on my way to my office at the Standard Building. I hope, if my staff hasn't gone home for the day, to say some goodbyes, and clean out my desk and generally take care of personal matters."

"And you don't want us tagging along," Wild said.

"Right."

"Then how about a statement?"

"I just landed this job, boys. I haven't had a whole hell of a lot of time to reflect."

Lawrence pushed his glasses up on his nose and said, "Are you kidding? You didn't have wind of this? It's been in the air all week."

"I don't have any political contacts, fellas. Nobody told me, 'cause there was nobody to tell me."

"A statement, Mr. Ness," Fritchey said.

"Let's just say my first duty is one of fact-finding. After that I don't know what I'll do, but I hope to take action first and talk about it later."

" 'Action first, then talk,' " Wild echoed, smiling a little, scribbling. "That'll do. That and bein' your own chief investigator. See you tomorrow, kid."

And the rest of the reporters had followed Wild's lead, leaving Ness alone to exit the massive City Hall and walk through the cold night-like afternoon, to his old office where Doris and other staffers waited with flowers and a resignation to sign.

"Some of them won't miss me," he said.

"What?" Eva said.

They were sitting together in the warmth of the fire, naked, his arm around her shoulder, snuggling her to him.

"I'm not popular with everybody on the Alcohol Tax Unit," he said.

"Hedges, for one, will be glad to see me go."

"I'm sure he's just jealous."

"I don't think so. Just a clash of styles. Hedges is a good cop, but he's an old-fashioned one. He doesn't understand police science. All he knows is the third degree and stool pigeons and stakeouts."

"I'm so glad you're out of that awful, dangerous sort of thing."

"What do you mean?"

"Well, you're the safety director. You're an executive, now."

"I suppose I am."

She gestured with both hands. "That's where you've been heading, isn't it?

You didn't go to college to be a policeman. You studied to make something of yourself, and you have."

"Well, thanks, honey."

"I'm so proud of you. So very proud of you."

She hugged him. Her flesh seemed cool and warm at once.

He said, "To be honest, baby, it's still going to be dangerous."

Her eyes grew as round as a silent movie queen's. "Why would it be dangerous?"

For a moment he considered telling her about Burton's "ticking clock." About the possibly suicidal career risk he was taking.

Instead he said only, "I'm up against a very crooked police force. I was hired to clean it up. That's not going to make me popular."

"I see."

"We'll have plenty of protection. You needn't worry."

She said nothing. She was looking at the dwindling fire.

"Really, sugar. There's nothing to worry about."

"Good."

"Of course we'll need to move into the city."

Disappointment painted her face. "Move? From here? But I love it here—my garden, swimming ..."

He smiled, gently. "You're not going to be doing any gardening or swimming in this weather, now, are you? We don't have to sell the place.

We don't even have to rent it out, if you don't want to. We can spend weekends here, particularly when the weather's nicer."

"How can we afford that?"

"The mayor as much as promised us an apartment, as a fringe benefit."

"No rent, you mean?"

"No rent."

She shrugged. "Well, I suppose it's best. We are awfully far from the city."

"I knew you'd see it when you thought about it for a minute."

Eva smiled bravely. "Can't expect to make a step forward like this, without some sacrifices."

"That's right."

"You will be on a more regular schedule than you've been?"

"Honey, uh, this won't be a nine-to-five job. It's going to require long hours."

She looked at him for several moments. Then she nodded.

"It's a big job," he said. "You got to stand by me on this. Things'll settle down, after the first few months."

She nodded again. Their gray cat, Big Al, hopped up on the couch and Eva scratched the animal's neck.

"You don't know the best part. The Mayor said I don't have to ride a desk all day long. He's given me a 'completely free hand,' as he puts it."

"What does that mean?"

"Well, I'll be my own chief investigator. I can get out in the field. I won't just be bogged down with boring administrative duties all day."

"I—I see." The cat was purring under Eva's touch. But Eva wasn't purring.

"Honey, are you all right?"

"I'm fine, Eliot. Why, uh, are you doing that?"

"Doing what?"

"Your own investigating. That doesn't sound like something ... an executive does. Do public safety directors do that?"

He grinned. "It's unheard of, or anyway that's what the reporters say. But I like investigating. Your husband's a detective, honey. You wouldn't take that away from him, would you?"

"No. Of course not."

"Besides, who can I trust but myself, to look into this damn thing? I can't ask the cops to help. It's the cops I'm investigating!"

"I understand."

"I knew you would."

Eva gathered her clothes. She didn't get into them, but she held them before her modestly. The cat hopped off the couch and disappeared into the darkness. "Are you coming up to bed?"

"Not just yet. I have to look over some material the

mayor sent home with me."

"Will you be long?"

"No. An hour. Or two."

She smiled tightly. "Good night, Eliot."

"Good night, honey."

She walked away. He watched her go, admiring her sweet plump rear as she went. She hadn't kissed him good night, but he didn't notice.

Then he put on his clothes and built himself a Scotch-on-the-rocks from a cart in the living room. He gathered the books Burton had given him and began to read, turning on a floor lamp nearby, as the fire had gone out.

CHAPTER 4

That same evening, on the East Side of the city, in a working-class neighborhood where Americans who still thought of themselves as Eastern Europeans huddled in sturdy but paint-peeling two-story, two-family frame houses, a fifty-year-old Slovak laborer named August "Gus" Kulovic, a tall but powerful man with a long horsey face and a pleasant manner, was saying what a wonderful place America was.

He was, after all, in the company of a government agent, Special Agent Sidney White, who was here to repay Gus the money the Depression had cost him. Uncle Sam cared about Gus Kulovic. So said Special Agent Sidney White.

At first Gus had been frightened. The knock at his door two nights before had been loud enough to wake the dead, even to wake Gus Kulovic, despite his bad hearing— which was getting worse and worse—a disability that dated back to the Great War. Yes, Gus had served his adopted country in the trenches overseas. He had not been wounded, but the shelling, the thunder of the shelling, had taken its toll on his poor ears.

Nonetheless, Gus had jumped from the sofa where he'd been napping after dinner, and his wife Marija, ten years younger than he, a plump plain woman who looked pretty to Gus, had come running from the kitchen, where she'd been doing dishes, apron flapping. The banging on the door had even summoned fourteen-year-old Mary, the youngest of their four children and the only one still at home.

"Do you owe money, Poppa?" the girl said sassily. She had her hair in braids and wore a calico dress. Cute as a button, Gus thought. A young skinny version of her mother. Despite her joking, the girl seemed a little frightened. The knocking was loud and insistent.

"We are not in debt, dumpling," Gus said, patting her shoulder. "Go back to your schoolbooks."

She made a face and went, but truth be told, she liked school. Gus was proud of her—she would be the first of his brood to finish high school.

He opened the door and a thickset bulldog of a man in a gray overcoat and a dark blue hat was raising a formidable fist to knock again.

"Yes?" Gus said. He was irritated by this interruption, but he kept his expression neutral. The man was too well-dressed to be a salesman, so he might be someone important. No use offending.

"August Kulovic?" The man's voice was low and resonant, like a radio announcer. He seemed "official" to Gus.

"August Kulovic is me."

The man, whose complexion was gray, remained as expressionless as stone as he withdrew a billfold and flashed a gold badge, returning it to his suit pocket.

"Sidney White," he said. "Special Agent. Could I have a word with you?"

"Of course," Gus said. He ushered the stranger into the modestly furnished flat, which took up the whole upper floor of this house on East Sixty-fourth Street. The most distinctive thing about the place, at the moment, was the good-sized Christmas tree with electric lights (Gus preferred candles, but Mary had cajoled him) over by the windows.

"Is there trouble?" Gus asked.

Agent White smiled. It was wide and white and reassuring, an odd smile to find in the midst of that round gray face with the dark eyes and bushy eyebrows.

"You're in no trouble, Mr. Kulovic. None at all. In fact, I'm here to help you."

Marija had disappeared but now she returned, without her apron. She had obviously been listening. She said, smiling stiffly, "Would you gentleman enjoy some tea and cookies?"

Agent White removed his hat and smiled again and said, "Very much, ma'am. It's so kind of you."

Marija's tentative smile relaxed some and she was gone again.

Gus took Agent White's coat and hung it on a rack near the door. He showed him to the couch, where they sat beneath a framed print of an East European landscape showing snow-capped mountains and a blue sky.

"It is kind of you, Mr. White, to offer to help me."

"It's the government that wishes to help you, Mr. Kulovic. It's Uncle Sam who wants to help."

"I see," Gus said. But he didn't.

"You're a veteran, aren't you, Mr. Kulovic?"

"Yes," Gus said, quiet pride in his voice.

"Uncle Sam hasn't forgotten that."

"Neither has August Kulovic."

"Nor should he. You've been steadily employed for some years now, haven't you?"

"Yes. Since I got home from the war, I work for East Side Rapid." He worked maintenance on the train line. But his hearing loss was getting more and more severe, and he didn't know how much longer he would last.

Marija entered with a tray of china cups, a teapot, and a plate of *rocliky,* filled butter cookies, which she smilingly served. Before she departed, Agent White spoke to her, thanking her, but Gus couldn't hear the words.

It was at this point that Gus realized Agent White had from his first word been speaking up for him. Even the G-man's knock had rattled the rafters, as if he'd known before arriving of Gus' hearing problem.

But Agent White knew of many things where August Kulovic was concerned.

"You have money with the Bailey Building and Loan," Agent White said, sipping his tea.

"Yes. How is it you know this?"

"I'm with the government, Mr. Kulovic."

"What branch?"

"I'm not at liberty to divulge that. It must remain secret. National security. You understand."

"Yes," Gus said. But he didn't.

"What we are doing at my agency must be done confidentially. Not everyone qualifies. Someone like yourself, a veteran, is given special consideration. You understand?"

"Yes," Gus said. And that he understood. That seemed only fair.

"It's a big country, and a lot of people have financial woes. This Depression has hit a lot of folks hard. Take yourself, for example. You put three thousand dollars into your building and loan society. And then hard times came, and your building and loan, like so many others, was forced to go on a restricted basis. The market value of your passbook was reduced to about fifteen hundred dollars."

Gus put down his tea cup. He looked hard into the dark

eyes of the agent.

"How do you know these things?"

The G-man smiled and shrugged. "It's my business to, Mr. Kulovic." Then the smile disappeared. "These facts and figures are strictly confidential. You needn't worry."

"I worry all the time about losing half my money."

"How would you like to get your whole three thousand dollars back, dollar for dollar, in cash?"

"I would like it fine. I need that money. I want to buy a house for my old age."

"And so you shall. You just give me that passbook and you'll have your money back in sixty days. Maybe sooner. Every penny of it."

Gus scratched and shook his head. "I want the money, all right, Mr. White. But how are you going to do it?"

"Don't you worry. That's our business."

"Whose business?"

"The government. We are, in a limited, selected manner, aiding and assisting passbook owners in distress, by giving them dollar-for-dollar value in return for passbooks. And we give bonds as security for the passbooks."

"Bonds?"

"Yes. You needn't turn over the passbook, now. I can come back in a few days with your security bonds, and you can sign some documents."

Gus sighed, gestured with his palms up. "Mr. White, I don't read or write good. I don't have education."

"Can you sign your name?"

"Yes, but ..."

"That's all that's necessary. May I stop by Thursday and discuss this further?"

"Yes, I ..."

"Good. I'll have the necessary documents with me."

Agent White stood and extended his hand to Gus, who stood also and shook the hand.

"I must be going," Agent White said. "I have several others to contact. Some of them your friends, no doubt."

And the G-man was gone.

Gus hadn't known what to think. Hope was bursting in him, but he had spent too many hard years—among them these last Depression years—to give in to this unfamiliar feeling.

His wife was worried, too.

"Who is this man?" she said.

"He had a badge."

"When he comes back, ask to see it again," she said, shrewdly.

"I don't know much about business or anything," Gus said. "But this sounds good."

"Ask to see the badge."

Tonight Agent White had come calling again. They sat on the same sofa, but instead of Marija's tea, they drank from the whiskey bottle Agent White had brought, tucked away in a briefcase along with his important papers.

"A toast to you, Mr. Kulovic," Agent White said, and they clicked glasses.

"To August Kulovic, who soon will have his savings back!"

They had several more drinks and several similar toasts.

"Oh," Agent White said, "I almost forgot. I brought along your security bonds."

From the briefcase Agent White withdrew several long sheets of paper.

Each of them had a gold seal, which looked very official to Gus. A word starting with the letter "G" was at the top of each page.

"Beg your pardon, Mr. White," Gus said, and rose. He went to Mary's room, where the teenager was sitting at a small desk doing her math homework. She was not yet in her pajamas, and so Gus did not hesitate to ask her to come out into the living room.

Agent White frowned as the girl entered the room.

Gus picked up the documents from the couch and handed them to his daughter. He asked her what the word starting with "G" was.

" 'Guarantee,' Poppa." She was studying the papers, flipping through them, making a face. "This paper says something about cemetery lots. Are you buying cemetery lots?"

"Dumpling ..."

"Why are you buying cemetery lots, Poppa?"

Agent White rose and gently snatched the documents from the girl's hands.

He said to her, "Excuse me, but you have to be careful with these." He smiled apologetically at Gus. "They're for your protection, remember. You've got to give them back to me when we pay you your money. If you start reading them, you'll get them dirty. They're no good if you get fingerprint marks all over them."

Mary looked at the G-man with narrowed eyes and smirked and said, "Poppa ..."

"Go to bed, Mary."

She sighed. "Okay, Poppa. G'night."

"Good night, dumpling. And thank you for your help."

But she was gone.

"She's a bright girl," Agent White said, as Gus sat back down.

"She's going to finish high school," he said.

"Maybe college," Agent White said. "You can consider that when you get your savings back."

"That is true."

Agent White poured Gus another drink and toasted the girl's future.

"You need to hand over that passbook," the G-man said, "and we can send it in to Washington and get everything fixed up."

Gus was shaking his head. "I don't need a lot of graves. What would I do with them?"

Agent White laughed, softly. "Why, you don't understand, Mr. Kulovic. We're not selling you any cemetery lots. We just want you to be protected while we're getting your three thousand dollars for you. These lots are a surety bond."

Gus nodded, slowly. "They're just . . . security."

"Right. Exactly. All you have to do is hold onto this security and give it back to me when I bring you your money."

"I would like my money. I need it."

"Of course you would. And you should have it. Uncle Sam wants you to have it."

Gus thought of Marija, sewing in the bedroom. He said, "Can I see your badge again?"

"Why, certainly, Mr. Kulovic.

The badge was a polished gold and seemed very, very official to Gus.

Satisfied, he handed it back to the agent.

Agent White leaned close, conspiratorially, and said, "What I'm about to tell you is strictly confidential. You must turn that passbook over to us, immediately if not sooner. Your building and loan society is on shaky ground. It might have to close up. We can't help you, once it's shut down."

"You can't?"

"That's the one limitation of our agency. We can only sign up distressed passbook holders while they're part of an active savings and loan."

Gus had a sinking feeling, amid all that whiskey. "What if they go under tomorrow?"

White smiled tightly, reassuringly. "Once you've turned your passbook over to me, and we've signed these documents, you're safe."

Gus finished his latest glass of whiskey.

"This is a wonderful country," Gus said, "America."

"Uncle Sam cares about you," Agent White said. "That's the God's honest truth."

Gus sighed, smiled. He glanced at the large Christmas tree with its fancy electric lights.

"*Vesele Vianoce,*" *Gus said.*

Agent White didn't understand.

"Christmas come early this year," Gus said.

Then he went and got his passbook and gave it to Agent White.

Who agreed with Gus about Christmas coming early.

CHAPTER 5

The Central Police Station at Twenty-first and Payne, in a West Side industrial district, was a four-story sandstone fortress nearly as gray as the bitter-cold overcast morning, a box with walls five feet deep. The ornate bronze trim of the building did not make it any less forbidding.

Eliot Ness pulled his city vehicle, the black Ford sedan the Mayor had promised, up the ramp next to the massive building and left the car in the elevated parking lot there. He glanced up. On the fourth floor the windows were barred—jail facility. Just the holding tanks, actually. The gray stone wedding cake of a building just down the street, the Cuyahoga County Criminal Courts Building, housed the county jail, considered one of the most modern jails in the States. An underground tunnel, which Ness had traversed more than once, connected the two buildings.

And the two buildings, police headquarters and the court/jail facility, were impressive structures, to say the least. Effective civic symbols of the law at work. It struck Ness as more than a little ironic that they served such a corrupt, broken-down, out-of-date police department.

He walked up the steps between the globes on twin poles at the Twenty-first Street entrance. Once past the small vestibule, he was in a narrow hall with a curved one-story ceiling, yellow plaster walls, and slate floor. Cops, both in uniform and plainclothes, were sleep-walking the tunnel-like hall, with about as much spring in their step as a Hooverville mattress. No one recognized the city's new safety director. Ness had a hunch it wouldn't have mattered if they had.

The chief's office was on the left just down the hall and Ness stepped inside, took off his hat, smiled at the pleasant, middle-aged receptionist and said, "Eliot Ness to see Chief Matowitz."

She looked up with a bland smile, blinking behind glasses. "Do you have an appointment . . . did you say 'Ness'?"

"Yes, I did."

Her smile turned nervous, and she said, "Excuse me a moment," and moving in a birdlike manner she went into the inner office, briefly.

Soon Ness was ushered into the wood and pebbled-glass office, which was similar to his own at City Hall but slightly smaller, where the beefy, six-foot, fifty-three-year-old Chief of Police stood watering the pots of plants and flowers that lined the inside of a frosted windowsill.

"Mr. Ness, I'm flattered that you've dropped by." The chief set his watering can on the edge of a polished mahogany desk uncluttered by work and came around to extend his hand for Ness to shake, which he did. The hand was moist, from the watering can, not from sweat. In one corner was a birdcage on a stand, where a parakeet chirped.

Chief Matowitz had a broad, lumpy, friendly face and blue eyes that seemed distant behind his wire-framed glasses. He was wearing his chief's cap, a lighter blue than his crisp uniform with its gleaming silver badge, dark blue tie, and red lapel flower.

"I had a call from Mayor Burton first thing this morning," the chief said, pulling up a chair opposite his desk for Ness, "and was assured that my position is secure. I was relieved to hear that."

"You've put in thirty-one years of service to the department," Ness said, sitting, unbuttoning his topcoat but leaving it on. "That's nothing to sneeze at."

"I want you to know," the other man said, resuming the watering of his potted plants and flowers, "that I'm behind you one hundred per cent. Whatever it takes. Don't hesitate to call on me."

"That's good to hear."

"There's a lot of fine boys in our department. You hear a lot of scuttlebutt to the contrary, but don't you believe it. Why, I can quote you chapter and verse, comparing statistics of crime figures in other cities of similar size to our fine city, and you'll see our department is doing a top-notch job." His voice was shaking with emotion, or seemed to be, as he added, "The Cleveland Police Department is the finest in the world. I'm proud of my boys."

Ness shifted in his chair, his irritation barely in check. "Chief, we have one of the worst departments in the world. And rooting out the corruption that makes it that way is my top priority."

The chief balled his free hand and shook the fist and did his best to look determined. "And well it should be. Those rotten apples can spoil the whole barrel."

Ness sighed and cleared his throat. "I feel we should discuss the situation."

"So do I," Matowitz said forcefully. "So do I." He placed the watering can on a window sill and moved to the para-keet's cage, where he began feeding the bird bread crumbs.

"Do you have any ideas, Chief?"

The chief turned momentarily away from his chirping bird to look at Ness blankly. "Ideas?"

"I thought you might have some suggestions on where our investigation might begin."

"What investigation is that?"

"Into our corrupt goddamn department."

The chief's face took on a thoughtful look. "Let me get back to you on that. I'd like to check with my staff on that one."

Ness shifted in his seat again. This guy was driving him batty. "Chief, I'm going to be moving very fast. You're going to have to play some heads-up ball, here."

Matowitz moved away from the bird cage. He walked behind the desk and sat. Ness was not sure whether the chief's plant-watering and bird-feeding reflected a lack of concern, or masked his nervousness. Or maybe the guy just wasn't playing with a full deck.

"I have heard bad things about the fourteenth and fifteenth precincts," the chief admitted, twiddling his thumbs. "Rumors, mainly. The Detective Bureau hasn't been able to confirm anything."

"The Detective Bureau is something I wanted to discuss with you."

"Oh?"

"Chief of Detectives Potter strikes me as a problem."

The chief's expression turned grave. "Inspector Potter has many friends, Mr. Ness."

"Friends in the Davis administration. Not Burton's."

"He's still a powerful man ..."

"I'm not surprised. The word I heard back at the Alcohol and Tax Unit was that Potter is the guy to see if you want your gambling resort or bookie joint protected."

"That's a serious allegation."

"And I don't intend to make it, not publicly."

"You don't?"

"No. Not yet, anyway. I'm going to transfer Potter. Maybe even promote him. But he's not going to head up our Detective Bureau anymore."

Ness knew that Potter had been running the show in the department during the two years of Mayor Davis' feckless administration, and that Matowitz, a holdover from an earlier regime, had been more or less a figure-head.

"You could run into trouble, Mr. Ness," the chief said. "The former mayor is still a powerful figure politically."

"I know. I know all about the free-for-all that the city council's going to turn into. And I don't really care."

Matowitz's expression darkened. He seemed to be taking Ness more seriously now, and, if nothing else, had stopped twiddling his thumbs. "If I might say so, this is nothing to take lightly, Mr. Ness."

"Chief, I'm not a political appointee. I'm beholden to nobody, except Mayor Burton, and he only got me to take this job by promising me a free hand. So we're going to shake things up, understood?"

The chief didn't seem to, but he said, "Understood."

Ness sighed. He didn't dare mention Burton's ticking clock. If Matowitz got wind of the fragility of Ness' position, then the chief could lean back and do nothing except water his plants and feed his birds and wait for Ness to fail.

Ness tried again, a different tack. "I looked over your record this morning before coming over. It's impressive. Impressive as hell."

That threw Matowitz a little. He almost mumbled his thanks.

"You're a good cop," Ness said. "And, I think, a clean one."

The chief said, tersely, "No one has ever suggested that George Matowitz was on the pad."

"You have one of the most distinguished records of any detective in the city," Ness went on. "Perhaps the country. You were dogged in your work, chasing killers to Mexico, and to Sicily. Hoodlums feared you. You were a boxer and a wrestler and you put those skills to use on the street."

Ness stopped there. He could see in the older man's sagging face that he'd made his point, that the chief had discerned the unasked question: *how could a hard-nosed, first-rate cop like you turn into an ineffectual, incompetent chair-holder?* This man had, after all, been a cop for almost as long as Ness had been alive. Would time do that to him, too? Did years inevitably put the fire out?

And the chief answered the unasked questions. He smiled, but there was sadness in the smile, and his hands were folded in a dignified manner as he said, "You're a young man, Mr. Ness. You're going places. When you get there, you will be better fit to judge."

"I didn't mean to sit in judgment."

"You're new to the city, Mr. Ness. I've been here a long time. Since I was six, since my father brought us over from Hummeno, in Austria-Hungary."

His parakeet was chirping in the corner. The eyes behind the glasses grew even more distant, though they seemed to smile. "I remember Hummeno. Especially the orchard next door, and the fields where poppies grew." The eyes stopped smiling. "Cleveland wasn't as pretty. I remember selling shoes on Public Square and selling papers in front of May's Drugstore. There were a lot of fistfights, so I could maintain my . . . economic integrity. They called me 'greenhorn,' and I guess I was, but I took care of myself. It was a continual scrap for existence, your veritable survival of the fittest. But I made it. I learned to speak English. Do you hear an accent, Mr. Ness?"

Ness shook his head.

"I went to school, and I was good at my studies. I was a janitor, and an errand boy, a grocery delivery boy, finally a streetcar conductor, coming up in the world.

Then I got into the police department, and I started going to night school. I guess I had about every job in the department—sub-patrolman, sergeant, lieutenant, captain, inspector, acting chief, director of Police Training School, Detective Bureau chief—and I was the first officer in charge of Cleveland's mounted troops. I took a civil service exam for every rank and no one, no one, ever beat me out in an examination." He was shaking a lecturing finger now. "I kept taking night school, too, Mr. Ness. It took me twenty years, but I passed my bar exam a few years ago—1928 to be exact. And in 1931 became chief. Chief of Police of a great city."

"You're to be congratulated," Ness said, meaning it. "You made the American dream come true. And worked hard to do it."

A firm jaw jutted out of a face long since gone soft. "That's right. I worked hard to get where I am. I would like to stay where I am."

"And rocking the boat isn't a good way to do that."

"That is quite right. I don't wish to rock the boat. I merely want to do my job."

Ness laughed shortly. "That's a coincidence. I merely want you to do your job, too."

Behind the wire frames, the eyes tightened. "Are you suggesting, sir, that I'm not?"

"I'm suggesting nothing. I don't give a damn about yesterday. How you chose to stay afloat while the Davis administration was in power is between you and your conscience. But I'm putting you on notice today: following the path of least resistance is not going to help you hold onto your job. I'm your boss, and I say the boat needs rocking. And you, Chief Matowitz, are going to help me rock it or you'll find out how easy it is to drown on dry land."

The chief thought about that.

Then he began to nod, slowly. "Where do we begin?"

Good, Ness thought.

He said, "We cut out the politics and graft and favoritism, where promotions are concerned. Here on out, the only qualification for promotion will be ability and performance. Seniority be damned."

"All due respect, Mr. Ness, that will go over like a lead balloon."

"Well, start pumping it up with hot air then, Chief." From what he'd heard today, Ness figured hot air was something Matowitz wasn't short of. "What a man does— not how long he's been on the city payroll, or who he knows—is going to be the basis for advancement in this department."

"Inspector Potter ..."

"Let me worry about Potter. Good God, man, wouldn't you like to get out from under that bastard's thumb?"

The chief swallowed. Then he half smiled, like a kid caught in a lie, and nodded. "I would."

Ness pointed a finger at Matowitz. "What would you do, what's the first thing you'd do, if you didn't have to worry about that bastard Potter?"

The chief shrugged, then his expression darkened again. "I guess I'd break up that little political clique they got going over in the Detective Bureau. Do you know what kind of salaries they're pulling down?"

"Best pay in town," Ness nodded. "Better than a uniformed captain."

"What if I wanted to transfer some of those guys out

of there?"

"You're the chief. Do it."

"You think I could?"

"I think that it would be a hell of an idea. I was going to suggest we transfer lieutenants and sergeants all over town, in every precinct."

The chiefs eyes got very wide and he looked as if the wind had been knocked out of him. Then he managed to say, "You're talking about hundreds of cops."

"That's right. And it would upset hundreds of apple-carts. The kind that have those rotten apples you were talking about."

"That would mean the bent cops would be uprooted. They'd have to start all over in a new precinct."

"Only we won't give them a chance. What do you say, Chief?"

Suddenly Chief Matowitz seemed very businesslike. His mouth was a thin straight line that barely opened for him to say, "Give me till tomorrow morning. I'll have the transfers ready for you to sign."

Ness smiled and nodded and rose. He buttoned up his topcoat and put on his hat. The parakeet was really making a racket.

"I think your bird is hungry," Ness said, just before he went out.

The chief was standing at a wooden file cabinet, digging some folders out, which he tossed on the polished desk top, finally cluttering it with some work.

"He can wait," the chief said.

CHAPTER 6

Reporter Sam Wild of the *Plain Dealer* had spent the morning at the Central Police Station gathering reactions from cops about the Ness appointment. Those reactions were pretty much as he expected: indifferent as dish water. "Wish him luck. He'll need it." "Sure, we'll cooperate. Why not?" Cleveland cops had seen safety directors come and safety directors go, but things usually didn't change much under the surface. Most safety directors didn't seem to mean anything to cops. Just a different name painted on the same old door.

So Wild was pleasantly surprised, in the tunnel-like first-floor headquarters hallway, to bump into Ness himself.

"Well, Mister Director of Public Safety," Wild said, grinning. "Bearding the lions in their den, I see."

Ness stopped and smiled faintly, as both uniformed and plainclothes cops walked by in either direction, none of them paying him any heed.

Walking again, Ness said, "Just had a little chat with the Chief of Police."

Wild smirked. "What'd he do, tell you about his brave 'boys' and his flowers and his birdie?"

"No," Ness said.

The safety director was walking quickly. Even a long-legged guy like Wild had to work to keep up.

"Give us a break, here," Wild said. "How about a quote?"

"Too early," Ness said.

"I thought sure you'd have a press conference this morning."

Ness kept walking. "I told you boys last night, I'd take action first, and talk later."

"Yeah, yeah. That made a swell quote, but that's yesterday's news. Newspapermen got to eat every day, you know."

Ness stopped again. "Would you excuse me, Mr. Wild?"

"Well, sure."

And then Wild realized why Ness had stopped.

Inspector Emil Potter, Chief of the Detective Bureau, had just come in the Twenty-first Street entry, toward which Ness and Wild had been so briskly moving.

Potter was a man in his mid-forties with black hair and shaggy black eyebrows and a Dracula-pasty face. Nonetheless, he had a hearty, hail-fellow-well-met manner. He was about five nine but broad-shouldered, and looked like he could change a tire without a jack. His hat was in his hand and his dark gray topcoat flapped as he walked. When he saw Ness, the skin around his eyes tightened.

The two men faced each other. Wild stood just to one side of Ness, taking it in.

"Good morning, Director Ness," Potter said, with a smile that struck Wild as about as sincere as a street-walker's come-on. "This is the first chance I've had to congratulate you on your appointment."

Potter reached out a big hand, which Ness took, smiling back with similar insincerity.

"Much appreciated, Inspector. I left a message for you with your secretary."

"Oh?"

"Yes. I'd like to speak with you this afternoon at three o'clock."

Potter made a *tch-tch* sound. "Sorry. I have a meeting with my sergeants at two-thirty. Why not stop down to my office now, and we can chat?"

Ness checked his watch. "That's white of you, but I have an appointment at eleven with Traffic Commissioner Donahue about these record traffic fatalities we've been racking up."

Potter nodded. "That is a major problem."

Ness smiled blandly. "Good. You may be able to help me out in that area."

Potter, not following this, shrugged and said, "Anything I can do, Director."

"You can start by being at my office at three o'clock."

Potter's eyes narrowed, the shaggy eyebrows twitching. "I thought I'd explained . . . my meeting ..."

"Cancel it. See you at three."

And Ness tipped his hat and moved on.

Potter stood there glaring at Ness, but Ness didn't see. Wild did, but quickly picked up his step and fell in with Ness.

"Nice piece of work," Wild said.

"How's that?"

"You're makin' Potter meet with you on your turf, not his."

Ness' smile was barely perceptible. He offered no other answer. They passed through the vestibule and out into the cold air.

Wild followed Ness down the steps, their breaths billowing like smokestacks.

"Headed back to City Hall?" Wild asked, digging his gloveless hands in his topcoat pockets.

"That's right."

"How about giving me a lift?"

"How about taking a streetcar?"

"Give me a break, Ness. I gave you one."

Ness stopped and looked at Wild, his expression impassive. "Really?"

"Yeah, I put in the good word for you. I was the first guy who mentioned you to Burton."

Ness dug under his topcoat in his pants pocket. "Let me see if I have a dime for your streetcar fare."

"Hey, City Hall's my beat. Give me a lift, for Christ's sake. I'm freezing my ass off out here."

Ness studied him, sucked in a long cold breath and let it smoke out. "Okay. But no press conference."

Wild shook his head, waved his hands. "Anything you say is off the record."

Ness thrust a gunlike pointing finger at him. "I'll hold you to that."

They walked up the cement ramp to the black Ford in the elevated parking lot. Ness had left the car unlocked and Wild climbed on in.

Wild sat and watched Ness, who was starting the car up. "What are you going to do to Potter?"

Ness looked at Wild carefully. "Off the record?"

"Yeah, yeah. Off the record."

Ness looked in his rear view mirror as he began backing up the Ford. "I'm going to promote him."

The sedan rolled out onto the brick street in front of Central Headquarters, turning left on Twenty-first. They rumbled along, turning left on Superior, as Wild continued to grill Ness.

"Why are you promoting Potter?" Wild asked. "He was Mayor Davis' boy, so he's no pal of your boss."

Ness drove casually, one hand on the wheel. "Wait and see."

"Why do I get the feeling you're going to take on the

whole goddamn police force?"

Ness glanced at him, smiled again, very slightly. "I'm planning to take on the Mayfield Road mob. That's who I'm planning to take on."

Wild laughed hollowly. "The Mayfield Road mob. You make it sound ominous."

"Isn't it?"

"They're just a bunch of savvy wops giving the public what it wants."

"Is that right?" Ness' voice was as flat as stale beer.

"Hell, every city has its version of the Mayfield mob."

Ness stopped for a red light and gave Wild a hard, cool look. "And every city has its version of a police force. My version isn't going to look the other way where gambling's concerned." He turned his gaze on the red light. "The Mayfield Road mob has been raking in some two hundred thousand dollars a week on gambling. The numbers racket alone is pulling in better than half that amount."

Wild shrugged. "Times are hard, Mr. Ness. Isn't the numbers game a harmless enough way for the average Joe to dream about hitting it big?"

The light changed and Ness moved through the intersection, the bricks beneath the Ford's tires making a steady hum. The heater in the car was going.

"I don't much care whether gambling's right or wrong," Ness said with a small shrug, his eyes on the road. "Matter of fact, I like to gamble—or I wouldn't take on a job like this. I'm no reformer. I'm a cop."

Wild shook his head. "The Mayfield mob is just the Italian branch of the Cleveland Syndicate. It's the Jews and the micks who are the real power—Horvitz, McBride, McGinty, Rothkopf, Kleinman—"

"Kleinman's in jail."

Ness was making a point, Wild realized. It was Ness' squad of "revenooers" who had sent Kleinman away.

"He'll be out soon enough," Wild countered. "Anyway, you'll never nail the likes of Mo Horvitz."

"You may be right," Ness admitted. "Horvitz and some of the other big boys are moving into legitimate business. But the Mayfield Road group isn't. And they aren't just 'wops.' "

Wild looked over, with a nasty smile. "You refer, of course, to policy guys like Frank Hogey, and gamblers like 'Shimmy' Patton and 'Gameboy' Miller."

Ness nodded, eyes on the road.

"Hogey's fair game, I suppose," Wild said. "But he's got police protection up the wazoo. And Patton and Miller are operating outside the city limits. How do you expect to do anything about them?"

"Not all their operations are outside my jurisdiction," Ness said, matter-of-factly. "And the ones that are—the Harvard Club, the Thomas Club, in particular—I'm siccing Cullitan on."

"The County Prosecutor? He isn't even a Republican!"

"No, he's just a good prosecutor. And isn't that a novelty?"

Wild laughed with quiet sarcasm. "So Patton and Miller and the gang move from bootlegging to gambling, and you follow along right after 'em."

Ness glanced sharply over. "That's right. Because gambling on this scale brings the likes of the Mayfield mob into financial power, and with financial power like that they can *own* a safety department. They can own the courts. You end up with cops on the beat and captains in the precinct house that don't know what laws to enforce, what persons they dare to arrest. Since a cop moving up in rank depends on not making mistakes, he can get cautious and complacent and pretty soon you have a city where criminals get away with murder, literally, while cops sit with zipped lips, twiddling their thumbs, trying not to step on any toes."

"Like Chief Matowitz, you mean."

"I didn't say that."

"Do you deny it?"

"If we were on the record I would."

"Why don't you go on the record with me, then? I think my readers would be interested in your views."

"When I have something to say, I'll say it."

"For a guy with nothing to say, you've been pretty talkative."

"For a reporter off the record, you ask a lot of questions."

Wild shrugged, grinned. "I'm just a curious sort of guy. You remember me from Chicago."

Ness grinned back. "Sure I do. You were a pal of Jake Lingle's."

Ness was referring to the notorious murdered newsman who after a brief period of martyrdom proved to have been in Capone's pocket, a major scandal for the Chicago newspaper world a few years back.

"I knew Jake," Wild said, trying not to sound defensive. "That doesn't make me a crook."

"It doesn't make you an archbishop, either."

"Don't look a gift horse in the mouth. I can give you some leads now and then."

"I'll appreciate that. I can tell just looking at you you're a public-spirited citizen."

"Banana oil. Aren't you wise to who you're chauffeuring around? Simply the best police reporter in town."

"Why, is Clayton Fritchey riding the running board?"

"Very funny. But I got a good memory, too. I remember Chicago myself. For instance, how you liked seeing your name in print, especially when it was in headlines. 'Eliot Press,' we used to call you."

That only seemed to amuse Ness. "Really," he said archly.

"Yeah." Wild jerked a thumb at his chest. "Treat me right and I'll treat you right. You can't afford to be on the bad side of the fourth estate. You ain't political. So you'll rise or fall on your press clippings."

Ness said nothing, but he did throw a sideways glance at Wild, and smiled a little himself.

"You know I'm right," Wild said. "Burton brought you in for publicity value: 'Former G-Man Appointed Safety Director.' The public eats up this G-Man shit with a spoon."

Ness smiled wryly, a secret lurking in his steel-gray eyes that Wild wished he could get at.

"I'll grant you part of my job is a cosmetic one," Ness admitted. "But right now I have to stay off the record for two reasons: I don't want to alienate the rest of the press; and I haven't had a chance to do anything yet. Give me a chance to get the lay of the land, for Christ's sake."

"That's fair enough, I guess. At least you aren't pretending you weren't hired for your press value."

"I was hired," Ness said, "to make the new administration, the reformers, look like they're getting something done. I'm helping 'em keep their campaign promises."

"Just like Chicago," Wild said, nodding. "You had to show the public that gangsters in the Windy City weren't immune from some good old-fashioned law and order. That there were a few cops in the world that couldn't be bought. And you pulled that off, while the tax boys did the less flashy work that really put ol' Scar face away."

Ness nodded.

Wild went on: "But I don't think you're very likely to have such luck with the Mayfield mob, frankly. And if you plan on cleaning up the police force, you'll need a broom bigger than God's."

Ness was driving with both hands on the wheel now,

turning right on Sixth. He didn't look at Wild as he asked, "If you think I'll be a washout, why come along for the ride?"

"It'll be fun seeing you try to do the impossible," Wild said good-naturedly. "There'll be some dandy headlines in it for both of us, while you do."

"You seem pretty convinced I'll fall flat on my face."

"Or thereabouts." Wild shook his head. "I just don't think you know what you're up against."

"Care to enlighten me?"

"Sure. Why not." Wild smiled tightly, smugly. "Ever hear of the 'outside chief?' "

Ness said nothing for a moment, the car humming along. Then: "No."

"The 'inside' chief,' of course, is Matowitz. The chief within the department. Inside the system."

"You're not suggesting Matowitz is corrupt."

"Hardly. He put those blinders on all by himself. Nobody paid him to. Matowitz isn't the point."

"Well, get to the point."

Wild shrugged with one shoulder. "It's just a rumor."

"A rumor."

"A rumor. Backroom talk. To the effect that a very high-ranking police official is on the pad."

This time Ness shrugged. "That would be no surprise on a department as ... troubled ... as this one."

"Don't worry," Wild smirked. "We're still off the record. If you want to call the department 'corrupt,' be my guest. I won't repeat it in print."

"Make your point."

"The point, simply, is this high-ranking cop is said to be the 'outside chief.' The chief of the 'department within the department.' "

Ness' eyes tightened. "The department within the department, huh?"

Wild smiled patiently, as if teaching a child. "The crooked cops know each other. They protect each other. They're a department within, and yet outside of, the department. And their 'chief—whoever he is—directs things, makes assignments, passes the graft around even-handedly and keeps everything and everybody in line. So rumor has it."

"I see."

"Are you sure you haven't heard this rumor before?"

"Not in such detail. Never that there was a so-called 'outside chief.' "

Wild lifted his eyebrows, set them down. "It's just a rumor. I wouldn't print it in the paper."

"I understand," Ness nodded. "Thanks, Wild."

"And their ties to the Mayfield Road mob are, well, obvious."

"That much I knew."

"I figured you had to know something. Now. What are you going to do for me?"

Ness thought for a moment, then, eyes still on the road, said, casually, "I'm going along with a squad of cops on a betting-joint raid tomorrow. How would you like to be the only reporter along for the ride?"

"It beats a streetcar all to hell," Wild grinned.

"I ask only that you don't make a sap out of me," Ness cautioned. "I'm just tagging along to check out their procedure. See if the raid goes off without a hitch."

"Or whether somebody tips off the place," Wild said, nodding.

"Right. It won't make a big story for you, but it'll be a start. Anyway, just stick around. Be patient. There's going to be plenty of dandy headlines for you in the next couple of months. I can just about promise you that. Now, here's City Hall."

CHAPTER 7

—

Eliot Ness had never really seen a fire before.

That is, not a fire in the sense of a burning building, like this modest, run-down two-story frame house that was managing somehow to retain its structure while the inside of it burned, the flames having eaten away much of the roof to lick the night sky. Now that the fire was more or less under control, the flames no longer rose from the top of the house. Instead, a strangely white column of smoke climbed into the overcast sky to make it even more cloudy, while flames twitched in the otherwise dark and broken windows of the house, like the flickering within the eyes of a jack o' lantern.

Ness had been here almost from the beginning. He'd even pitched in with getting the old people out of the house and onto the cold street. Many of them were in robes and even pajamas but neighbors had come out bearing heavy coats to help the shivering, bewildered old folks; some of them were barefoot, and neighbors rustled up shoes and slippers for impromptu footwear. Most of these now-homeless elderly were wheezing from the smoke, several were crying, and a few vomited onto the frozen ground.

Two were dead. Two old men who'd shared a room in the back of the house, on the ground floor, where the fire had started. Incinerated. Their bodies, the charred logs that had been their bodies, were removed by firemen who'd carried them out of the steaming, smoking building, cradled in their arms like black babies, to be deposited in asbestos-lined wicker baskets, and put in the back of a Black Maria, bound for the morgue.

It had shaken Ness. A fire striking one small building—a dilapidated house passing as a refuge for the aged, just another shabby frame house on the East Side, in a working-class, mostly Slovak neighborhood—made for a full-scale disaster.

Especially in Cleveland, where the fire department was using equipment that was modern only in the sense that horses weren't pulling it. Ness had taken the safety director's job because of its relationship to the police department, to law enforcement. He had not, frankly, given the fire department much thought.

Thus far he'd had only one brief meeting, on Thursday morning, with Fire Chief Grainger. All else had been police matters. The mayor's two-month ticking clock made that the top priority. This included dealing with Potter, who'd seethed silently at the news of his "promotion," and the betting-parlor raid, on which he'd allowed Wild to come, where as expected someone had phoned in a tip-off, queering the bust.

Tonight, Friday, he was learning that the fire department was just as troubled as the police. Corruption wasn't the problem. The men Ness had seen tonight did their jobs bravely and relatively well. However, he'd also seen fire hoses with low pressure due to leakage, patched hoses that wouldn't fit hydrants without some imaginative jury-rigging, and a hook-

and-ladder truck so decrepit that it arrived after the two police squads and the pumper truck and the ambulance.

Ness had been on his way home this Friday night, after a long afternoon of meetings with various commissioners and department heads, when he heard on his one-way police radio the call go out for police backup on a fire at an old folks' home at 933 East Seventy-eighth Street. It seemed like a good opportunity to check out the fire department in action. It was already ten o'clock, and he had a brief thought of Eva waiting for him well into the evening, but he dismissed it.

He had pulled up in the Ford and leaped out and pitched in, helping those old people out the front door. The frame house was distinguishable from its neighbors only by its state of dilapidation, a small sign saying JOANNA HOME that hung from the roof over the porch and, of course, the fact that it was very much on fire.

"I'm the safety director," Ness had snapped at the team of three firemen who were trying, with little success, to get the pumper truck in operation.

"Where the hell's your hook-and-ladder?"

They looked at him and shrugged, in unison, and went back to their work. It would have been amusing, if the air hadn't been filled with the crying and coughing and rasping and puking of the dozen or more old people, trooping out of the house like refugees, aided by fire fighters and neighbors.

The hook-and-ladder arrived minutes later, and Ness identified himself to the battalion chief who rode on board, a middle-aged potbellied Irishman with a nose as red as the fire.

"Where the hell have you been, Chief?"

"Director Ness, I'm sorry—but you can only get to a fire so fast when your truck's so old it can only climb hills in reverse gear. Now if you'll be excusing me, sir, I have a fire to put out."

Ness had no answer to that, and when he got a look at the ancient, rusted-out hook-and-ladder, he could only sympathize.

The fire fighters did a good job, considering. They began by quickly, thoroughly wetting down the houses on either side of the burning one. The street was filled with curious neighbors, including those who'd fled the homes bordering the Joanna, and the two police squad cars, which Ness had beat to the scene by several minutes, another fact that didn't sit well with him, began crowd control procedures, keeping them back on the other side of the street. The front of the house became a wall of ice as water from the hoses froze on contact. The whole scene was a nightmare of hot and cold, fire and ice.

"These goddamn winter fires are the worst," one soot-rouged fireman told Ness, in a panting, hoarse voice.

Ness understood. He had watched the frustrated fire fighters, kneeling over the frozen-up hydrants, using blow torches to melt them down—fighting fire with fire.

One group of firemen was in the house, while another group climbed ladders, smashing out upper windows, having already done so on the first floor. They seemed somewhat scattered in their efforts, with many of the younger men frantically asking older ones what to do next. The battalion chief to whom Ness had spoken seemed to be the only one with authority, and he was busy directing the outside hoses.

The fire fighters had decided the building was now empty. A fortyish, rail-thin woman was in charge, but it had not yet been pinned down if she was the owner or not. Mrs. Winters proved to be as cold as her name.

"This'll cost me a pretty penny," she disgustedly told Ness, who had inquired after the old people, getting from the gray-robed woman an exact count of the number of "patients" at the home.

"If you're thinking of repairing this place," Ness said, "I wouldn't count on it."

Her witch's face contorted. "You think the damage is going to be that bad?"

"I think your 'home' is an obvious fire trap and you're out of business."

She scowled and moved away, disappearing into the crowd of neighbors.

The Salvation Army contingent showed up in a beat-up truck and an old flivver. From the truck the uniformed men and women began dispensing doughnuts and coffee to the elderly victims, and using the flivver to shuttle them to a nearby hospital. It disturbed Ness to see that the Salvation Army was better organized and more efficient than either of the public departments under his command.

Chief Grainger showed up when the fire was well under control, a second hook-and-ladder and another truck already on the scene. A sturdy blue-eyed, white-haired man of fifty-five, Grainger was in full uniform and looked pretty spiffy. Ness wished the department had a single fire truck that looked so fit for duty.

"My men have got things in hand, I see," the Chief said proudly as he approached Ness, where he stood in the middle of the street watching the fire.

"They do," Ness admitted. "On the other hand, I think the neighbors putting together a bucket brigade might have done about as well."

The two men were bathed in the shadowy flickering of smoke and flames from across the way.

Chief Grainger bristled, but kept his tone respectful as he said: "My men are dedicated public servants, Director Ness."

"I know they are. I'd like to see what they could do with equipment manufactured after the turn of the century."

Grainger shrugged, and smiled humorlessly. "We do what we can with what we're given."

Despite the truth of that, it struck Ness that Grainger was copping out. "It's going to take more than new equipment to overhaul *this* fire department, Chief. I've seen less than a crack team at work here tonight. More training is obviously needed. I may not be an expert about firefighting, but I know that much."

"Training takes money, too," Grainger said.

"Agreed," Ness said tersely. "And I want your detailed budget request as soon as possible. Make that part of it."

"First thing Monday soon enough?" Grainger asked.

"That would be helpful."

"You think we'll get what we ask for?"

"We'll know in a couple of months, won't we?"

The Chief nodded glumly and tipped his cap to the safety director as he left to join his men, not pitching in, just observing and cheering them on.

Ness checked his watch. It was almost midnight and he hadn't even called Eva. Damn.

He was heading for his car when the mayor's limousine pulled up, sliding a little on the glassy street, iced over from the fire fighters' hoses. His Honor, dressed in a tux, an expensive gray topcoat draped over his shoulders, stepped out of the back seat, as the police driver held the door open. Mrs. Burton remained in the car, a vague shape in a white stole. The crowd of neighbors began smiling and chattering; a few hollered hellos to the mayor, and he smiled tightly and waved back at them.

"I was on my way home from a banquet at the Hollenden," Burton explained to Ness. The mayor, in white tie and tails, was an incongruous figure in this neighborhood, standing in an ice-slick street before the burning ramshackle frame house. "I heard an old-age home had caught fire. I thought I should check it out ..."

Just yesterday Ness had ordered a police radio installed in the mayor's car, at His Honor's request. He had also presented Burton with a gold Safety Department badge, which had pleased the mayor, who seemed to have a child-like enthusiasm for cops-and-robbers stuff.

"Fire's under control," Ness said.

"Fatalities?"

"Two," Ness said, and gave particulars, as many as he knew, anyway. "And thirteen more inhaled a lot of smoke. The Salvation Army's helping us get them to Mount Sinai and Glenville General."

Burton nodded gravely. He looked over at the burning house across the way. "When I heard an old-age home was on fire, I envisioned something else."

"Me, too. I wonder how many of these rattraps are passing for nursing homes."

"We'll have to find out."

"And we will. You know, we have to talk money."

The mayor snorted. "Is there any other subject?"

"The fire department's in sad shape."

Ness began giving details, but Burton interrupted, saying, "Let's get away from the smell of smoke." He gestured down the street, past the thinning crowd of gawking neighbors. "Let's walk and talk.

"You've obviously seen why my overriding concern is getting our budget past the council," the mayor said, as they strolled down the dimly lit streets lined with ramshackle frame houses.

"I can certainly see why we need money for the police department," Ness said. "Money other than the graft some cops are pocketing, that is."

"You've spent the past two days on the prowl, haven't you, Eliot?"

It was the first time Burton had called Ness by his first name.

"I spent most of the afternoon in my office. But yes, I've been out and about. Went on a sorry excuse for a book-ie-joint raid this morning. Toured some of the precincts."

"What have you seen?"

Ness shrugged. "A bunch of sloppy, poorly trained cops who are low in morale, to say the least, some of whom—perhaps many of whom—are so corrupt they make a Chicago cop look like St. Francis of Assisi."

"These are rank-and-file cops you're talking about. Any sign of corruption higher up?"

"Not specifically, but I heard an interesting rumor."

He told Burton about the so-called "outside chief."

"Damn," Burton said, his voice breathy. "If such a man exists, and you could nail him ..."

"You'd have your top-ranking corrupt cop for the pa-pers, and at the same time we'd knock the pins out from under our 'department within the department.' We'd ac-complish something substantial."

Burton had started to smile just thinking about it. "The city council wouldn't dare withhold your budget requests."

"I'd think not. And all I have to do is turn that rumor into a man. And find him, and arrest him, and make it stick."

"And do it by early March," Burton added, the dreamy expression gone.

"Sorry you took this job?"

"No."

"You seem less enthusiastic than you were in my office Wednesday. What do you propose to do at this point?"

Ness stopped. "Well, to do anything much, I need money, now."

Burton's face tightened. "I thought you understood that we don't get any money until you produce."

"I'm not talking about money on a budget level."

"What level, then?"

Ness gestured in frustration. "I need to be able to hire men outside the department. I need to be able to bring people in when I need to."

"Men? People?"

"Investigators. Including private detectives. I know some pretty good operatives. A friend of mine in Chicago might come in handy now and then. I can't get this job done if I have to draw from the police department for my staff."

Burton sighed. "Hardly."

They began to walk again.

"These investigators would mostly work undercover," Ness said. "So we need new faces. They can't be a part of the current system. Oh, sure, I can call on rookies for occasional help—young kids who haven't lost their fire yet, who became cops for some reason other than a pension and/or a chance to tie into some graft."

"But your investigators can't be rookies."

"No. And they may come and go, like I said. I'll only need a handful, but they'll have to be paid."

The Mayor stopped and stood with his arms folded; he rocked on his feet a while and thought. "What if we could come up with something like the Secret Six, in Chicago?"

"Businesspeople, you mean?"

The two men stood in a pool of light under a street lamp.

"Merchants," the Mayor said. "Industrialists. I have friends in the Chamber of Commerce and the American Legion who are good and tired of being shaken down."

Burton had long been associated with the Legion, having been its county chairman.

Ness raised a hand. "They could have no say over my actions."

"None at all." Then, thoughtful, Burton said, "But I think perhaps I could put together a secret fund for your investigators. A slush fund of sorts. Perhaps just to tide us over until we get our budget. Assuming we do, of course. And it wouldn't be bottomless, by any means."

Ness smiled tightly. "Just so I can get my feet wet in it."

Burton's eyes narrowed; he gestured with a gently lecturing forefinger.

"Any investigators you hire will draw a public salary, but they'll be listed on the city's payrolls as laborers. We'll supplement their salaries with money from our new Secret Six."

"That would be just about perfect, Your Honor."

Burton smiled a little. "Don't get your feet wet just yet. Let me see if I can get something like this off the ground, first. You, uh, haven't made Inspector Potter very happy, now, have you?"

"All I did was promote him."

"Interesting promotion."

"I hope you don't mind the way I handled it. If I could've busted him on corruption charges, you'd have had your top-ranking bent cop to feed the press. At this stage, though, all I know for sure about Potter is he plays political games. He'll be investigated, but I had to act sooner than that. I had to get him out from under me, now."

"No, no," the Mayor said, patting the air with his hands. "I wholeheartedly approve. I'm pleased. Even amused."

Ness had put the inspector in charge of a traffic survey designed to study placement of traffic lights, boulevard stop signs and other matters "materially affecting traffic." Stressing the "high priority" of dealing with traffic problems, Ness had announced to the press that the investigation needed to be done "intelligently" and there-fore the "highest technical intelligence" available in the entire department needed to be employed.

Hence, the safety director had relieved Inspector Potter of his duties as chief of the Detective Bureau, and placed him at the head of the survey.

"The papers treated you kindly, where the Potter ouster is concerned," Burton commented.

They began to walk again, heading back.

"They did like it, yes."

"That's the kind of publicity we're looking for. That's the kind that can get me that slush fund you need. That's the kind that can help us get our budget past even an un-willing city council."

Ness stopped again. "You say that as if I've generated some other kind of publicity, as well."

The Mayor stopped, too. "Uh, then, I take it you didn't see the last edition of the *Plain Dealer?*"

"No."

"It's in the car," Burton said. "I'll show you."

They walked quickly to the limo, where Burton got the paper from the front seat and handed it to Ness. A head-line said,

FORMER G-MAN'S
FIRST RAID
A FIZZLE

Under Wild's byline, the article went on: "Director Ness accompanied police in a raid on a barbershop and came up empty-handed. Ness found a man with earphones listening to a radio broadcast of a horse race, but there were no betting slips and no evidence that money was being wagered. The celebrated gangbuster, it would seem, may find Cleveland a tougher nut to crack than Chicago."

"That son of a bitch," Ness said, under his breath. He thrust the paper back at Burton. "That's what I get for trusting a guy who ran with Jake Lingle."

"What is the, uh . . . scoop? If you'll pardon the expression."

"The scoop is, I invited Wild along on this raid as a favor. I didn't organize the raid. I just went along to observe procedure, and see if a department leak would sink the thing. Which it did, of course." He pointed at the newspaper Burton held. "Wild knew that. Playing it like it was my raid that went sour is a cheap damn shot."

"We need good press relations, Eliot. Obviously."

"I'll handle this in my own way."

Burton shrugged. "That is our arrangement."

The fire across the way was still going. Flames licked up in a few windows, but the column of smoke was narrowing.

Ness forgot his departmental problems, for the moment, including that SOB Sam Wild. He looked over at the house, the basic structure of which had somehow survived the fire.

"Two men died in that house tonight," Ness said.

"A shame."

"Sure, it's a shame. But we also have to find out why."

Ness bade the Mayor goodnight and went home to see if his wife was still speaking to him.

CHAPTER 8

When Joe Fusca, alias Special Agent Sidney White, pulled his sporty blue Packard up in front of the paint-peeling, ramshackle two-story clapboard on East Sixty-sixth, he could scarcely believe his eyes. This was hardly a classy neighborhood, sure, but this eyesore was the bottom of the barrel.

The pits.

Hard to believe there was a twelve-grand passbook in a shack like that, ripe for the picking.

It was Monday evening, a little before seven, and Joe was pretty much over it. He'd killed before, in Chicago, but that had been different. That had been mob stuff. You had to prove yourself to those guys if you were going to stay on the in with them. You just didn't say no when they asked a favor.

And it was other mob guys he'd hit, after all. It was in the family.

Friday night had been a whole 'nother deal. It had given him the willies, doing that. It was creepy, it was dangerous, and, anyway, the two old guys he bumped off were just looking out after their own best interests. Which was more than you could say for most of the bazoos on his sucker list.

Most of these lilies were so ripe for plucking it was almost
a duty to get there and do the job before somebody beat
you to it. People that stupid didn't deserve money. People
who saved money for a rainy day when they were in the
middle of a goddamn downpour simply had to be relieved
of the burden of their dough.

But those two old birds at the Joanna Home, Great
War veterans both, had tumbled to the scam. The way it
was set up, promising the money within sixty days, was
supposed to give the salesmen like Joe that long to fully
work a neighborhood, and move on. Only those two old
boys had got talking between themselves, after turning
their passbooks—one for $5600 and another for $3200—
over to "Agent White." They took a streetcar down to the
Hanna Building where the Memorial Developers, Inc.,
office was located, just a boiler shop, really, and started
complaining. They were talking about going to the county
prosecutor, and the boiler-shop boys calmed them down
and said Agent White would do a follow-up call.

Agent White had. It had been his own idea to handle
it the way he had, but he'd heard no complaints from upstairs. He knew the lights went out at the Joanna Home
around nine, and he slipped in the back door a little before
ten. The geezers in question shared a room in back, and
they were both asleep in the darkness. Joe didn't even know
which one was which, as he crushed the skull of first one,
and then the other, with a sash weight. He splashed them
down with kerosene, a can of which he'd lugged in with
him, and splashed some more on the walls, particularly
around a light switch and a couple of electrical outlets that
were showing loose frayed wires. The Joanna Home was
a wreck, anyway—a lousy firetrap. It was a crime passing
the joint off as an old folks' home, Joe thought. The crooks

in charge would no doubt take the blame for the fire. That is, the faulty wiring would.

He'd lit two matches—one each for the already dead old men—and tossed them one by one at their targets, lurching back at the immediate flare-up, and ducking out back. No one had seen him as far as he knew. There was a one-story lean-to out back, a sort of annex built onto the house, where some of the old biddies slept (he'd picked up eight passbooks at the Joanna Home), and the lights were out there, too. He was safe.

But he'd had a bad weekend. He hadn't worked at all. He wasn't cut out to be no fucking torch. He was a con artist, not a killer. It made his stomach jumpy.

He just sat in his hotel room and listened to the radio and read every edition of every paper, looking for mentions of the fire. When the *Plain Dealer* reported the fire warden as blaming the blaze on a short circuit in the "old, rotten wiring, sending flames crackling up through the dead, dry timber of the walls into the attic," Joe felt relieved, but not at ease. He could only make it through the weekend by drinking his worries away. Straight Scotch, and a lot of it, had allowed Monday to finally roll around.

He'd felt hung over and shaky, but ready to have at the world again. He went down to the Hanna Building to get a fresh list of names. The way the scam operated was, like all great scams, simple. Neighborhoods were surveyed and blocked off. Slush money was paid to a savings-and-loan employee in the district for providing a sucker list of passbook holders.

Commissions were paid to the savings-and-loan bird dog whenever a salesman successfully scammed a passbook. With this system, a guy like Joe didn't have to go door to door. He could hit pay dirt every time he made a call.

There were different ways of going about it, on Joe's end. Some salesmen posed as bank presidents or big real estate operators, particularly those salesmen dealing with clients who could read. They would openly tout cemetery lots as a good investment ("everybody has to die sometime, and there's a big demand for burial plots") which was horsefeathers, of course.

Enough lots were available in the Cleveland area to bury the city's dead for the next three hundred years.

That was how the racket got off the ground in the first place: cemeteries laying off their excess lots cheap to the "sales organization" Fusca worked for. He was vague about who the big shots were. He had the name of a contact, some guy who ran a horse parlor on Ivanhoe Road, if he got in a jam and needed to lam out or hole up. Beyond that he knew nothing.

Except he knew it wasn't the Mayfield Road bunch. They'd tried to cut themselves in for a percentage a while back and got told to back off, by the cops no less. He didn't know who would have the kind of leverage it took to make the local mob back off like that, using the cops as muscle. Some crooked politician, maybe. Joe didn't really care.

All he knew was he was making good dough, a third of everything he hauled to shore.

Of course, Joe had less overhead than most of the salesmen. A lot of them worked in pairs. Those posing as bankers or real estate agents needed translators, as many of the marks didn't speak English. These marks Joe simply avoided. And in most cases it was necessary to employ yet another bird dog, namely somebody in the neighborhood, a respected businessman who spoke the mark's native tongue, to make introductions and pave the way. Or the cop on the beat, of course.

Joe cut out the middle-man with his G-man routine. The shiny gold badge and a little Uncle Sam went a long way with these dumb fucking hunkies.

And he got a kick out of using a G-man badge to bilk a mark. It was like getting back at the bastards for nabbing his brother Phillie.

Phillie had been the class act of all con artists. Joe admired and loved his older brother. Every Christmas, coming up soon now, he sat down and wrote Phillie a letter, and sent it off to the pen at Atlanta.

Everything Joe knew about conning came from Phillie. When they were little kids, Joe and his older brother had come over from Italy with their parents. Their papa was an honest man who almost made a living with an import cheese business in Brooklyn. When Phillie came into the nearly bankrupt business at age sixteen, it took him only a few months to turn things around by bribing customhouse weighers.

In 1915 Phillie got sentenced to a year in prison, but only served a few months. An eloquent letter from the parish priest ("the gallant" lad shielded his father from jailhouse bars, shouldering the blame on himself) won him a Presidential pardon. It paid, young Joe had learned, to put money in the collection plate.

The next family business, engineered by Phillie of course, was importing human hair from Italy to make wigs for American would-be Gibson girls.

This went very well, till the Burns Detective Agency proved the Fuscas had conned twenty banks out of nearly a million bucks by taking loans on hair shipments based on phony invoices.

The whole family was caught in New Orleans, boarding a Honduras-bound liner. Joe tried to throw twenty grand overboard, but it landed in a government boat. Phillie again gallantly took the rap for the family, winding up in the Tombs in New York City. He played stoolie for the prosecutors for a year, spying on other prisoners, and earned the gratitude of the law, and a suspended sentence.

Chicago and Prohibition came next. Phillie became a partner in a pharmaceutical manufacturing company, entitling him to five thousand gallons of alcohol a month for production of hair tonic and cough syrup. It was Joe's idea (Phillie was proud) to color and scent the products in such a way that a simple run through a still turned them back into high-proof straight alcohol. A little water, some color and flavoring, and you had stuff "right off the boat."

They had to tie in with the Capone crowd, of course, but there was money enough to be had by all.

At least there was until that goddamn Ness had busted the entire operation and put Phillie in stir. Another year and Phillie would be out, and Joe had no doubt great things would start happening again.

Until then he was on his own, picking up on whatever con he could. The Chicago outfit offered him work, but he didn't like all those deaths in the family. Anyway, he preferred grifting.

This cemetery scam was better than most. Cleveland wasn't the only place where this sting was playing. He first broke in his G-man act (fuck you, Ness) in New York, for another cemetery lot sales outfit. The New York cops had finally got wise, and he and two other salesmen had lammed. But Joe had heard about the Cleveland game, and so, here he was.

In front of a creaky old house on East Sixty-sixth.

Joe dug his hands in his topcoat pockets—Christ, it was cold—and made his way up the front walk, and around the side and climbed the rickety steps to what was more an attic than a second floor. Twelve grand, hiding out in a hovel like this. He knocked on the door. Yellow paint dropped off like ugly snowflakes.

The door opened and seventy-three-year-old childless widower Elmer Elsworth answered. A skinny prune-faced geezer in Coke-bottle wire-framed glasses, Elsworth was the first client Joe had encountered in the neighborhood who wasn't a Slovak.

"What can I do for you?" the old man rasped, squinting behind the thick glasses, smiling, immediately friendly. He wore a frayed plaid shirt, suspenders, and well-worn brown trousers. None of the clothing looked any too clean, and Elsworth's face was stubbled white.

Joe showed him the badge, identified himself as Agent White and asked if he could step in out of the cold.

" 'Course you can," Elsworth said, gesturing graciously. "Glad for the company. These winter evenings are mighty dull."

The interior was a shock. It made Joe wonder what made Elsworth so goddamn cheerful. With the exception of a worn easy chair, the room was bare of furniture. Across the room a fire burned in a small coal stove. The colorless wallpaper was ancient and peeling off walls that fell from a slanted, cracked ceiling. There were no curtains on the windows, just weathered shades, pulled down. The wooden floor was bare and dirty. In front of the easy chair was a crate, which served as a table for a plate of beans and a cup of coffee, Elsworth's supper, it would seem. On the floor, near the chair, was a large brass ashtray, a remnant of better days perhaps, filled with cigar butts. The smell of smoke and beans lingered in the air.

And on another crate was a lit candle, dripping wax. Somewhere in the darkness, perhaps behind a wall, perhaps not, was a chittering sound. Mice.

"Sorry it's so dark in here," Elsworth said. "Don't have no electricity. Place is wired for it, but I just don't care to spend the money. And, well, I'm legally blind, so the devil take it."

The room was fairly warm from the glowing stove, but it was obvious that otherwise there was no heat either.

"Can I offer you my chair?" Elsworth asked, gesturing toward it.

"No. No thank you. You sit. I'll stand."

"Mighty neighborly of you," Elsworth said. He bumped into the crate as he sat, jostling his beans and coffee, and asked Agent White if he'd like some Java. Agent White declined.

"If there's some way I can be of service to the government," Elsworth said, "just let me know. I was a babe in arms during the War Between the States, don't you know, and too old for the Great War. But that don't mean I'm not a good American."

"I'm sure it doesn't," Joe said. "Besides, the government is interested in helping you."

And Joe went into his spiel: he was collecting passbooks in restricted loan companies with the idea of forwarding them to Washington so Mr. Elsworth could get full value, all at once.

Elsworth sat blinking behind the thick glasses and gradually started to smile.

"I knew it," he said, "I just knew it."

"Uh, knew what, Mr. Elsworth?"

"I knew one day my ship would come in. Why, I scrimped and saved all these years . . . worked for White Motor Company for longer than you've been alive, I'd reckon. Retired some time ago, and I suffered privations, believe you me, preparing for my declining years."

Jesus Christ, Joe thought, these crazy old coots. What were they waiting for? Elsworth here has a twelve-grand passbook (worth six grand face value, at least) and he lives in a dirty, dreary attic, sitting in the dark, eating his plate of beans, dancing with mice, waiting for what? To get even older?

They didn't deserve their money. They didn't know how to enjoy it. They didn't know anything to do with money but save it. Let somebody have it who knew what to do with it.

Joe Fusca.

"Then you'll stop by in two days with my security bonds, Agent White?"

"That's correct. And I'll see you then. You don't have to get up to show me out. I know the way."

Elsworth pointed to the coal stove.

"I was just about to stoke up my fire," he said.

"You just relax," Agent White said. "Let me do that for you."

CHAPTER 9

On Tuesday morning, Eliot Ness sat at the scarred rolltop desk in his spacious wood-and-pebbled-glass office in City Hall, signing papers. Judging by the grin on his face, you'd think that paperwork was his favorite part of his new job. You would be wrong.

These papers were special ones. As he blotted his signatures one by one, he savored his executive position. He was very quietly, in an administrative way, shaking up the city's police department as it had never been shaken up before.

In the midst of this pleasant paperwork, Ness was interrupted by the buzz of the intercom on the desk.

"Captain Cooper is here for his appointment," his secretary's voice said tinnily.

"Good," Ness said, leaning into the little speaker box. "Send him in."

A tall, balding, round-faced cop of about sixty, Cooper wore a brown suit that looked slept in, and his tie bore a food stain or two. But Ness could grit his teeth and overlook a little personal sloppiness in a cop as hard-working and well-respected as this one.

Cooper, hat in hand, took the chair Ness offered him at one of the conference tables that took up the central part of the room, and Ness sat across from him. Cooper's face was almost as rumpled as his suit, though his light-blue eyes were incongruously benign and even becoming in the midst of his battered features.

"Captain Cooper, I'm naming you acting Detective Bureau chief."

Cooper opened his mouth, but at first couldn't seem to think of anything to say.

Ness went on. "And, if the work of the weeks ahead goes at all well, we'll drop the 'acting.' "

"I ... I want to thank you for the vote of confidence, Mr. Ness," Cooper said, beaming, seeming a little nervous.

"From what I've read and heard," Ness said, "it's not misplaced."

"I didn't think you'd see me as, well, the right material for your administration. I'm not exactly a criminologist or anything. Or a spit-and-polish type, either." Chagrined, he flipped his food-stained tie, like Oliver Hardy.

Ness smiled and said, "I'm looking for effectiveness and honesty in my cops. But if you want to spend some of your salary increase on dry cleaning, I wouldn't complain."

Cooper smiled on one side of his face. "I think I can swing that."

"Now," Ness said, "let's get down to it."

Ness filled Cooper in on the theory that a virtual network of crooked cops was working within the force. He didn't mention Wild as the rumor's source.

"If they are an organized group," Ness said, "it stands to reason they do indeed have a leader, a 'chief of their' department within the department.' I believe this so called 'outside chief' is among our sixteen precinct captains.

The most likely candidates would seem to be the captains in charge of the Fourteenth and Fifteenth Precincts."

"I'd have to agree," Cooper said, nodding.

"There's another possibility, of course: your immediate predecessor."

"Potter?" Cooper said, shocked. "Impossible. He's a political wheeler-dealer, but I don't believe for a minute he's crooked."

"We'll see. At any rate, we have to begin investigating."

"I'll put some of my men right on it."

"I don't know about using the Detective Bureau itself, just yet. Not till you've had a chance to get in there for a while and do some housecleaning. And I don't want this information in the hands of a lot of men."

Cooper gestured casually. "I know some detectives I can trust. Let me put them on the job. They can make some discreet inquiries."

"Okay, but let's make it extremely discreet. Let's do it from the inside. And with one man."

Cooper's sky-blue eyes narrowed. "How, exactly?"

"I've been making a lot of transfers, a lot of changes in assignment. I've got a raft of 'em going out." Ness nodded toward the pile of paperwork on the rolltop desk, itself a veteran of his Chicago wars. "Find me an honest detective, brief him, and I'll put him on that list, knock him back down to uniform, and place him in the Fifteenth Precinct."

"The most suspect precinct in town," Cooper said, nodding again.

"Exactly right. People are assuming that most of these transfers indicate suspicion, on my part, of either corruption or dereliction of duty. That isn't always the case, but it will give our undercover man a nice patina of disrepute. Of course he'll complain vocally about being 'demoted.'

And that should encourage any bent cops in the Fifteenth to invite him into their little club."

Cooper smiled tightly, and said, "If we can infiltrate their network with one of our men, we can bust the bastards wide open."

"One would hope," Ness said. "But you have to find the right man."

Cooper put a hand on his chin. "I think I may know just the boy."

Ness raised a lecturing finger. "Nobody is to know about him but the two of us."

Cooper nodded. "I'll talk to him. If he agrees, I'll have his name for you by tomorrow morning. Do you want to meet with him?"

"No. Let's not risk the contact. I trust your judgment."

Cooper, sensing he'd been dismissed, stood stiffly and extended his hand, a rather formal gesture for a rumpled cop with a food-stained tie. Ness stood and shook the hand, as Cooper said, "I'll try to be worthy of that trust."

"The cops in the department who earn my trust," Ness said, "are going to find me the best friend they ever had. Those who don't are going to have an enemy out of their worst nightmares."

Two cops yesterday, who'd been drinking on the job, had found that out; Cooper was well aware of that.

"I'll see if I can't stay on your good side," Cooper said, putting on his hat, tipping it, and going out through the inner office.

Ness returned to his rolltop desk and continued signing the transfer orders until the door from the outer office swung rudely open and Sam Wild strode in, irritated as hell, with Ness' secretary Betsy, an attractive brunette woman with glasses, right on his heels.

Ness swiveled his chair away from his battered desk and turned to look at the pair, as they skirted the conference tables, coming at him. He leaned back in his chair, bumping the desk behind him, and smiled just a little as Wild said, "What the hell's the idea? We had a deal," while Betsy spoke at the same time, some of her words aimed at Wild, "I told you Mr. Ness was busy, you need an appointment," and others at her boss, "I told him you were busy, that he needed an appointment."

Ness patiently waited for silence, ceasing to listen after the first volley.

Then he said, "Thank you, Betsy. I will see Mr. Wild."

Betsy's mouth tightened. She glared at Wild and strode out, not quite slamming the door behind her.

Wild smirked, then walked over and leaned one hand against the nearest arm of Ness' chair. His red bow tie was crooked; his brown jacket looked almost as slept-in as Cooper's suit had; he was hatless, his head of brownish-blond wiry hair looking as rumpled as the jacket. He was such a skinny, angular guy he made Ness think of a praying mantis. In Wild's case, preying.

"I see in the Press you were out in the field yesterday," Wild said.

"I was," Ness said.

"Fritchey had a pretty good story on it."

"I thought it read well."

"So you personally charged two uniformed officers with drinking on the job."

"Intoxication on duty."

"Whatever. Personally ordered their dismissal."

"That's right."

"What happened to our arrangement?"

"Where I treat you right and you treat me right?"

"That's the one."

Ness stood. "I'll tell you." He took off his coat and folded it and put it neatly on the desk behind him, next to the papers he'd been signing.

Wild laughed. "Workin" up a sweat signing those forms, are ya, Mister Director?"

"No," Ness said, and coldcocked him.

Wild went down like kindling. He sat there, all elbows and knees, rubbing some blood out of the corner of his mouth with two fingers, and gave Ness a round-eyed look of utter disbelief.

Betsy peeked in and her mouth opened wider than Wild's eyes. Ness gestured her out with one hand and gave her a look and she retreated, the door shutting with a click like a gun cocking.

Wild breathed some air out. He didn't get up. He sat there, looping his arms around his legs like a kid playing Injun-pass-the-peace-pipe, only peace wasn't what he had in mind.

"That's called assault here in Cleveland, Mr. Ness."

Ness unfolded his coat and put it back on. "Like we used to say in Chicago, Mr. Wild—prove it."

Wild got up, slowly, like a tent being raised. He dusted himself off and said, "Maybe I had that coming."

Ness sat back down and pointed to the door. Not the one Wild and Betsy had come through, but the one that opened onto the hall, the locked one on which the words SAFETY DIRECTOR'S OFFICE could be seen, backwards, through the pebbled glass.

"The press room is thataway," Ness said, and swiveled back to face his desk.

Wild positioned himself to one side of Ness, but didn't lean against an arm of his chair this time. "You think I made a sap out of you, with that story last Friday."

"You did your best to."

Wild's upper lip tightened over his teeth. "Well, hell,

you wasted my time, with that milk run. That wasn't news, except the way I played it. You tell me all sorts of stuff off the record, and I tell you about the 'outside chief' and everything, and what do I get for it? A raid that lays an egg. You could've handed me the Potter scoop, but instead you gotta be a big shot and announce it at a press conference. What good does that do me? Give me a real story and I'll make a hero out of you."

"Maybe I'm not looking to be a hero."

"Maybe I'm not looking to get laid tonight. Look, give me a story. Give me a real story. Give the mayor some headlines. You remember the mayor, don't you? Just down the hall, here? Come on! Earn your goddamn keep, Ness!"

Without looking up from his signing, Ness said, "You'll never get an interview out of me again, Wild, if you play me for a sap."

"What if you act like a sap? Am I supposed to lie about it?"

Ness laughed, looked at Wild. "Why, afraid God would strike you dead?"

"Well." He shrugged, thinking it over. "I slanted stories before, I guess ..."

Ness threw his pen down, sighed. "I don't expect you to slant your stories to make me into Jack Armstrong, All-American Boy. I just want a fair shake. And if you wanted to be on my side a little, well, I wouldn't lose respect for your sense of journalistic ethics."

"Such as it is," Wild said, smirking slightly, not so cockily as before.

"Such as it is. Sit down over at one of the conference tables, Wild. Get your notebook out."

Wild smiled and did.

Ness joined him.

"You want a real story. An exclusive."

"No. I want to quit my job and ride the rails."

"Well, if adventure is calling you, Mr. Wild, don't let me stand in the way."

"I want a real story," Wild said dryly. "An exclusive."

"Those papers I'm in the process of signing. They're transfers. Reassignments."

"Yeah?"

"The chief made some suggestions. I helped him some."

"Oh? What, to clean his bird cage?"

"No. Say what you want about Matowitz, but he was a great cop."

"Emphasis on 'was.' "

"I'm giving him a chance to show he still has it. And he's coming through for me."

"Recommending a few transfers, you mean? Big deal. This is your idea of an exclusive? Any theories on whether this cold front's going to move out? Has somebody in Cleveland finally seen the sun?"

"We got an all-points bulletin out on it."

"Not a bad idea. Transfers." Wild shook his head. "How many?"

"One hundred and twenty-two."

Wild looked up from his notepad. His eyes hadn't been this round since Ness knocked him on his can.

"Including," Ness said, "two captains, seven lieutenants, thirty-five sergeants, and thirty-one detectives."

"Holy Christ." Wild scribbled frantically.

"Also, twenty-four officers are on probation."

Wild let air out of cheeks puffed up like Old Man Winter's. "You're coming out and saying all these cops are on the pad?"

"No. If I knew them to be crooked, they'd be out on their collective ass. I'm just shaking things up, Mr. Wild.

Responding to the chief's suggestions, and my own observations in the field."

"How many precincts does this affect?"

"All of them. All sixteen."

Wild continued to scribble. He was grinning now. "This, Mister Director, is more like it."

"I just love to please you, Mr. Wild."

Wild looked up from the notepad. "You wouldn't want to let me know who your replacement for Potter's going to be?"

"Captain Cooper is acting Detective Bureau chief."

"Anybody else got this?"

"I made the appointment about five minutes before you burst in here. Is that exclusive enough for you?"

"It'll do," Wild grinned. "Cooper's a good man, I hear. Popular with the men, but not political. Suppose that's what you like about him. Is he going to land the job for real?"

"I haven't decided."

"Hey, Mister Director, let's not go clamming up all of a sudden."

"I'm not. I haven't decided. It's a key position. I'm not rushing into anything. But he's got the inside track."

The reporter shrugged. "Fair enough. When can I get a list of names and transfers?"

"That goes out to all of the press at once. All I'm giving you is the basic story. Your 'scoop.' And the Cooper appointment is a little bonus for you."

"Fair enough." Wild put his pencil and pad down. "You know, Ness, no offense, but you're really inviting a shit storm with all this."

"I have a hat."

"It better have a hell of a brim. Never mind your wholesale transfers of a hundred and twenty-some cops. Just those two cops you charged on intoxication will be enough to get your ass in a sling."

Ness smiled mildly. "I was hired to clean up this town. I'm starting with the department. Let's just call it my Christmas present to the city."

"Let's just hope somebody else's idea of a Christmas present isn't you in a ditch with a bow around ya."

"It's been tried."

"Yeah, and successfully."

"Not with me it hasn't."

"Oh, yeah. Right. I forgot. You're untouchable. Unkillable."

"Don't be stupid."

"Some advice, considering the source."

"You're suggesting I'm reckless."

Wild gestured with an open hand, and rolled his eyes. "I'm suggesting you're bucking civil service and public opinion, not to mention the politicians. One of those cops you dismissed is related by marriage to Councilman Fink, you know."

"Do tell."

"There'll be hearings. You'll have to defend yourself, like it was you who's on trial, Johnny-come-lately Ness, and not those longtime public-servant cops. It could be a real circus."

"Maybe I should bring a whip."

"Hell of a lot of good it'll do you on a high wire. Did you ever think about taking things a step at a time? You ever consider that firing and transferring and putting cops on probation right before Christmas is going to make you look more like Scrooge than J. Edgar Hoover?"

"Hoover's no friend of mine."

"And Scrooge is? Rome wasn't built in a day. It took longer than a day to fall, too. But, hey, do what you want—keep going a hundred miles an hour. It'll make great copy. But if you last longer than a couple of months, you'll be beatin' the odds."

Ness smiled again, briefly, and said, "Did you ever stop to consider that a couple months is about all the time I have, anyway?"

The skin around Wild's eyes tightened. "What do you mean?"

"Think about it."

Wild thought; said, "You want to go off the record for a minute?"

"Okay."

Wild slid his pad and pencil away from him on the table top. "This is all about money, isn't it? You have to come up with some phenomenal results before the council votes on the budget."

Ness nodded.

"So you're depending on the press to make you such a big deal that your budget requests can't be denied."

Ness nodded again.

"Then you got a funny idea of how to maintain good press relations," Wild said, with a wise-guy grin, touching the corner of his mouth where a little blood was caked.

"I'm not going to apologize for that," Ness said. "If you can't keep your word with me, I'll do my business with Fritchey and Lawrence and the rest."

"I'm not going to apologize either," Wild said. "But I won't make a sap out of you again. That much I promise. Look at it this way. You'll seem all the more a hero when you do start going out on real raids."

"Which I will," Ness said. "But first I have some transfers to sign."

Wild stood. "That's dangerous enough in itself. But if you really have to pull this off in a couple of months, you better find yourself some doors to kick down, in a hurry."

"I can usually find those, Sam."

"Maybe you'll get a couple for Christmas."

And Wild went out, and Ness went back to work, neither man knowing that the Christmas present they were both hoping for wouldn't arrive until January tenth.

T W O

JANUARY 10-30, 1936

CHAPTER 10

Blizzards in late December had turned the dark city white. And on Friday, January 10, the sun was rumored to have been seen shining in Cleveland, briefly, in the morning. Some attributed that notion to light from blast furnaces in the steel mills. Others figured the radiance must just have been another winter fire, albeit a particularly ambitious one. Very young children, confronted with a glowing ball of light in the sky, may simply have failed to recognize it.

For those who did, clouds soon rolled in from the west to make the point moot. Gray-and-white Cleveland settled in for another bleak day. As the afternoon faded into the subtle difference of evening, Assistant Prosecutor Charles McAndrew, slight, barely thirty, stood in the cinders of the parking lot of the massive Harvard Club, backed up by two assistants and ten plainclothes "constables." The constables were really deputized private detectives from the McGrath Agency.

The Harvard Club, a gambling casino run by Mayfield Road mob members, was just south of the city limits in the suburb of Newburgh Heights. That put it within the jurisdiction of County Prosecutor Cullitan, for whom McAndrew and the others were working, but outside the bailiwick of the Cleveland police.

Truth be told, McAndrew well knew that steering clear of the Cleveland police was just fine with Prosecutor Cullitan. And it had been on the suggestion of the top cop in town, Safety Director Eliot Ness, that Cullitan had turned to private detectives.

"It's the only way to avoid a tip-off," Ness had told Cullitan.

The local Newburgh cops were out of the question for the same reason.

And as for enlisting the aid of the county sheriff, well, that too was out of the question. Sheriff John L. "Honest John" Sultzman—that white-maned, folksy, self-styled friend of the people—had a strict hands-off position toward the law enforcement affairs of the communities within his county:

"My home rule policy is a sacred instrument in the hands of the people, who love liberty and freedom and who love to govern themselves!" What this meant was the sheriff left up to others as much of the law enforcement in the county as he possibly could.

Then there was the little matter of the sheriff's son having been held overnight in the lockup at the Central Police Station in Cleveland proper just the day before yesterday. The kid was drunk and his car climbed the curb and tried to climb a tree as well. A passenger was injured and the driver was booked, sheriff's son or not.

The previous administration would've helped the sheriff out on something like this. But Safety Director Ness was cracking down on traffic offenses, and didn't play politics (or anyway, that kind of politics) and so the kid went to jail.

McAndrew was wishing Ness and Cullitan weren't such damn hard-noses.

It'd be nice to have the sheriff's deputies behind him right now. He couldn't help but wonder, if any court cases came out of this, how it would look, using a bunch of private eyes as backup.

I'm a lawyer, McAndrew thought, wincing at the cold, and at the thought of what was ahead of him, not a cop.

He gave his men a tight smile and motioned for them to stay behind him in the drive of the parking lot, and he advanced up the porch steps of the barnlike building with the fancy, New Orleans-style facade that could not hide the structure's warehouse roots.

He swallowed. He sighed. He stared at the massive wooden doorway before him, with its speakeasy slot. He knocked.

The slot slid open and dark eyes with dark bushy brows and dark circles beneath filled the opening. At first blank, then bored, the eyes narrowed as they took McAndrew in, particularly the badge on his lapel.

"Yeah?" The voice wasn't as menacing as the eyes, but it came in a close second.

McAndrew held up his left gloved hand with the folded warrant.

"Better open up," he said. "This is a raid."

"Fuck you," the voice said, turning the first word into two-syllables, and the window slot slid shut with metallic force, like a soldier quickly cocking a carbine.

McAndrew stood staring at the door a while. The door stared back.

He turned to the dozen men below and shrugged. Beyond them was a vast parking lot filled with cars. A lot of people were inside the club. Citizens breaking the law, certainly, but did they deserve getting caught in the midst of something ugly which McAndrew's instincts told him was how things would go, here.

He was about to have his suspicions confirmed.

As McAndrew stood on the edge of the porch, the door behind him swung open and revealed the burly human being who went with the eyes, his several hundred pounds squeezed into a tux. Now McAndrew knew why they called them "monkey suits" (assuming the monkey was an ape). The thug gave McAndrew a shove and sent him tumbling down the half dozen steps to land in a heap on his ass in the cinders.

The deputized private cops and McAndrew's two assistants were momentarily stunned, but a few began moving forward, their hands digging deep in overcoat pockets for their pistols.

But the plug-ugly at the top of the porch stairs produced an automatic from somewhere and pointed it at them. They froze like a bunch of kids in a bad Christmas pageant.

"You got your job to do," the gorilla with the gun said, "and I got mine."

McAndrew picked himself up. "I have a search and seizure warrant for this place."

"You'll get your fuckin' heads shot off, you try comin' in here." He lifted the gun and waggled it, like a professor waving a pointer at his underachieving class. "Word to the wise."

He lowered the gun but did not put it away as he walked casually back inside, slamming the door.

One of the assistants, a guy even younger and more scared than McAndrew, approached. "What now?"

"Hell, I don't know. Bust into the place? It's full of citizens. If there's more like that monkey inside, we'll have a shooting war on our hands."

"Maybe we could wait for Cullitan to show."

McAndrew shook his head, feeling helpless. "He isn't going to like that."

"Why don't you ask to talk to the big boss? Instead of trying to reason with muscle?"

McAndrew nodded. "Good idea." He glanced at the phalanx of men behind him, and said, "No guns out, gentlemen. But be able to fill your hands quickly."

He went up the steps again.

He raised his fist to knock, but the door swung open before he could.

It shut just as quickly, and three men were standing there before him.

McAndrew backed up rapidly.

In the rear were two thugs in ill-fitting tuxes, each of whom had a Thompson submachine gun in his two hands. At the fore was a short, stocky man with a moon face and slicked black hair, who stood, arms folded, eyes hooded, cigarette dangling. He, too, wore a tuxedo, but he seemed at home in it. He was James "Shimmy" Patton, described in the warrant McAndrew held as "operator" of the Harvard Club.

McAndrew never really got a good look at either of the men backing Patton up. All he could seem to see was the blue steel of the choppers. His stomach was churning.

"What the hell is this?" Patton said. His voice was a surprisingly pleasant tenor, but this didn't take the edge off his words.

"Exactly what it looks like, Mr. Patton. It's a raid."

"You're not Cullitan."

"I'm his assistant. I have a warrant. Each of my deputies has a copy."

"Who gave it to you?"

"That's none of your business."

Patton was shaking with anger. "Well, why in hell wasn't I tipped off?"

"We aren't here to squeeze you for protection money, Mr. Patton. We're here to shut you down."

"The hell you will. If any of you try to stick your goddamn necks in that door, we'll mow you down with machine guns. As you can see, we've got 'em. And we'll use 'em."

McAndrew patted the air with his hands. "We don't want any bloodshed. Look, this is developing into a state of siege. We can't get in, and you can't get out."

"We don't want out."

"I would imagine your patrons do. They must be starting to be aware of what's going on out here. They'll be getting nervous."

"My patrons are my concern."

"I don't want any bloodshed. I suggest a truce. I'll allow you half an hour to clear your patrons out before I start the raid."

"The hell with that," Patton yelled, liquor on his breath. He poked a stubby finger in McAndrew's chest. "You aren't coming in here. If you do, you'll get killed!"

Patton turned and one of his chopper-wielding body-guards opened the door for him and the three men slipped inside.

McAndrew's assistant approached again. "Now what?"

McAndrew sighed. "Wait for Cullitan. And hope to God his raid is going smoother than mine."

*****

It was. In the nearby suburb of Maple Heights, at Thomas Street and McCracken Road, Sam "Gameboy" Miller's Thomas Club was being well and truly raided by County Prosecutor Frank T. Cullitan himself.

Cullitan was fifty-five years old, a big man with salt-and-pepper hair (mostly salt) and wire-framed glasses. Tonight he wore a dark topcoat with a dark tie showing, and a gray hat, the brim of which was not tucked down in front. His small chin jutted over a softer second one and his slightly bulbous nose softened his otherwise strong features. A quiet man who could turn into a powerhouse—just ask the seven murderers who'd gone to the chair, thanks in no small part to Cullitan's courtroom oratory—he was relishing this night of cops-and-robbers. He was glad Ness had prodded him into it.

The prosecutor, two assistants, and the other ten private-eye "constables" had arrived at five P.M., the time set for the simultaneous raids on the Thomas and Harvard Clubs. Like the other raiding party across town, they had arrived in a moving van and several cars.

Cullitan had marched up to the front door of the Thomas Club, a big brick affair that lacked the pretentious facade of the Harvard Club, and hammered at the door with the heel of his fist.

The speakeasy slot in the door slid back. Dark, alert eyes filled the space.

"What do you want?" the voice that went with them said.

"I'm Cullitan. The county prosecutor."

"You can't come in without a membership card."

Cullitan waved his warrant in front of the eyes in the slot. "Here's my membership card. It's called a warrant for search and seizure."

"What is this, a raid?"

"Exactly right. Open the door and I'll give you your cigar."

The window slid shut.

The door did not open.

Cullitan stepped back, glanced at his men huddled nearby, shrugged, and turned to face the door, folding his arms, waiting for something to happen.

Nothing did. Behind him, Cullitan heard muttering. The boys were chomping at the bit. He was heartened by the enthusiasm these hired hands were showing, but frustrated that he couldn't give them any more leadership than to just stand here and wait to see if his warrant would be honored.

Five minutes crawled by and Cullitan's Irish complexion began turning red.

"Are we the law or not?" somebody behind him said.

"The hell with it," Cullitan muttered, and pointed to a wooden bench near the door. "Would any of you men like to sit down and rest? Or would you prefer to use this little item as a battering ram?"

Several grinning volunteers stepped forward, hoisted the bench and began to slam it into the closed door, splinters and chips of wood flying. The door was solid and didn't give easily, but the men kept at it, with a steady jungle-drum rhythm that, Cullitan thought with a smile, must be playing hell on the nerves of the folks within.

Finally a voice from inside made itself heard above the drumming of the battering ram: "Okay, okay, okay!"

The eager private cops backed off and the door cracked open, revealing the pasty wedge-shaped face that went with the eyes seen in the speakeasy slot.

The guy said, "I'm tryin' to find somebody to talk to you. You'll just have to wait a little."

"Like hell," one of the boys said, and they dropped the bench with a thud.

One of them yanked the door open, another pushed the lookout out of the way, and the party of deputized private cops went in, followed quietly by a smiling Cullitan and two assistants.

The front part of the club was a dimly lit bar, but in back was a big, mostly undecorated room where a crowd of five hundred or more well-dressed, upper-class patrons, mostly couples, stood at numerous tables playing blackjack, roulette, chuck-a-luck, and craps. Slot machines lined one wall and were doing good business.

Cullitan and his crew went unnoticed at first, as they spread themselves out around the large room, where the action was so hot and heavy that gamblers were banked three and four deep around the tables.

The gambling din was considerable, but Cullitan was a trial lawyer and he could be heard when he wanted to be. He wanted to be. "Ladies and gentlemen, this is a raid!"

A woman screamed, but Cullitan cut off a general panic, saying "We'll be holding no one but employees and operators. Those of you who are patrons are free to go. Move out slowly and quietly."

A raider was posted at each exit to make sure no employee slipped by.

At the gambling tables, Cullitan and his men found stacks of silver dollars, used for chips, which were swept by the raiders into two large sacks. A dozen payoff windows lined one wall. On one side of them a door led to the office, a massive room behind the payoff windows, its back wall an immense chart posting racing results. Above the windows was a sign listing seven locations in Cleveland where customers could catch a free limo to the club, every fifteen minutes from noon to six P.M., seven days a week, encouraging daylight-hour patronage of the club.

Just inside the office, Cullitan found a telegraph switch panel with a key and a resonator, which he ripped out. A loudspeaker system which announced race results was removed as well. So were various casino supplies—sealed decks of playing cards being the staple—and an arsenal including sawed-off shotguns, revolvers, blackjacks, sheathed knives, and a tear gas gun. And six trays of silver dollars, approximately a thousand dollars' worth, and over fifty thousand in paper money.

"Gameboy Miller isn't here," one of Cullitan's assistants announced, coining in from the gaming room where the casino's staff was being rounded up. "None of the big wheels are here. All we drew is working stiffs."

That didn't bother Cullitan. He wasn't looking to prosecute anybody.

Pulling in these private eyes as his personal army of deputies could get his case tossed out anyway, not that judges in the pockets of the Mayfield Road gang needed any legitimate excuse. The point of the exercise was to close these clubs down. And in the case of the Thomas Club, Cullitan noted with satisfaction—watching his raiders dismantle and seize the equipment, loading it and the handcuffed employees into the moving van for the first of two trips—that objective had been met.

He left the mop-up to his assistants and took his car over to the Harvard Club to see how that raid had come off.

Only it hadn't yet.

He found McAndrew's raiding party huddled in front of and inside a Sohio gas station across the street from the Harvard Club, which was sheltered on either side by a wooded area.

"What the hell is going on?" Cullitan demanded.

McAndrew told him.

"Machine guns," Cullitan said, rubbing his chin.

"Nobody's left yet. The patrons are still in there. Maybe they're hostages."

"I doubt that."

"It's a Mexican standoff. I decided to wait for you."

"Damn. We need more men."

"What about yours?"

"They're already headed downtown with a vanload of gambling gear and arrests."

"Do you want to try the sheriff?"

"He wouldn't give us the time of day."

"What about your friend Ness?"

"We aren't in Cleveland."

"But this whole damn thing was his idea."

"Not really." Cullitan liked to think it was his own idea, but Ness certainly had been there rooting him on.

"Call him. What harm can it do?"

Cullitan looked across at the Harvard Club. "Why's it so dark?"

"Patton turned off the parking lot lights. That's why I moved my men across the street. Standing in the dark like that, waiting for the shooting to start was playing hell with everybody's nerves."

"Give me a nickel."

"What?"

"Give me a nickel," Cullitan said.

Time to call Ness.

CHAPTER 11

Eliot Ness sat in the gallery of the City Council Chambers—a vast, ornate assembly hall of dark wood paneling where even the dolts among the council could hear their pronouncements resonate—and fought sleep. All evening he'd been subjected to floor fights on procedural matters, stemming from the fact that Monday night's turbulent meeting had resulted in multiple roll-call votes. The final one, which took place just before dawn, was disputed, leaving two claimants to the council presidency. Mayor Burton had ties to Sonny D'Maioribus, the Republican who seemed to have won the presidency. But Democrat William Reed also believed himself the rightful winner and on Wednesday had filed suit in the Court of Appeals.

Tonight a president pro tem was being elected, to preside till the courts sorted it all out. But the heated battle of Monday night had deteriorated into bickering as Friday evening eroded.

Ness had been here Monday and had seen the whole fracas. He'd gotten into it, inadvertently. The onlookers in the gallery had seemed on the verge of rioting—pushing each other around physically, reflecting the verbal war on the chamber floor—so he'd sent for a riot squad to expel all the spectators. When the squad arrived, a big uniformed cop immediately grabbed Ness by the collar and ejected him first.

He almost wished that something that interesting would happen tonight.

The council chambers were just across from his office, and Ness was thinking about slipping over there. His administrative assistant, political appointee John Flynt was working on a summary of crime statistics that Ness was anxious to go over.

And, too, he really ought to get home. He'd promised Eva he'd be in no later than ten for a late supper. He'd been trying to be nice to her lately, because she'd been so disappointed when they couldn't get back to Chicago for a family Christmas. Also, Eva didn't seem too happy about their new apartment, nice as it was.

She also didn't seem to understand that his job included some duties beyond the work itself. Like attending city council meetings, for the next few weeks anyway, because Mayor Burton had asked him to. Budget hearings were coming up, after all. The mayor wanted his new, apolitical safety director's physical presence in those council chambers, wanted him to become a familiar face at meetings. The young cop who'd failed to recognize his safety director boss was emblematic of the need for newcomer Ness to make himself known.

The budgets Chiefs Matowitz and Grainger had come up with for their respective departments added up to a staggering three million-plus dollars.

The mayor's budget clock was ticking, and this was the second week of January, but Eliot Ness had spent most of his time thus far at his desk, in public hearings, and in city council meetings. Not in the field, where he belonged.

Not cracking down on the policy banks; not sniffing out the "outside chief." Sitting, like tonight. His frustration was chewing at him, just as he was chewing at his own thumbnail, his most noticeable nervous habit.

What had eaten up his time most, as Sam Wild had predicted, were the public hearings over the dismissal of the two intoxicated-on-duty cops.

Each cop, one a ten-year and the other a sixteen-year veteran, got a separate hearing, and both had worked up some public sympathy. Outside City Hall, school children paraded with placards pleading for their "big pals."

Character witnesses lauded the patrolmen as "upright men who merely strayed" and should be given a second chance.

At the hearings, Ness had cut through the bullshit with facts: both men had past records of drunkenness on duty, but had previously been no more than censured by the department.

"I won't put up with that," Ness had told the civilian review board. "In testimony, their fellow officers admit the first thing they did when handling these men was to disarm them. In London, where police aren't armed, drunkenness on duty is sufficient cause for immediate dismissal. Here, in this country, in this city, a drunken cop is a menace because he has a gun on his hip."

It had played well in the press, which noted that dismissals of this sort were a "notable departure" from the actions of previous safety directors, arid Burton had been pleased. But at the same time, the mayor pointed out that a powerful enemy had been made of Councilman Fink. He was a small, natty, rodent-like man who scowled at Ness when their eyes met in council chambers, and he was also the brother-in-law of one of the busted cops.

Ness was just nodding off when he felt a tap on his shoulder. He glanced up and realized that his assistant,

Flynt, was leaning in from the row behind him.

John C. Flynt, a thirty-seven-year-old lawyer whose bearing and appearance were slightly military, apologized for the interruption.

"But," he whispered, with a lift of one eyebrow, and a twitch of his tiny waxed mustache, "Mr. Cullitan is on the phone. He says it's urgent."

Ness, embracing the interruption, slid out of the pew and followed the dark-haired, dapper Flynt across the hall into the office.

He sat at his desk and picked up the phone. "What is it, Frank?"

"Eliot, we need your help. This Harvard Club raid is turning into a disaster. I need at least twenty men for backup before I dare make another move."

Ness had a lot of respect for Cullitan. The hardnosed prosecutor was a Democrat, but was no more political than Ness, conducting his election campaigns without Democratic party funds or contributions from lawyers or anybody else who might have an ulterior motive. He was an ally.

"I'd like to help," Ness said. "I realize I got you into this."

"I'm not saying you did. I have to shoulder the responsibility on this one."

"Well, you are out of my jurisdiction. I don't have to tell you I hold no authority past the city limits."

"I know," Cullitan sighed. "But what in hell can I do? Just tuck my tail between my legs and go?"

"What exactly is the situation there?"

Cullitan told Ness.

"Machine guns," Ness repeated coldly, standing.

"McAndrew only saw two, but I'd wager that's just a hint of their firepower. It's a big place. They'll have a big staff."

"Let me see what I can do for you."

"Thanks, Eliot."

"Give me the number of the phone you're calling from and stay right by it."

Cullitan gave him the number, and they hung up.

Ness sat again and called Sheriff Sultzman's office at the county jail.

"Let me speak to the sheriff," Ness said after identifying himself.

"Sheriff Sultzman's not in his office," a bored male voice replied.

"Where is he?"

"Home sick with the croup."

"I see. Who am I speaking to?"

"The chief jailer."

"Does the chief jailer have a name?"

"Sure. Edward Murray. This is Edward Murray."

"Mr. Murray, Prosecutor Cullitan is at the Harvard Club with several of his staff and their lives are endangered. As a private citizen, I'm calling on you to send deputies out there to protect the prosecutor."

"Sorry, but we can't send men out there without a call from the mayor of Newburgh."

"The mayor can't be reached." Ness hadn't tried to, of course, but what good would it have done? The Harvard Club had operated wide open in Newburgh Heights for over five years.

"Well, I don't know," the jailer whined. "The sheriff has his home-rule policy, you know."

"Will you go out or won't you?"

"I'll have to call the sheriff and call you right back."

"To hell with that. Have you got another line?"

"Yes."

"I'll stay on this one while you call him. I'll wait on

the phone."

"Okay."

Several minutes crawled by. Ness gritted his teeth, pounded a fist on his desk, listening to silence.

The jailer returned. "No, we won't go out there."

Ness slammed the receiver into the hook, then quickly dialed again.

"Frank," he said into the phone, "I've exhausted all legal means."

"Yes? And?"

"And I'll be there as soon as I can."

Cullitan sighed his relief. "Thank you, Eliot."

"Just do me one favor."

"Yes?"

"Try not to start without me."

Flynt, who'd been standing by hearing only Ness' half of these conversations, seemed a bit puzzled.

Ness said, "Get your topcoat and pistol and wait for me here."

Flynt's eyes went wide for a moment. "If I understand what you're up to, the legal ground is shaky."

Ness just looked at him.

Then Flynt was off to his own office for his coat and gun.

Ness returned to the Council Chambers, walked up to Mayor Burton's chair, and leaned in and, *sotto voce,* told His Honor the tale.

"This doesn't sound like our business, Eliot," Burton said reluctantly.

"These sons of bitches are parading around in public with machine guns," Ness whispered harshly, "making the law a laughingstock. Am I supposed to put up with that?"

Burton's broad brow creased. "You can't step in officially."

"How about unofficially?"

Burton shrugged, smiled faintly. "There's nothing stopping you from going out there as a private citizen."

Ness grinned. "Thanks."

"Eliot." The Mayor raised a cautionary finger. "Watch your step. This will attract publicity. Make sure it's the kind we're looking for."

Ness nodded and went out in the hall and down to the next door, which said PRESS. Inside he found Sam Wild, Clayton Fritchey, and half a dozen others, most of whom were sitting at a table playing poker, money openly on the table.

"Gambling's illegal in this town, fellas," Ness said.

Wild smirked. "Prove it."

"Meet me at the Harvard Club in half an hour or less," he told them, "and I will."

He shut the door on the startled faces and strode back down the hall and into his office, where Flynt waited in his topcoat, pistol in hand.

"Put that in your pocket or something," Ness said, irritably. He went to his desk and unlocked and opened the bottom drawer. He withdrew a shoulder holster which held his .38 Police Special. He got out of his suitcoat and was unbuttoning his vest when he thought better of it.

"No guns for us," Ness said, putting the .38 and harness back, rebuttoning the vest buttons, and slipping on the coat.

Flynt was puzzled again. "Why not?"

"That shaky legal ground you mentioned. We're going out as private citizens. Actually, you don't have to go at all."

Ness explained the situation.

"Well, of course, I'll go," Flynt said, without much enthusiasm. "But shouldn't we have some firepower?"

"I think we'll be able to scrounge some up. Let's go."

Ness drove directly to the Central Police Station. It was just after ten o'clock and the shift was changing. He walked down the tunnel-like first-floor corridor, with Flynt following along, into the locker room. Cops, some still completely in uniform, others in various stages of undress and putting on their civvies, froze, conversations trailing off, as the presence of the safety director was felt.

Ness stood there in his fedora and camel-hair topcoat, his gold "City of Cleveland—Director of Public Safety" badge on his lapel catching the light, hands in his pockets.

"I need some volunteers," he said. "I only want those who are going off duty to consider this."

He explained the situation at the Harvard Club.

"The press will be there covering what we do," he said. "I mention that, because this department has a reputation for being on the take. I thought some of you might like to demonstrate you're not part of that."

As men began to step forward, Ness spoke more loudly than was his usual style, saying, "Understand this: the city's responsibility for you ends when you cross the city limits. If you're killed, it won't be considered in the line of duty. Your families might wind up off the pension rolls."

That sobered the volunteers, and Ness added, "I won't hold it against any of you if you don't go."

But without exception they all did, twenty-nine patrolmen, ten motorcycle cops, and four plainclothes dicks. Sirens screamed as the five squad cars Ness had ordered went speeding down Harvard Avenue with his own black Ford sedan in the lead.

The sidewalks were filled with hundreds of gawkers, some from nearby residential sections, but many from the casino itself, patrons who'd moved to their cars and then stuck around to watch the raid.

Ness pulled into the Sohio station where Cullitan and his stalled wrecking crew waited. The sirens of the squad cars wound down as they too pulled into the gas station, their cargoes of cops staying aboard. The motorcycle cops remained mounted, engines rumbling.

Ness climbed out of his sedan and shook Cullitan's hand.

The prosecutor smiled. "The cavalry arrives at last."

"Any action?"

"I had a little shouting match with Shimmy Patton. I told him it was my job to close the club, and he suggested I quit my 'goddamn job.' He repeated his quaint threat to blow the head off anybody who steps foot inside. 'You got your goddamn homes to protect, and I got my goddamn business to protect.' "

"Mr. Patton is nothing if not colorful. So the state of siege remains?"

He shrugged. "Well, the patrons are out. Must've been a thousand of 'em. We didn't try to stop them—we didn't want to stop them. Unfortunately, some of the equipment from inside, and of course money, may've been carried out under bulky overcoats. Trucks were pulling out of that parking lot along with the cars. We couldn't really monitor who was leaving. Besides, my warrants don't cover seizure of property outside the club itself."

The crowd of onlookers was encroaching upon the gas station command post, and Ness put several cops in charge of moving them back. When that was done, he got back in the Ford and drove slowly across the street into the now largely empty parking lot before the sprawling barnlike Harvard Club.

The squad cars and motorcycles followed, and Cullitan and his men trailed on foot.

All of the cars and the motorcycles lined up in front of the casino, the headlights cutting at angles through the darkness of the cinder lot, hitting the building like small prison searchlights looking for escaping cons.

"Leave your lights on!" Ness ordered, as he walked from his Ford up the steps of the Harvard Club.

Behind him, uniformed cops were piling out of the squad cars, falling in with Cullitan's private-eye constables. Ness was unarmed, but his cops were armed to the teeth: sawed-off shotguns, tear-gas launchers, riot guns, revolvers and nightsticks.

Ness knocked on the door.

Eyes appeared in the speakeasy peephole.

Ness said, "I have a search warrant. Open up."

The peephole slid abruptly shut.

"If that's how you want it," Ness said, and raised his foot and, with his heel, kicked.

The sound, a splintering crunch, was strangely satisfying to Ness, as was the feel of the physical effort of punching his foot into the wood, the pull of the muscles in his leg.

He did it again.

And again, and that kick was the one that tore off the lock, springing the door, but a safety chain caught it. He kicked once more and the door flew open.

Ness stepped inside onto whorehouse-red carpeting and a big guy in a tux, no gun apparent but with hands open, came at him with a look that was supposed to be mean but seemed to Ness more on the order of constipated.

He flipped the guy.

Now two more men approached, even bigger than the thug he'd given the jujitsu treatment to. They were wearing tuxedos and Thompson submachine guns. These two, Ness would later learn, were Shimmy Patton's body-guards, the ones who'd threatened McAndrew earlier.

Ness just stood there, his hands empty. He said, "I'm Eliot Ness. I'm unarmed. I've got a warrant. Killing me would be about the surest ticket to the hot seat I can think of. You guys ambitious to burn?"

They apparently weren't.

Because they looked at each other, and, helping up the guy Ness had thrown, retreated quickly into the casino room.

Ness stepped outside into the headlight-streaked darkness and called out to Cullitan.

"All right," he said. "Your men can go on in and serve their warrants now. We'll back you up."

As Cullitan moved by, Ness cautioned him: "A couple of hoods inside have machine guns, so take it easy. I don't think they're in the mood to use them, but you never know."

Sam Wild and other reporters from all the papers—photographers, too—showed up soon thereafter.

But all that was left for the photographers to shoot was a huge, pretty much empty room where open steel beams and catwalks looked down on a cement floor littered with paper, a U-shaped blackjack table, and a few baize dice tables. A gigantic race chart blackboard also remained, but otherwise, the casino had been stripped, the roulette wheels, slot machines and such having somehow been carted away. While the front of the Harvard Club held a well-appointed restaurant and bar, echoing the New Orleans appearance of the building's facade, the sprawling interior of the casino had all the atmosphere of the warehouse it once had been.

Perhaps a score of strong-arms remained, in blue cheeks and tuxes. No guns were in evidence. Patton and a clutch of bodyguards were grouped around the blackjack table. Cullitan sent two of the private eyes over to cuff them, and one thug threw a punch. A private eye punched back and punches from both camps began flying.

Ness crooked his finger and gathered one of his cops and waded in, pulling Patton and his men off the two constables, and Patton jerked away from Ness, saying, "Don't you try to slug me! You do and you won't get out of this place alive."

"Really."

"Lightning's liable to strike you, buddy." Patton brushed himself off. "You guys act like gentlemen while you're in here, or you'll wish to hell you had."

"I see."

Patten looked at Ness.

Ness looked at Patton.

"I gotta get my coat," Patton said, and scurried away, ducking into a doorway, followed by several of his "boys." The door, marked OFFICE—PRIVATE, slammed.

Ness laughed to himself, and shook his head.

Meanwhile, Press photographer "Shorty" Philkins had climbed up on top of a stool to snap some pics, and picked as his subject one of Patton's boys who hadn't managed to flee to the office. Said subject quickly kicked the stool out from under Shorty, who fell hard on the cement floor.

Sam Wild, standing nearby and taking some notes, crossed over and swung a haymaker that started at his knees and ended on the chin of the thug, who went down on the cement harder than Shorty had.

There was no love lost between the Harvard Club's surly staff and the gloating reporters, whose papers had been harping about wide-open gambling in greater Cleveland for years, paving the way for raids like tonight's.

So, when the remainder of Patton's strong-arm squad went rushing over to thump Wild, the rest of the reporters picked up on that, and went rushing over themselves, fists flying and folding chairs getting folded over heads and backs. Ness had to go wading in again, some of his uniform boys backing him up, helping him try to pull the foes apart, only it just wasn't taking.

Finally Ness turned to one of the cops and held out his hand, palm up.

"Loan me your service revolver, would you?"

The cop, a surprised young rookie, obeyed.

Ness fired the gun in the air.

Reporters and hoods froze in mid-swing.

Ness smiled at the group and waggled a finger of his free hand at them, as if to say, "Settle down, kids," handing the smoking gun back to the startled cop.

Then he called Flynt over and had him herd the thugs into one corner to get them cuffed.

Ness wandered over to Wild, looking down at the sprawling, sleeping hood, who Wild had coldcocked, starting it all.

"In Chicago," Ness said, "we call that assault."

"Good thing we're in Cleveland," Wild said with a grin, rubbing his bleeding knuckles.

Shorty Philkins was still on the floor as well, but not out cold.

"You might want to get a picture of this," Ness said to Shorty, helping him up, then heading for the office.

With several of Cullitan's constables backing him up, Ness stood at the door and said, "I can kick this one down too, if you like, Shimmy. Or maybe knock this little window out and send some tear gas in."

Brief silence.

And the door opened.

Inside were three of Patton's boys, who when patted down proved to be unarmed, though two were the original machine-gunners. A chair with a box on it stood next to a high, open window through which Patton apparently had fled. The office was as stripped as the casino: four large safes squatted along one wall with their doors open and their insides emptied. The floor was littered with betting slips.

Up above, an unoccupied machine-gun nest opened off one of the catwalks. From this cubbyhole, with slits for gun barrels, both the office and the main gambling room could be protected from a holdup or raid. It had gone unused tonight.

In the yard at the rear of the building, constables led by Assistant Safety Director Flynt and backed by Ness' cops found two moving vans, not unlike the ones the constables themselves had arrived in. One of the vans was pulling out; the other was partially loaded with gambling equipment but was unattended.

Ness stood in the big empty casino and shook his head, smiling at his own expense. He couldn't help but think of the Sweeney Avenue still, his last raid as a Prohibition agent, which had netted him a big, mostly empty building. Now his first gambling raid had netted him much the same.

"If you're thinking this raid's a flop," Cullitan said, coming up to him, "you're very wrong."

"Oh?"

"I wasn't looking for cases to prosecute. You weren't looking for arrests. We were looking to shutter this place. And the Thomas Club. And I think we've accomplished that."

Ness nodded. "I think we have. I think we've made life a little miserable for the Mayfield mob tonight."

"What about tomorrow?"

"Tomorrow I'll issue arrest warrants on Shimmy Patton, Gameboy Miller, and the other club operators. I'm still not looking for arrests, just encouraging the sons of bitches to stay out of Cuyahoga County."

Soon Ness slipped away. He was just a private citizen, after all. No arrests to make, no property to seize, for him. He felt good. He'd seen some Cleveland cops behave like cops tonight, even if they hadn't officially been cops at the time. He had little doubt that the press would play this up in his favor, which would give the Mayor precisely the publicity fodder he'd been looking for to kick off the battle of the budget. More important, to Ness at least, he'd gotten to kick down a door and tangle with some toughs. His heart had raced and adrenaline flowed.

It beat the hell out of a city council meeting.

CHAPTER 12

Eva Ness, née Jonsen, sat in her modern apartment feeling like a stranger in what was supposed to be her own home.

She should have felt grateful, she knew, for such a lavish place. At least it seemed lavish to her, lavish compared to any standards she knew. In fact, the apartment was much smaller than their house in Bay Village, which they had not gotten around to renting yet. Good thing, she thought. The apartment consisted of two bedrooms, one of which Eliot had converted into a study, a kitchen, a living room, and one bath. Plenty of space, but not spacious.

Square footage wasn't the key thing; the location was. Their massive brick gingerbread-trimmed apartment complex fit right into this upper-crust area. The problem was, Eva didn't. What was she doing here, on the West Side of Cleveland, just a block from the lake? The only thing between them and Lake Erie was the even more expensive neighborhood along the lakefront.

They'd been on the lake in Bay Village, too, but that community was comfortably middle-class, and their house was nothing next to the big, fancy homes of Lakewood and

Rocky River that separated Bay Village from Cleveland. This location was uncomfortably top-hat for her. She had tried, for almost two weeks now, to feel at home. They had moved out right after Christmas (she'd begged Eliot to have Christmas at Bay Village, and he'd given her that) and ever since she'd been, well, she'd been miserable.

She hated these strangely modern furnishings—the pastel colors, chrome trim, rounded surfaces, the air-brushed paintings of flowers. She much preferred the comfortable, homey furnishings at their Bay Village home, some of which they'd brought with them from Chicago. She was ashamed of herself for feeling this way, since the place wasn't costing them a cent.

Eliot described it as a "fringe benefit." The mayor had insisted they move to Cleveland, and some rich friend of his had provided this apartment, already furnished. She and Eliot paid only the utilities and phone.

It was a dream come true. Why, then, did it feel like a nightmare? Why was she giving into these crying jags? It was more than just homesickness, though even now she had a pang at the thought of having missed Christmas with her family.

Partly, it was the crushing boredom. There was so little housekeeping to do; Eliot was home so infrequently, he didn't get much of anything dirty, outside of his clothes, and the bulk of those went to a Chinese laundry. And she was almost afraid to touch anything in this shiny pastel palace. She read movie magazines and romances; she sewed; and she listened to the radio—*Just Plain Bill* was her favorite program.

Eva had liked her life better when she was working. She missed that. It made her less mad at Eliot because she could hardly blame him for preferring the hustle and bustle of an office to a dull life at home.

He wasn't mean to her. He didn't have a mean bone in his body, at least that she'd ever seen. She marveled sometimes when she heard, or, more often, read in the papers, of his exploits. It seemed to have so little to do with the quiet man she—almost—lived with.

She thought, sometimes, about asking Eliot if she might go back to work.

After all, they had no family for her to take care of. But he made a good living, and she assumed he'd be too proud for that. It wouldn't look right for a man with a job like his, she felt. So she never asked.

Back home in Chicago, in the early years especially, being with a man like Eliot Ness had been thrilling. Even though as his secretary and then his wife, she was on the sidelines, she felt a part of him. He was going places. Name in the papers all the time; fancy education; respected by important people in the community.

But after they'd been married a while, she began to hate his work. She began to hate the loneliness of waiting for him to get home, and especially to hate the nervousness, the anticipation, the wondering whether anything bad had happened to him. Was he bleeding in an alley somewhere? Was he dying, or dead? The Capone gangsters had threatened them at home many times; the couple had, in response, and more than once, moved. Eliot was shot at more than once. She hated it. She hated it.

When things began to wind down in Chicago, she had been relieved. But the year that followed, when he was chasing moonshiners around the woods of Kentucky and such, was the worst yet. He admitted that himself. He'd come home shaking.

"Sometimes I wish I was still up against Capone and machine guns," Eliot had said to her, in a rare discussion of his job. "Those crazy hillbillies with their squirrel guns can spook a fella."

But the Cleveland job, with the Alcohol Tax Unit, had been easier, less frightening. Certainly Eliot got into scrapes and was doing dangerous police work, and kept his usual long hours. But it didn't seem so intense, somehow.

It seemed more like a regular job.

And she could tell Eliot was getting bored with the Prohibition work. He'd admitted to her that his job "wasn't about anything," several times. He told her he hoped to land a job as police chief or commissioner in some smaller city, or put law enforcement behind him entirely and go into private business.

Hearing him say that had made her so happy. She felt they could build their marriage at last. His long hours, his dangerous duty would be behind him, a part of his youth. It was time for Eliot to grow up. And he seemed to know it.

When she first heard the news about his appointment as Cleveland's safety director, she thought heaven had opened up for her. But as soon as Eliot had enthusiastically reported that he wouldn't be "desk bound," that he could still get out and investigate and "shake things up," she knew she was in for the same old hell on earth.

Such feelings made her feel guilty. She knew it was her responsibility to make a go of the marriage. She knew she should support him in what he was doing. He was doing important work. He was still going places, and the papers had been full of him ever since his appointment was announced.

Right now, in fact, as she sat on an uncomfortable sofa in the shiny, pastel apartment, sunlight filtering in through sheer patterned curtains, putting shadowy X's on her lap and legs, she had in her hands the morning paper, which was again full of Eliot. She had read the article again and again till her eyes blurred. She read it over morning coffee, and then she took the car and drove to the nearest drugstore where she bought the other papers, and she read their versions of the Harvard Club raid as well.

She took time out midmorning to do a few personal things, and then she read the papers some more, and then she fixed herself an egg salad sandwich for lunch, drinking a glass of milk with it, feeling like a little girl.

Shortly after that came the threatening phone call.

"Your fuckin' husband's a dead man," the voice had said.

She hung the phone up, quietly, the foul word bouncing off her. Such phone calls had been coming regularly, since they moved in. Eva had mentioned them to Eliot and he had told her not to worry. He had said they had something to do with his throwing two drunken cops off the force.

"I'll get our phone number changed," he had told her, but he hadn't.

She wondered if this call was about the drunken cops, or whether it had to do with the raid last night. Not that it mattered. Such calls would continue, for old reasons, and for new ones that Eliot's future actions would provide.

She had not cried today. Instead, she had trembled with something that she barely recognized as rage, and she had felt oddly empty. These and other reactions, other emotions, ran through her, but she had not cried. She went over and over the newspaper stories of how her husband, the city government executive who ran the police department and the fire department, had gone kicking down doors and scuffling with bandits and facing men with machine guns, unarmed.

How he had very possibly broken the law by taking a "battalion," as one of the reporters put it, of Cleveland's finest across the city limits to get involved in a messy, dangerous business that was none of Eliot's business, none of the cops', and none of Cleveland's.

Oh, but the papers loved it. Every one of them. Eliot had proven that the advance notices of his G-man bravery had not been exaggerated. He was a man of action, Eliot Ness was. Fearless. Like something out of the movies.

Last night, when he got home after midnight, he had said only, "Sorry I'm so late. Stupid city council meeting, and then something else came up."

She'd found him in the kitchen, checking to see if she had anything ready for him to eat, which of course she did, cold cuts and cheese on a platter in the Frigidaire.

"Didn't mean to wake you," he'd said, with his shy grin, as he took the platter to the white kitchen table in their oh-so-modern kitchen, the blindingly white kitchen that reminded Eva of an operating room. She missed their breakfast nook so.

"I wasn't asleep," she told him, sitting with him. She'd dressed in a pink robe and looked nice—at least she hoped she did. She'd made an effort to.

"I'm starved," he said.

"You want a beer with that?"

"Is there some cold? I didn't see any."

"There's some in there. You just didn't dig around enough."

He laughed. "Some detective I am, huh?"

She opened and handed him the bottle of beer; he wasn't one to use a glass. "You want some bread with that?"

"No, thanks, honey." He was folding the slices of meat and cheese, gobbling them. He usually had better manners than this, but he was clearly tired and, as he said, starved.

"What came up?"

He looked at her, puzzled.

"You said something came up," she said. "What?"

He waved it off. "No big deal. A lot of buildup and not much payoff."

"Why don't you tell me about it?"

"Just boring stuff. You know. Work."

"I see."

"You better get back to bed. It's the middle of the night."

"I missed you."

"I missed you, too, baby."

She got up and put an arm around him and kissed his cheek. "Come to bed. Don't sit up and read."

"Is that an invitation?"

"Sure is."

"Okay. How can I refuse a siren like you? Give me a few minutes to finish stuffing myself."

"Sure."

"And I'll just take a glance at the evening paper."

"Fine."

She went to bed and waited. Fifteen minutes later, she got up and found him in the living room, asleep in his chair, the paper in his lap.

She'd let him sleep. Now she was glad nothing had happened last night.

She loved him, and she loved the way he made her feel; he was no rough-and-tumble guy where lovemaking was concerned. If they'd had a sweet night together last night, it would make what she had to do today, this afternoon, even harder.

He worked till noon on Saturdays, and then had lunch at the Theatrical Restaurant with some of his reporter friends. She knew he would show up around mid-afternoon and take a nap. Then the couple would spend Saturday night together. In Bay Village they had friends they'd play cards with. They hadn't made any friends in the apartment building yet, and last.

Saturday, their first Saturday in the apartment, he'd taken her to some fancy banquet where they met a lot of politicians and businessmen.

She'd enjoyed that. She liked dressing up, meeting important people, basking in her husband's celebrity. That was nice, it was fun, and so were most of their Saturday nights together. But it wasn't enough. It could not make up for the rest of her life, in this pastel prison.

At three o'clock he came in. He was cheerful, as she helped him out of his topcoat and hat, which she hung in a pale green closet.

"How would you like to go to a show tonight?" he said, putting his hands on her shoulders. That boyish grin, that lock of hair that wouldn't stay off his forehead. God, she loved him so.

"You hate going to the movies, Eliot," Eva said.

He took his hands off her shoulders, and shrugged his own. "I don't hate it. It's just not my favorite thing. Have you started supper yet?"

"No."

"Maybe we could take in a restaurant then. There are some pretty fancy places in this neck of the woods. Or we could drive downtown. They serve a mean steak at Stouffer's. I hear."

"That's very nice, Eliot. Sit down."

"Sure."

She sat on the sofa. He sat next to her.

"Is something wrong?" he asked.

"I read the papers."

He noticed, for the first time, the pile of papers on the round glass coffee table. "Why the extra editions? Isn't the *Press* enough for you?"

"I read about your . . . adventure last night."

He snorted. "That was nothing."

"No, it wasn't. It was a very dangerous something."

"It wasn't dangerous at all."

"Those men had machine guns."

"They didn't use them."

"You were unarmed."

"The men behind me weren't. The men behind me could've invaded a small country."

"I don't find that very reassuring."

"Eva, Evie, it's my job. It goes with my job. We've been through this a hundred times."

"You're the safety director of the city of Cleveland. You don't have to go kicking down the doors of gambling places. You don't have to get in fights and play with guns."

"I'd hardly call it playing with guns."

"I don't really think of it that way myself. Eliot, I've loved you for a long time. And for a long time, I've had to put up with what you do."

"What I do for a living, you mean."

"With what you do. I think it's more than making a living. I think you need the excitement. You're like some-body who has to drink. But with you it's not drinking. It's kicking doors down and so on."

"That's just silly, Eva. I just do my job, that's all."

"And you're good at what you do, Eliot. I'm very proud of you. Sometimes, when I see you with all those important people, I feel I'm holding you back."

"Now that is silly."

"I know you're smarter than me. I know ..."

"Who says I'm smarter than you?"

"You've been to college. You're a brilliant person, Eliot. That's one of the things that made me fall in love with you."

He touched her arm. "I thought maybe some of that 'excitement' in my life, that you've been complaining about, might have been a factor, too."

She nodded. "I was caught up in that, I admit. I was thrilled by your . . . exploits. But I was younger then. So were you."

"We're not old, Evie, not by a long shot."

"I want children, Eliot, before I am old."

He smiled just a little. "We've been trying. We'll keep trying. It's not such rough work, now, is it?"

"Eliot, please don't make light of it. I know you want a son. I know this is serious with you."

"Look, we'll keep trying. We'll adopt if necessary."

"I don't want to talk about that now. It's too late for that."

"Too late?"

"I don't want to hurt your career."

"My career?"

"This is a bad time for a divorce."

"Divorce?"

"I think we should just live apart for a while."

"Evie, please, let's not ..."

"I've made up my mind on this, Eliot. I'm moving back to the house in Bay Village. If you like, I'll attend some of the public functions, the social things. No one has to know. I don't want to hurt you."

"You are hurting me."

"I don't mean to. I don't think you've meant to hurt me either. Have you?"

"Of course not," he said forcefully, squeezing her arm.

"Of course not," she said sadly, warmly, gently moving his hand off her arm.

She got up and went to the bedroom and got her coat and handbag and the suitcase she'd packed that morning.

She walked toward the door with the suitcase and he quickly followed.

His hands were open in a pleading gesture, as he said, "But you'll be all alone out there."

For the first time tears came to her eyes. She felt the moisture quivering there.

"Oh, Eliot," she said, and went out.

CHAPTER 13

The Euclid Avenue Arcade provided a shortcut between Euclid and Prospect, the facing tiers of shops and offices separated by a four-hundred-foot esplanade covered by a massive glass-domed roof. Sunlight filtered through the Old Arcade, transforming it into a greenhouse for people. The ornate brass railings and balconies were tarnished and some of the streetlight-style lamps had gone dark, and every now and then a shop was shuttered. But Depression or no, the Arcade was an impressive, well-walked place.

Sam Wild sat at a small round table along a balcony on the third level. He was near the Stouffer's Buttermilk stand, an ice cream parlor, one of many such indoor "open-air" cafes in the Arcade. He was eating an obscenely large and gooey hot-fudge sundae with whipped cream, nuts, and a cherry.

People strolling by, particularly fat ones, would occasionally frown at the skinny Wild, who would just smile at them, flashing the smear of hot fudge on his mouth like a badge. He wasn't vicious, but he did have a little mean streak.

It was the last Thursday in January, mid-afternoon, and Wild was waiting for Eliot Ness. Ness was unusually late, five minutes, and Wild kept looking for a sign of him. And there he was, standing at the nearby ice cream counter in his topcoat and fedora, ordering something.

A cup of coffee. Wouldn't you just know it.

Ness walked over with the steaming cup of coffee and sat across from Wild, who smirked in the midst of a hot-fudge bite and said, "Pretty adventurous of you."

Ness removed his hat and unbuttoned his tan topcoat. He looked a little haggard, his eyes red and faintly circled. He'd aged since December. "I'll leave the hot fudge sundaes to the younger generation."

"I think we're about the same age."

"Chronologically. What's this about? Why can't we meet in my office?"

Wild pushed the nearly empty dish to one side, used a paper napkin to remove the chocolate badge.

"Sometimes," he said, arching an eyebrow, "a public place is more private than a private office."

"What's that supposed to mean?"

"It means I don't trust anybody at City Hall except you."

"I appreciate the vote of confidence." There was no sarcasm in Ness' voice. "But," he added, "I do trust my staff."

"I don't know if you should."

"Oh?"

"Your second-in-command Flynt's a political hack. An appointee to appease Rees, his personal pal." Rees was the chairman of the Republican Executive Committee. "Flynt campaigned for Burton, and he worked for Rees' law firm as a claims attorney for insurance companies."

"That doesn't make him a crook."

"Maybe not, but it has a familiar ring. Flynt's doing favors down party lines. Last week he gave out half a dozen jobs in the police garage to political pals, thumbing his nose at civil service."

Ness winced in thought. Then he said, "The tip's appreciated. I'll look into it."

"I realize you're stuck with Flynt, for the time being anyway. But watch your back."

Ness nodded. Smiled faintly. "Didn't know you were so concerned about honesty in government."

"Who, me? I expect a little honest graft to be going on. Especially when a wholesome, clean-cut administrator like you would rather play G-man than run his department."

Ness seemed to take no offense at that. Still smiling his barely perceptible smile, he said, "I told you right at the start, Wild, that fact-finding was my first mission. I've barely been in office a month, remember."

"And barely been in your office. What facts you been finding lately?"

He shrugged. "Just what you'd expect. That we've got an undermanned, inadequate, and demoralized police force."

"That's not news."

Ness smiled again, privately, ironically. "A few nights ago," he said, "driving home, I was listening in on the police radio, and heard a burglary call. By the time it was answered by a squad car, I had time to commit six or seven other burglaries."

"Gee, I didn't know you were moonlighting."

Ness sipped his coffee, his expression turning sober. "Just making a point. D'you know, I found one poor copper patrolling seventeen square miles of the city on foot? He shook his head. "Just yesterday I tried to find out what the hold-up was on replacement parts, so we can get some of these broken-down police cars repaired. The factory rep was polite enough, but explained he just couldn't help it. Seems after twenty years, they discontinued making replacement parts for the model in question."

"Yeah, well, they don't make replacement parts for the broken-down cops in this town, either."

"Some things just need flat-out replacing."

Wild was well aware that Ness was referring to the twenty-one rookie patrolmen he'd sworn in earlier that week. Ness had gone over each and every application with a care that bordered on obsessiveness. Despite the time pressure he was under, Ness had interviewed each candidate personally. Wild supposed this mirrored the approach Ness had put into assembling his ten-man "untouchables" squad back in Chicago. These rookies, Wild knew, were important to Ness; they were the future. Ness' plan, his dream, was to replace the old guard with a new breed of cop.

Even now it was on Ness' mind. He said, "You know, I saw it in Chicago, and it's been the practice here, too. Police department appointments and promotions bought and sold, patronage and payoffs. That leads to a department rife with sloppy, out-of-shape cops. I know what I want out of my cops ..."

Wild waved at Ness to stop. "Don't tell me, don't tell me, 'A good officer should be a marksman, a boxer, a wrestler, a sprinter, a diplomat, a memory expert and, at least, a high school graduate. And most important, he should be honest.' "

Another twitch of a smile. "I'm impressed. Flattered, even. That seems an exact quote."

"It oughta be. You've worked it into half a dozen speeches around town in the past two weeks. Do you ever sleep, by the way?"

"I squeezed some in last year."

Wild leaned back in his metal chair. "I hear, on top of all this, you got some labor problems, too."

Ness sighed. "Yeah, we know the produce haulers are

getting shaken down, for one thing. I've got the Vandal Squad on it. I put Captain Savage in charge and if any-body can get the job done, he can."

"The labor boys hate Savage. And he hates them."

"You're telling me. I had a call from McMahon today."

McMahon was executive secretary of the Cleveland Federation of Labor.

"You told anybody about this call yet?" Wild said.

"Press, you mean? No. It just happened."

"You prepared to tell me about it? The particulars, I mean?"

"Sure. Why not?"

"Whaddya know—pay dirt." Wild got out his notepad and a stub of a pencil. "Spill."

Ness shrugged again. "Not much to spill. He bitched about Savage being 'bitterly prejudiced' against the unions. They have some sort of committee that wants to make a report to me about it. I said I'd listen, but that Savage was going to continue as head of the Vandal Squad in any event."

"Why don't you put Savage someplace else? It'd be the politic thing to do."

"You want me to behave like you say Flynt does? Hell with it. Savage is a good, honest cop. I have to get behind every one of that breed I can identify. And the Vandal Squad is where he's made his mark."

"Some of that mark was made strike-busting."

Ness frowned. "He hasn't done any strike-busting for me. Look, I'll tell you what I told McMahon. Savage's principal assignment is investigating and suppressing window smashings, bombings, and other kinds of violence, which no legitimate union should have part of, anyway."

Wild took down the quote and shut his notepad and said, "Thanks. You're going to get an anti-union reputation, my friend."

"It won't be deserved. I'm anti-racketeering."

"You make me yearn for the good old days."

"What good old days is that?"

"The good old days when there was a difference between the two."

Ness laughed deeply. "You're such a goddamn cynic,
Wild. What makes you tick, anyway?"

"Curiosity. The same thing that killed the cat is what
keeps Mrs. Wild's little boy lively. See, it's trying to figure
out what makes a Boy Scout like you tick that keeps me
interested in this ol' life."

"You really think I'm a Boy Scout?"

"Actually, no. I think you're an ambitious young guy.
A guy on his way up. But you got a problem, and it may
hold you back."

"Which is?"

"You can't get Chicago out of your blood."

"What's that supposed to mean?"

"You shouldn't have taken this one on, Ness. It's career
suicide. You got a month, maybe a month and a half, to
get some Hollywood results, or you're screwed, right?"

Ness said nothing, which to Wild was an admission.

"You've already used up a month of your limited time,
and you've done okay. You made some nice headlines,
and the mileage you got out of the Harvard Club is a good
start on what you need to get accomplished, I'll grant you.
But where are you where your dirty cops are concerned?
They're not exactly gonna blow the whistle on each other.
How are you going to manage an investigation into a closed
shop like that, let alone find out who their 'chief' is?"

"It can be done."

Wild wiped some fudge off his face with a paper napkin. "In a year, maybe. Not in a month and a half."

"And that makes me a career suicide." For the first time Ness sounded irritated.

Wild shrugged. "It's that problem I mentioned before."

Ness laughed hollowly. "I can't get Chicago out of my blood, you mean."

"Yeah. You had such a good time chasing Capone's boys around back alleys and driving trucks through doors and playing cops and robbers, you just can't quite give it up."

Ness looked into his coffee as if an answer might be there, to some question or other. "That's what my wife says," he said softly, almost absently.

"I don't think I've ever met your wife."

"I don't think you have at that."

Ness drank his coffee and looked out over the balcony, down to the lower level where shoppers strolled under the shadows of flapping flags of all nations.

Wild didn't need to be sent a telegram to tell him to drop the subject of Mrs. Ness, although he couldn't help wondering if the circles under Ness' eyes were from problems at home or from the long hours he put in. Of course, those factors might be related. What the hell. Wild went on to other matters, to the reason he'd asked Ness to come here today.

"What do you know about cemeteries?"

Ness' eyes widened at the apparent non sequitur. "People are dying to get in?"

"I mean the cemetery *business,* " Wild said. "Real estate. Little bitty pieces of real estate."

"I don't know anything about cemeteries, other than I know some people who wish I'd move into one."

"Suppose I told you that you aren't the only guy in Cleveland playing G-man?"

Circles or not, Ness' eyes became alert. He sat forward and said, "Enlighten me."

"A Slav from the East Side, a railroad worker named August Kulovic, came to me with his fourteen-year-old daughter in tow. Seems before Christmas he gave his passbook worth fifteen hundred bucks to a so-called G-man calling himself Sidney White."

"Gave it to him?"

Wild explained the scam to Ness, who sat listening intently, his expression darkening.

"The only reason Kulovic got suspicious," Wild said, "was his daughter. She can read. She read the 'surety bonds,'—even though the Kulovics had been warned not to handle bonds 'cause if they got them dirty, they'd be worthless. And Miss Kulovic found out her father had bought some overpriced cemetery lots."

Irritation tugged at the corners of Ness' mouth and eyes. "Why do you know about this, and I don't?"

"Well, you do now, thanks to me. But Kulovic first went to the cemetery itself and was told they didn't own these lots. A sales organization did. That sales organization's office was no longer at its listed address, in the Hanna Building, no less . . . although I'll bet they're still in town, doing business under another name. Anyway, Kulovic called the cops and they sent him to the Better Business Bureau, who said they couldn't help him. He went to several lawyers who didn't want the case. No-body to sue, since the cemetery companies had done nothing illegal laying off some of their plots to an investor. Finally, the poor old guy did the smartest thing he ever did. He left government and business and lawyers behind and came to the fourth estate. He dropped by the paper, and I happened to be in my office instead of covering City Hall that day, and if you've wondered why my shining face has been so scarce the last couple of weeks, I've been busy putting together one hell of a story."

"Which breaks when?" Ness' eyes were narrow. Their placid gray did not lessen the intensity of his gaze.

"Soon. Of course, I'd have a better story if I could lead with your statement to the effect that you plan to tackle this nasty little sting. I've been digging, Ness. I turned up and talked to half a dozen other victims, and that's just the tip of the iceberg, I'd wager. This is just one neighborhood. I bet they're hitting all over town."

Ness was nodding. "Systematically hitting ethnic neighborhoods, taking advantage of devalued passbooks and their illiterate holders. I think your instincts are right."

"One other nasty angle."

"Which is?"

"In some instances, the neighborhood cop has paved the way for the scam artists to make contact with their marks. Vouched for them."

"Bent cops again," Ness said, tightly.

"They're a common denominator in this burg. Anyway, those are the facts. So what's your pleasure?"

Ness lifted an eyebrow. "Why don't we go over and talk to Cullitan about this?"

Wild shrugged. "If that's how you want to go."

"I hate to say it, but his men could investigate this better than any cops I could come up with at the moment. This sounds like the makings of a grand jury investigation to me."

Wild grinned. "That'd make a swell lead for my story. But for your purposes, isn't a grand jury a slow way to go?"

"Cullitan's in my corner; he'll move fast if I ask him to. Do you have a list of the victims you've uncovered so far? Kulovic and the others?"

"Sure." Wild got out his notebook, flipped to the proper page. "You want me to copy 'em down for you?"

"No, thanks," Ness said, reading Wild's list. His eyes

narrowed. "Jesus," he muttered.

Wild had never heard Ness say that before. It made the reporter sit up.

"Do you know what neighborhood this is?" Ness said.

"More or less," Wild shrugged. "Middle of the East Side."

"Remember the Joanna Home fire?"

"Sure. That old folks' home. Burned right before Christmas. Two old goats got themselves incinerated."

"They weren't goats. They were men."

"Jeez, excuse me, Saint Ness. I'm such an insensitive lout."

"You are at that. And you don't have much of a nose for news, either."

"What are you talking about?"

"All your victims are elderly, or at least getting up there, and they all live in this same Slovak neighborhood."

"Right. So?"

"The Joanna Home is smack in the middle of that same neighborhood. The two elderly victims of the fire were Slovaks, just like the victims of your sting."

Wild waved that off. "I thought the fire warden said that house was a firetrap, that the fire started in some faulty wiring and went up a wall into the laundry room and that was that."

Ness didn't reply. Instead he took the reporter's notepad and from inside a jacket pocket took a pen and a small spiral notebook, in which he copied the names and addresses of the victims.

"You really think its arson," Wild said.

Ness pushed the notepad back across the small table and tucked his notebook and pen back in his pocket.

"Let's keep that angle out of your story, for right now, okay?" Ness smiled, but it wasn't very convincing. "It's just a hunch, this arson thing. Let's just leave it at that."

"What's in it for me, if I do?"

"You'll be the only reporter along for the ride when I make my policy raids soon."

"You're moving against Frank Hogey?"

"I might be."

"Hot damn. You got yourself a deal." Wild didn't have to think that one over. The cemetery scam was an investigative piece, not news, and no other paper in town was onto it. "Where to now? Cullitan's office?"

"Not just yet. First let's go out to August Kulovic's place on East Sixty-fourth. You've got some pretty fair staff artists at the *Plain Dealer,* don't you?"

"Yeah," Wild shrugged. "So?"

"So we're going to take one of 'em with us. I'd like a picture of Agent Sidney White."

"Good idea," Wild said as he and Ness left together, leaving melting ice cream and half a cup of coffee behind. "From what I hear, he looks a hell of a lot more like a G-man than you do."

CHAPTER 14

The next evening, Friday, was bitterly cold and windy and starlessly bleak.

All in all, a good night to stay inside and hope that tomorrow would be more suited for making merry, or Mary, whichever the case might be. The citizens of Cleveland seemed to know just how vain a hope that was, however, because thousands of men and women, young and old, weren't waiting for a better tomorrow. They were crowding into the Hollenden and Carter Hotels tonight, for F.D.R.'s Birthday Ball, paying a buck a ticket to dance "so that crippled children might walk."

Most of the action was at the Hollenden, on Superior Avenue near Public Square, and not just this evening. The fourteen-story, red brick Victorian structure, all towers and bay windows, had been built in 1885 by the owner of the *Plain Dealer*. It was the hub of Cleveland's downtown social life, only a stone's throw from City Hall and diagonally across from the *Plain Dealer* building. The Hollenden drew newspapermen, politicians, lawyers, and, it was said, the higher-ups of the so-called Cleveland Syndicate.

Whether any of the latter were among the three thousand or so people now crammed into the hotel's ballroom was anybody's guess.

Eliot Ness, who of late had been frequenting the hotel's taproom, the Vogue Room, had never seen a gangster—or reputed gangster—in the Hollenden, but the rumors persisted.

But tonight, gangsters weren't much on his mind. Nor had he put on this tux because he felt like dancing. He had thought about calling Eva, to take her up on her offer to attend social functions with him, but couldn't quite bring himself to pick up the phone.

At first he had hoped time would heal their marital wound. As the days passed into weeks, he began to enjoy the solitude. It only occasionally felt like loneliness to him. He missed her; he did miss her. And he entertained thoughts, particularly at night alone in the double bed, of making it up to her somehow. Putting the marriage back together.

But he didn't know how to change the way he lived, or more specifically, the way he worked. Or perhaps it wasn't that he didn't know how to; he didn't want to. He wasn't a homebody, that wasn't his style. Perhaps Evie would miss him, too, and come back, willing to accept him on his own terms.

Perhaps when these crucial months of his new job were past, when the Mayor's ticking clock had run out, he could find a way to fit her back into his life.

Had he invited her along tonight, he'd have been distracted from the important work there was to be done. He was fund-raising, and it wasn't for crippled children.

He needed that Secret Six type of slush fund desperately. Without the support of a trustworthy investigative staff, his task was hopeless. Maybe it was hopeless even with such a staff, but at least he could give it the old college try.

It was now almost midnight and Ness' arm hurt from shaking hands and his face hurt from smiling. The crowd was mostly "the people," which is to say middle-class working folks dressed up in their Sunday best, enjoying a rare one-dollar night in the Hollenden's elegant Crystal Room, basking momentarily in the elegance of mirrored walls and shimmering crystal chandeliers and dim lighting that made ordinary people look like movie stars. Never mind that in the middle of all this formal elegance, wall-to-wall jitterbuggers were trucking to Ben Bernie's Boys playing "The Music Went Round and Round."

But amidst such common folks were bigwigs of every stripe. Ness had smiled and shaken hands with his potential adversaries among the local labor leaders, a small army of whom were in attendance. Lieutenant Governor Mosier was there. So were Board of Education members, and a slew of Ohio legislators, headed by Senator Metzenbaum. Smiles to all, handshakes all 'round, and possibly a warm, even witty remark or two.

It was hard work. Cold as it was outside, Ness was sweating in here, and not just because the place was packed.

Mayor Burton, who was threading through the crowd with his wife on his arm, found Ness and said, perhaps for the twelfth time, "There's someone you must meet."

So Ness went over to smile and shake the hand of James McGinty, vice president of the Cleveland Railway Company. He'd already done the same with several chairmen of the board and executives from National City Bank, Cleveland Trust, Cleveland United National, White Motor Company, Cleveland Builder's Supply, Industrial Rayon Company, Stouffer's Restaurants, Corrigan-McKinney Steel, and the Hollenden Hotel itself.

"You're doing a great job," McGinty said. Ness thanked

him, but couldn't find anything warm—let alone witty—to say. Nonetheless he stood making small talk with McGinty and his wife, nearly yelling to get his voice heard over the orchestra.

Burton had slipped away, leaving Ness to his own devices. This kind of glad-handing bullshit was hard for Ness. He enjoyed parties and people, and in small groups could get along with just about anybody. But in a crowded, forced situation like this, he felt the world closing in on him.

At twelve-thirty he managed to find his way to the men's room. He'd had a lot of champagne tonight. He was standing at the stall relieving himself, when he looked over and saw with some anxiety that the man standing next to him was Mayor Burton, which was not a relief.

"Not in here," Ness said.

Burton, similarly occupied, glanced over at Ness, not understanding.

"There's nobody in here," Ness said, "that I have to meet."

Burton laughed, doing the little dance that follows male urination, and zipped up. "This is important work you're doing tonight. And you've done a good job."

Ness stayed at it; he'd had a lot of champagne.

"I'm not so sure. I'm lousy at politics."

Burton frowned. "Don't think of this as politics. I don't. Not exactly."

The men stood at sinks washing their hands.

Burton said, "The men you've met tonight are impressed with you. And you know what that means."

Ness smiled. "I'll have my undercover investigators."

"Right. That is, the slush fund to pay them."

Ness stopped smiling. "I don't want to be beholden to these people."

The colored restroom attendant handed them warm towels and they dried their hands.

"You're thinking about those labor leaders you met tonight," Burton said.

"That's right. They have a right to expect me to be unbiased. They have a right to look uneasily upon a safety director who's in the pocket of business."

Ness and Burton handed their towels back to the attendant, and the mayor took care of the twenty-five-cent tip. The two men stood by an unoccupied shoeshine stand within the restroom and talked. Burton smoked one of his trademark Havanas.

"Your fears are understandable," Burton said, "but I wouldn't worry about being in anybody's pocket. We're not talking about businesses looking for special treatment. We're talking about businesses that want their city cleaned up. They want to be protected from shakedowns by crooked unions, sure. You don't, object to that, surely?"

Ness shook his head. "No. No, I don't object to any of it. Just as long as I have a free hand."

"They want their city cleaned up. What's wrong with that?"

"Nothing."

"The Expo is ready for launching. They don't want Cleveland to be some nightmare city nobody wants to come spend money in."

The mayor was referring to the Great Lakes Exposition set for the coming summer and fall. Local business had underwritten the million-dollar cost of the World's Fair-type expo.

"Watch your step, Your Honor," Ness said. "They tried the same sort of 'clean-up' in Chicago a couple of years ago, and Mayor Cermak got killed for it."

Burton seemed puzzled by the remark. "I thought Cermak was killed by some deranged assassin. And if the madman had been a better shot, we wouldn't be here tonight celebrating the President's birthday."

"According to inside sources," Ness said, "including a friend of mine, Roosevelt wasn't the target of the hit. Cermak was."

"What do you mean, 'hit'?"

"He was assassinated. By the mob."

The mayor smiled uneasily and flicked ashes from his Havana. "Are you trying to scare me, Eliot?"

"No. I want you to know what we're up against. If we take on the Mayfield mob, assuming I can clean up the police force to the point where that's possible, things may get bloody. These gangsters are capable of manipulating events. They can kill you, and nobody but you and them will ever know who did it. And you won't know for long, because you'll be dying at the time."

"Are you drunk?"

"I never get drunk," Ness said, smiling, patting His Honor on the shoulder.

"I'm a Prohibition agent."

The mayor rolled his eyes and said, "I'm glad you're having a good time. You aren't driving yourself home, are you?"

"I have a police chauffeur lined up. And I'm not drunk."

"Good."

"And if you have anybody else you'd like me to meet, that'd be just dandy."

"I don't think that'll be necessary, Eliot." The mayor grinned and put out his cigar. He made an "after you" gesture, and the two men left the men's room, parting company.

Ness moved out toward the dance floor. His intention was to make his way around the edge and find his way out of this crystal sardine can. Along the way he bumped into a very pretty blonde.

"Excuse me," Ness said.

The blonde smiled, a one-sided, crinkly smile, and a stunning one at that.

Her eyes were a startling dark blue. Barely under thirty, she had a healthy, apple-cheeked look and her lips were painted stop-sign red, only the effect was "go." She wore a simple pink off-the-shoulder gown, revealing a creamy complexion and breasts that might have been a little large for her otherwise slender frame. He didn't mind.

"You're Eliot Ness," she said.

"That's right. Do I know you?" he asked, wishing he did.

She stuck her hand out, like a longshoreman. "I'm Gwen Howell. Gwen Cooper Howell."

Ness still made no connection, but did shake the small, warm hand, which was definitely softer than a longshoreman's.

"My father is John Cooper. Captain Cooper."

"Of course," he said, smiling. "I heard the Captain had a pretty daughter. Don't you work in City Hall somewhere?"

She made a face at his mention of a job she obviously didn't like. "In the Clerk of Public Service office."

"That's just down the hall from me. Why haven't I run into you before?"

"I've seen you around. You've never noticed me. You're always preoccupied."

"Maybe you don't go to work in that gown."

"Hardly ever," she said, smiling again. "I wear my hair up and I have these glasses ..."

"You're the classic case of the secretary the boss overlooks."

"I wish you were my boss. I'm so bored where I am. Just clerking."

"Maybe I can do something about that. Do you have a table? Are you with someone? Your husband, perhaps?"

"I have a table. I am with someone. I don't have a husband. Anymore."

"I see. I'm sorry."

"No need to be sorry. He isn't dead, unfortunately. I caught him in bed with another woman."

Her frankness startled him more than the color of her

eyes. Maybe she'd had too much champagne, too.

"What asylum is he in?" Ness asked.

She liked that. "My husband—former husband—was a lawyer. He specialized in divorces. He specialized in divorcées, too."

Ness arched an eyebrow. "Interesting way of looking at the lawyer/client relationship."

"He told me he was just comforting them in their time of need."

"A pity he went into law. Medicine could have used his humanitarian instincts."

She shrugged. "He defended himself in the divorce. Fool for a client. I get a handsome alimony check. Not as handsome as you, but what the hell."

Definitely too much champagne.

"Where are you sitting?" Ness said, taking her arm.

She gestured, and he escorted her. Her father, a widower as Ness recalled, was sitting alone at a postage-stamp table that held several empty champagne bottles and glasses. Cooper beamed when he saw Ness, and stood to shake his hand.

The big, balding, moon-faced cop seemed about as at home in his tux as the bodyguards back at the Harvard Club had in theirs. His sky-blue eyes, a much lighter blue than his daughter's, were a little bloodshot. He, too, seemed to have had too much champagne.

"You're the best goddamn safety director this town ever had," Cooper said. "The very best. Sit down."

Everybody sat down, Gwen across the table from Ness and her father between them.

Cooper said, "I can't tell you what it means to me, this vote of confidence."

Earlier that day, Ness had appointed Cooper head of the Detective Bureau, after several weeks as acting head.

"Don't mention it," Ness said. "I knew you were the man for the job."

Cooper leaned over. "Since we spoke today, our boy reported in."

Cooper, apparently a touch tipsy, was referring to the detective who'd been busted down to uniform to go undercover. This topic had no place in a very crowded hotel ballroom.

"He's found nothing yet," Cooper said, "but . . ."

Ness said, "Let's not talk business here, Captain."

Cooper was immediately embarrassed. "I didn't mean to speak out of turn."

"You didn't. Pour us all some champagne, Captain. It's the President's birthday, after all."

"That it is," Cooper said, and poured a round of bubbly.

Out on the dance floor, with soft, sweet-smelling Gwen in his arms, Ness felt light on his feet, but maybe that was just his head. They were dancing to "The Nearness of You."

"I think Daddy's a little smashed," she said, fondly if a little embarrassed.

"Your dad's a good cop," Ness said flatly. "And besides, we seem to be just this side of smashed ourselves."

"Where's your wife?"

"Uh, this isn't widely known, Mrs. Howell, but my wife and I are separated."

"For how long?"

"Just a couple of weeks."

"How do you like bachelor life?"

"I don't know yet. You're the first girl I've had in my arms since I became one."

"A girl?"

"A bachelor."

"I've been out with men since my divorce. A lot of men."

"How long ago was your divorce?"

"Over a year."

"Lot of boyfriends, huh?"

"Not really. I haven't been with one since my husband."

"Been with one?"

She smiled wryly. "You know. They call it 'sex.' "

"Oh. Is that what they call it."

"How about you?"

"I've never been with a man."

"I see. And you haven't been with your wife for two weeks. That must seem like a year to a man like you. Or is that your finger?"

"How many hands do you think I have?"

"How many do you need?"

"I guess that's up to you, Mrs. Howell."

She whispered in his ear. "Did I see you talking to the manager of this place?"

"Of the Hollenden? Yes."

"Do you know him well enough to ask for a room?"

"I think so."

"Why don't you, then?"

"For us, you mean?"

"Maybe it's a bad idea. Maybe in the morning, when this champagne wears off, we'll feel ashamed."

"Maybe."

"Want to risk it?"

"What about your dad?"

"Think we can find him a ride home?"

"I have a cop who can drive him home. Do you live at home with him?"

"Yes. But I've stayed out all night before."

"You said you hadn't been with a man in a year."

She put her cheek next to his as they danced. "I lied," she said.

THREE

FEBRUARY 3 - MARCH 7, 1936

CHAPTER 15

The sun was shining in Cuyahoga County at one o'clock on this Monday afternoon, but it didn't warm William Wiggens. William—Willie to his friends, at least one of whom hadn't been particularly friendly—was just a body in ditch, and a snowy ditch at that. He lay face down at an odd, askew angle, like a child making a shape in the snow. His topcoat was black and so was his hair; he was hatless. He looked vaguely crumpled, like a discarded piece of paper. The splotches of blood on the snowy ground were turning black.

"We've got to quit meeting like this," Nathan Heller said, Nate to his friends, one of whom was Eliot Ness.

Heller, a sturdy six-footer in a brown topcoat and a darker brown hat, had just stepped from the squad car that had delivered him, at Ness' request, to this desolate rural spot outside Pepper Pike Village, Cleveland's easternmost suburb, just beyond Shaker Heights. A Pepper Pike patrolman, bundled in a light blue coat, stood nearby with several Cleveland cops in darker blue coats, their breath smoking.

Ness was down in the ditch where Wiggens had fallen. He was bending over the body, having a look at the bullet wounds on the man. Or boy, really—Wiggens was barely past twenty.

Ness stood with a sigh. "Young," he said. "So goddamn young."

"Not so young," Heller said. "You don't get any older than dead."

Ness nodded, and glanced at Heller, who took off his hat and riffled his head of reddish brown hair. His father had been Jewish, but it was his Irish mother he took after. He had dark blue eyes and was, Ness supposed, handsome, in a rugged sort of way. One corner of Heller's mouth often pulled into a half grin, which gave him a wise-guy appearance. Ness had known Heller a long time, and knew the man's flip cynicism was largely a self-defense mechanism.

"Don't you get a little tired." Heller asked, putting the hat back on, that half smile tugging at his cheek, "of poking at corpses in roadside ditches?"

Ness laughed, but it had a hollow sound. "This isn't the same. A gangster like Prank Nitti bumping off another gangster like Ted Newberry makes a certain kind of sense."

"That sounds funny, coming from you."

Ness shrugged. "Those boys were playing for high stakes, and they weren't really 'boys,' either. This poor kid was just an independent policy writer."

Heller, hands shoved in his topcoat pockets, looked down unbelievingly at the corpse sprawled nearby. "Since when do you get killed over the numbers, for Christ's sake?"

Ness held up two fingers. "There's two ways, in Cleveland. The Mayfield Road mob has a foolproof, profit-every-day system for the numbers racket: they avoid any 'losing' days in their lottery by franchising individual operators who take the financial risk while the mob takes the cream of the profits. Any operators who come up short on a losing day wind up like Mr. Wiggens here."

"Dead in a ditch," Heller nodded. "Is that what Mr. Wiggens did?"

"Not necessarily. According to Captain Cooper, my man on the Detective Bureau, Wiggens was an independent. He wrote policy without a mob franchise. That's the other way you can die over the numbers in Cleveland."

"How do you happen to have all this information at your fingertips? And, God, how I hate playing Watson to your Sherlock Holmes."

"Elementary, my dear Nathan. Wiggens' blood-spattered car was found mid-morning, about a mile and a half from here. A shiny new blue Chevy coupe with a bullet hole in the rider's door. We've been looking for him ever since."

Heller knelt over the body, as if playing Holmes himself. He looked at the wounds. Wiggens had been shot in the left temple, and in the left side, under the shoulder.

"Powder burns," Heller said, standing, dusting snow off his topcoat with gloveless hands. "The bullets enter high and exit low."

"And how do you read that?"

He shrugged. "He knew the guy who shot him. Car was probably stopped and the guy was talking to him, standing on the running board, with Wiggens behind the wheel. And then the shooting started."

"One guy, then?"

"One guy shooting. Two guys in all. If they dumped his shiny new car half a mile from here, somebody had to drive it, while somebody else drove the car they came in."

Ness was nodding. "That's how I read it, too. Willie used to work for Frank Hogey, who was the most powerful numbers boss in Cleveland, till the Mayfield gang muscled in. Now Hogey's in their pocket.'

"So at least one of the hitters was probably somebody

Wiggens knew when he was working for Hogey."

"Yeah. And that's how this young man came to be dead today."

They climbed up out of the snowy, bloody ditch.

"This isn't your bailiwick, is it?" Heller asked. "Not that that would stop you."

Ness said, "Cullitan called me. He's working with somebody from the sheriff's office on this, and asked me to put some men on it, to keep the sheriffs boys honest."

"So you're helping out."

"Actually, Cullitan's helping me out. He knows this killing has more to do with Cleveland than Pepper Pike or Shaker Heights."

"Yeah," Heller said, the wry half grin back again, "these ritzy suburbs ain't exactly Little Italy."

"Not hardly. They don't play the numbers in neighborhoods like these. It's wall-to-wall golf courses out here."

"The only number they're interested in playin' is 'fore,' "

"Exactly. Let's stroll down this country lane a ways, shall we?"

Heller shrugged, and whispered, "Why the need for privacy? There's nobody around here but us cops."

Ness didn't dignify that with a response. He walked down the gravel road and Heller walked alongside him.

Nathan Heller was the president of the A-l Detective Agency in Chicago, a small, one-man office that was doing good if unspectacular business in these Depression days. Ness had met Heller around '31 or '32, when Heller was still on the Chicago P.D., and was, in fact, the youngest plainclothes officer on the force. He had gotten there by graft, of course, but had suffered a dose of conscience when his idealistic father, an old union man who hated the cops and hated his son's becoming one, blew his brains out with Nate's automatic.

Nate had, you see, given some of the graft money to his father, whose modest West Side bookstore was in trouble. Suicide had been the old man's response. Not long after, Heller had been called upon to get his badge even dirtier and had instead chosen to leave the department and go private.

Heller, a relatively honest cop by Windy City standards, was one of Ness' few contacts on the Chicago police force, and Ness had been sorry to lose him as a dependable source. But just the same, Ness had helped his friend get started in the detective business, putting him in touch with some of his former clients, particularly one retail credit firm from his own private detective days.

Last night, when he picked Heller up at Union Station in the belly of Terminal Tower, his old friend had wondered what he was doing in Cleveland.

"You got cops and detectives up the wazoo," Heller told him, as they climbed one of six sets of stairways leading to the terminal's concourse.

"What does the great high muck-a-muck of the Cleveland coppers need one lousy private op from Chicago for?"

The sound of trains behind them made it necessary for Ness to nearly shout his answer, which considering the nature of the conversation made him feel uneasy.

He said. "I can trust you, Nate."

Heller, carrying his own bag, glanced at Ness and the familiar half smile started as he seemed to consider a wisecrack. But he left it unsaid and the smile faded.

"I'll help any way I can," he said. "Just don't expect me to move to this one-horse town."

Heller's remark seemed more than faintly ridiculous, as they were presently walking through the Steam Concourse, a vast chamber forty-some feet high, with a skylight the size of a football field, an array of huge bronze chandeliers, marble walls, and mammoth Greek columns. But it was hard to impress somebody from Chicago.

"How long can you stay?" Ness asked.

"A month," Heller said.

"A month is perfect," Ness nodded. "Can you spare that long?"

"I got Lou Sapperstein holding down the office for me."

"Oh? And where does that leave the pickpocket detail?"

"Who cares? Lou put in his twenty years and got his pension and got the hell out. It just don't pay to be a cop in that burg, not when you got a conscience."

"Is he working for you?"

Heller laughed. "That'd be sweet! My old boss, working for me. That'll never happen. He's planning to open up his own little office, but till he does, he's willing to hold down my fort."

"Your agency's in good hands."

"Yeah, yeah, but I'm not staying in this hick town a day longer than a month. Understood?"

"Understood."

"Now, what exactly am I doing here?"

Later, Ness explained in detail at his Lake Avenue apartment just what his situation was—including the search for the "outside chief" and His Honor's ticking clock.

"If we land our budget," Ness said, balancing a glass of Scotch as he leaned back on the uncomfortable modern couch, "I plan to put together a permanent staff of investigators. I've already sent word out to some federal men I know to see if I can entice them out of Uncle Sam's employ."

"And if you don't get your budget,' Heller said, "it's a moot point. You'll be warming the safety director's chair till Burton tries again next year."

"Essentially. But I'd find something to do."

"I'm sure you would. Brother! What a job you signed on for. This is reckless, even for you."

"Time is running out," Ness admitted, "but we've had some nice headlines already." He smiled. "And I've got my slush fund."

"Now that you got that," Heller said, with a little shrug, glass of rum in hand, "you should be able to go to town. But isn't this a little like being on the take?"

Ness frowned. "What is?"

Heller smiled. "Settle down, settle down. All I mean is, these businessmen are going to want something for their dough. Stands to reason."

"Cleveland isn't Chicago, Nate."

"It ain't the Land of Oz either. It's a nasty little place, where apparently the cops are so corrupt they make the boys back home look like priests. Of course, I've known priests with mistresses and kids, so what the hell."

Ness swirled his Scotch in his glass. "Look, Nate. I appreciate what you're saying, and I've been over that with the mayor. But taking money from legitimate citizens, who have certain civic concerns, to fund undercover police work, is slightly different from taking graft from goddamn gangsters."

Heller gestured magnanimously. "Hey, I don't mean to be critical. My shorts aren't entirely white either. Just watch it. There ain't no such thing as something for nothing."

"I'm not naive, Nate."

"I know you aren't. But sometimes you can be real selective about what you choose to see and hear."

Ness shrugged.

"You're sure it's okay I stay here?" Heller said.

"There's a couch in my study. Folds out into a bed."

"It's swell of ya, but—"

"I can use the company."

Heller studied him. "Are you and Evie really tossin' in the towel? I find that hard to believe."

"We're just separated."

Heller leaned back on the couch, his smile reflective. "Remember when I was dating Janey? The four of us would get together. We always looked to you as the ideal couple."

"Well, that was foolish, wasn't it?"

Heller sipped his rum. "Guess it was. I see selectively sometimes, myself. Hell. Janey and I didn't work out either, did we?"

Ness sat forward. "How is business back home, Nate?"

"When you change the subject, you really change it."

"Would you be interested in moving here? Taking on a job as my chief investigator? For now it has to be temporary, of course, but with some luck, in a month or so I may be able to offer you a permanent position."

Heller smiled, and it wasn't a wise-guy smile at all. He said, "That's damn nice of you. And I take it as one hell of a compliment that you regard my abilities that high. I wasn't sure you did."

"I do."

"Fine, but I don't want to get married. Much as I love ya, pal, I like being my own boss. If you pull this off, you'll be top dog in this town. But as soon as this angel of yours, Burton, bites the mayoral dust, as he will one day, you're probably going to be out of work just the same. And where would I be?"

"I think I could see to it that your job was secure."

"Maybe you could do that, but then I'd be right back in the middle of a police department again, wouldn't I? Where graft and corruption breed like flies on horseshit. Don't look at me like that. You look like a cross between a cocker spaniel and Jackie Cooper. I hate that. I'm complimented, and I'll help you out, but I ain't movin' here. I don't like this place." Then he added, "It's too damn cold," as if Chicago wasn't.

"I appreciate your help, Nate, even in the short term."

"Besides," Heller went on, "you already got a chief investigator: you. That's the only chief investigator you'll ever hire."

But for the short term, Nate Heller was indeed working for Ness, and first thing this Monday morning, Ness had sent him to the Salvation Army shelter where the Joanna Home residents were still being housed.

As they walked slowly along the gravel road, about a quarter mile away from the body of William Wiggens, Ness asked Heller, "What did you find out?"

"Half a dozen of the Joanna Home old folks did in fact invest in that cemetery scam of yours," Heller said. "Only none of 'em know it's a scam. They think the government's going to turn their passbooks into gold. They think they're holding 'surety bonds,' for Christ's sake."

"Were the two old men who died also investors?"

Heller shrugged. "Nobody seemed to know. I don't think your phony G-man approached them as a group. He talked to them one or two at a time."

Then with sarcasm he added, "Confidentially."

Ness clicked his tongue. "That's the standard pattern. I talked to one of the victims myself a few weeks back. Gus Kulovic, the guy who blew the whistle to my pal on the *Plain Dealer.* "

"Whoever hustled that neighborhood was one smooth scam artist."

Ness lifted an eyebrow. "Well, we got a good sketch of him by having Kulovic work with a cartoonist from the paper."

"I don't suppose you i.d.'ed the finagler, or you'd have said."

"We didn't i.d. him, no. He's got a round, bulldog mug. Looks familiar to me, really rings a bell, but I just can't place him."

"Maybe it'll come to you. You know a lot of crooks."

"That I do. But I never knew a con artist who could turn around and pull off something like this . . . murder by arson. Con men by nature aren't violent criminals."

Heller made a face. "Spare me your criminology crap. If I've learned anything in this business over the years, it's that people are capable of about anything."

"These Joanna Home refugees you talked to," Ness said, getting back to the facts and away from Heller's bleak philosophizing. "Did any of them hear the two victims complaining about the so-called surety bonds?"

"No. And these old folks were pretty sharp. It's not a bunch of geezers with Swiss cheese for memories. They still got a lot on the ball, most of 'em. But not enough, unfortunately, to see through this scam."

Ness sighed. "Like you said last night—sometimes people hear what they want to hear, see what they want to see."

Heller nodded. "In times like these, if somebody tells you the money you invested before the crash can magically come back, you want to believe, you desperately want to believe it."

"Cops helped it happen." Ness stopped. The wind was chilly, carrying flecks of ice. "That same *Plain Dealer* reporter, Wild, came up with half a dozen instances where a cop in the neighborhood vouched for the G-man."

"Have you pulled those cops in and questioned "em?"

Ness smirked humorlessly. "Yeah, and they played dumb."

"Yeah, but they aren't." Heller nodded back toward the ditch and Wiggens.

"Your policy racket couldn't be flourishing like it is without cops, plenty of 'em, looking the other way. That 'department within the department' you were talking about."

"Exactly," Ness said. "Which is why I want you to go over to the McGrath Detective Agency." He dug in his pocket for a list, which he handed to Heller. "Those are twenty McGrath cops who accompanied Cullitan and me on raids against the two biggest casinos in Ohio. Both of which we shut down."

Heller nodded, looking over the list briefly, then folding it and putting it in his billfold. "And nobody from McGrath leaked news of the raids," Heller said.

"Right. So they would seem trustworthy. But I've arranged with the agency for you to go over the employment records of each man. Check the background of each thoroughly. Phone around to prior employers. Check all their references."

Heller was nodding.

"Whittle that list down to half a dozen men," Ness said, "and those six will be your little squad of investigators."

Heller smiled in his smart-ass way. "And what is my little 'junior untouchable' squad going to do?"

"Well, for one thing, you're going to tap the phones of two precinct captains, my own executive assistant, and a few other city officials."

The smirk disappeared. "Jesus. That isn't exactly like tapping Capone's line outside the Montmartre Cafe. What if I get caught at this? These are city employees."

"I know. But the mayor gave me a free hand, and anyway, you won't get caught. This approach did work against Capone, remember."

"You can't use it in court."

"No, but it can sure tell us the lay of the land. Look, I don't particularly relish being a sneak—"

"So you brought me in to do your dirty work. Is it okay if I feel less complimented now?"

"Fine by me. You still interested in the job?"

Heller shrugged. "Money's money. Where are you getting the equipment? That stuff's expensive. Don't tell me, some of your federal pals?"

"Yeah. They loaned me some Pam-O-Graphs. You can attach them to telephone lines and monitor conversations. I'll expect comprehensive field notes from all of your men."

"I bet you will." Heller sighed. He glanced up at the sky, where clouds now blotted out the sun. "You're wading into murky waters, friend. Crooked cops who been that way since Prohibition passed. Gangsters who murder some pitiful punk over the numbers racket. Anybody take a shot at you yet?"

"No. I get the occasional death-threat phone call. Same old stuff—'we'll cut off your wang and dump you in a ditch.' That old song."

"Yeah. And I'm sure they're just kiddin'. Your Mr. Wiggens didn't get his wang cut off, after all. Of course, when you're in Mr. Wiggens' condition, having a wang is small consolation, right?"

Ness looked at the sky. Where had the sun gone? It seemed like dusk and it was early afternoon.

Heller shook his head. "Let's walk on back. This fucking cold town of yours, I'm getting frozen stiffer than that stiff in the ditch."

They walked back.

"Thanks for coming, Nate."

"Ten bucks a day," Heller said, "and expenses."

Ness smiled and nodded. He opened the squad car door for Heller and the officer drove the private detective back to the dark city.

CHAPTER 16

The Murray Hill district, a somewhat isolated compact area often referred to as Little Italy, was considered home turf for the Mayfield Road mob, although many of the chieftains had moved to better, less claustrophobic digs farther to the east. The closely grouped brick buildings tended to be narrow across the front while going back endlessly, built on the slope of Murray Hill Road itself, or the intersecting slope of Mayfield Road. The cold kept people indoors. In warmer weather, old men would sit on the steps of neighborhood shops arguing politics—national more than local—while younger ones would discuss work, or rather their lack of it. Although the neighborhood produced the occasional lawyer or doctor, as well as a good number of successful merchants, the majority of Italian men here were manual laborers. But about the best a laborer could hope for in these times was working a couple weeks a month for the W.P.A. for seventy bucks or so. During the day, in weather like this, the only activity on the street was the usual stream of women and children going to and from Holy Rosary, praying for better times. Nonetheless, crime wasn't much in evidence here, even at night. You might see some teenage boys playing craps under a dim street light, and occasionally a kid might steal coal from a railroad car to heat the family home. But that was about all. The speakeasy days were over.

In a cozy, unpretentious restaurant called Antonio's, a second-floor walk-up over a *grosseria Italiana* on Mayfield Road, Eliot Ness sat at a small round table. A thick red candle, its steady flame providing a modest glow in a room dark with atmosphere, dripped wax onto the red-and-white checkered table cloth. Across from him was Gwen Howell. They touched wine glasses.

Gwen looked as lovely as she had that first night at the Hollenden, even though this was the end of a long work day. She still wore the same light blue woolen sweater over a pale pink silk blouse and black skirt that she'd worn to the office twelve hours before. But she'd let down her lighter-than-honey blonde hair so that it brushed her shoulders. And she'd tucked her glasses away in a purse and freshened her lipstick, which again was stop-sign red. She looked like a million.

Ness told her so.

"Thank you, boss," she said, as their glasses clinked.

Across the room, serenading a couple at another table, a man in a waiter's tux played "O sole mio" on the violin with lots of vibrato.

"My pleasure," Ness said, smiling at her, quite taken with her.

Gwen sipped her red wine. "You said you wanted to celebrate. What's the occasion?"

He sipped his. "Your first day on the job, of course."

"Now that I'm your secretary," she said, "will we need to go to out-of-the-way places like this?"

Two evenings last week they'd wined and dined—late evenings, of course, since Ness tended to work till at least seven and often much later—at the Vogue Room at the Hollenden. They'd wound up in bed in a room at the hotel on both occasions. The morning after the President's Ball at the Hollenden, they did not wake up ashamed, nor had they felt compelled to blame their conduct on the champagne. Theirs was a grown-up affair from the start, and was now in full swing.

"No," Ness said. "We'll still take in the Vogue Room. And the Bronze Room at the Hotel Cleveland, too."

"What about reporters? They're thick as flies around those places."

"I'm thicker than that with them—the newshounds, that is. They'll leave me alone."

"What makes you rate?"

Ness shrugged. "Friendship and headlines, not necessarily in that order."

She smiled wryly, a single dimple's worth. "So you don't think being seen out with your new secretary is going to make the papers?"

Ness shook his head. "Why, does it bother you being out with a married man?"

"It would if you weren't separated. Have you talked to her lately? Evie, I mean."

He looked into the glass of wine. "We speak on the phone. Once a week or so."

"If you don't want to talk about it . . ."

"I really don't. What about your father? Does he know you're seeing me?"

She smiled less wryly, shrugged. "I think so. We haven't talked about it. I think he'll approve."

"He may not like you're seeing a married man."

"I think he'll understand your situation. He thinks the sun rises and sets on you, you know. He sees you like some white knight who's charged into gray ol' Cleveland, to clean up his beloved police department."

Ness laughed, softly. "Horseback riding is one sport I stink at. Ah, here's the waiter."

Antonio's reminded Ness of his favorite restaurant in Chicago, Madame Galli's in Tower Town, in that there was no menu, just spaghetti served with a choice of entrees: chicken, squab, filet mignon, or lamb. Gwen chose the lamb, and Ness ordered the filet. The middle-aged waiter, whose broken English charmed Gwen, was abrupt but polite and wrote nothing down as they ordered. Then he disappeared into the kitchen.

"Are you always out of the office as much as you were today?" she asked Ness.

"I'm at my desk more than I like," he said. "But we did have a good afternoon out in the field today, yes."

"You certainly seemed in a good mood when you got back. You still do. Are you sure it's my first day at work we're celebrating?"

He laughed a little. "I'm celebrating this afternoon, too. We pulled a little raid."

"A little raid?"

"Well, not so little."

It had, in fact, been the first successful raid of a Cuyahoga County policy bank in anybody's memory. With no notice at all, Ness had bundled two squads of Cooper's detectives into unmarked cars, with Sam Wild along for some press coverage, and drove to the headquarters of policy king Frank Hogey, located in a deceptively crummy-looking two-story house on Central Avenue South East. Ness shouldered the door open and Cooper's dicks followed him in, arresting Hogey, his two brothers, and a woman, apparently living with Hogey. His "housekeeper," he said—a twenty-one-year-old redhead with a cute, sulky face and a nice shape, for whom any red-blooded man would gladly provide a house for keeping.

When Ness barged in, Hogey had been standing at the open door of a squat square safe in the study-cum-office of the house. He'd tried to shut it, but Ness stopped the door with his foot and Hogey with a right cross.

Hogey, a stocky guy of forty or so, had sat on the floor and licked blood out of the corner of his mouth and thought about it. The floor around him was littered with clearinghouse slips and long rolls of adding-machine tape, curling like wood shavings.

A little over two thousand dollars was found in the safe, as were the day's records. Most policy operators burned their records nightly, so, not surprisingly, no others were found.

"This fella Hogey is the biggest numbers operator in the city," Ness explained to Gwen. "He's tied in with the Mayfield Road mob now."

She looked both amused and dumbfounded. She pointed out toward the street. "As in that Mayfield Road out there?"

"Right," Ness smiled. "We're in the midst of their home territory. This place used to be a speakeasy."

"And you frequent it?"

"Sure. Why not? It's legal now. Have some more wine."

He poured for her and she smiled and shook her head. Then her expression turned serious, interested. "What's so important about this guy Hogey? Will he go to jail a long time?"

Hogey, who also ran a chain of butcher shops, was a former Police Court bondsman who knew his way around the legal system.

Ness lifted an eyebrow. "Probably he'll just get a slap on the wrist and a fine. The judges are so corrupt we can't hope for more. But by raiding him, we're putting him on notice."

"What sort of notice?"

"That he'll be raided again. And again. That his life

will be made pretty much miserable, from here on out."

"That sounds like harassment."

"That's exactly what it is. If the courts aren't behind me, what other recourse do I have? I'd like to catch Hogey on a murder rap, but that'll never happen."

"A murder rap?"

Ness nodded. "Just a week ago today, a former policy writer of his wound up dead in a ditch."

"My. I think I read about that in the paper . . . ."

"Yeah. From the evidence at the scene, it's clear the guy was shot by a friend or associate. From other things we know, we believe Hogey and his people were responsible, probably bumping the guy off at the Mayfield Road mob's behest."

"I'm glad you're naturally soft-spoken," she said, rolling her eyes, glancing about the restaurant, "or we'd probably be in a ditch by now ourselves."

He grinned, and swirled his wine in his glass. "Not everybody in Murray Hill is a part of the mob. I promise."

"So you raided Hogey to get back at him for the murder? It didn't have anything to do with this policy racket?"

"Well, I had Hogey on my mind because of the murder, yes. But cracking down on policy is a priority, anyway."

"This policy you're talking about . . . that's what they call the numbers racket, isn't it?"

"Right."

"I don't even know how you play the numbers."

He shrugged again. "It's simple. The bettor takes a 1,000-to-1 chance that he'll pick a set of three digits between 000 and 999, as they'll appear on some prearranged daily newspaper statistics. Locally, they key off racetrack results. A winner gets, at most, a 599-to-1 payoff."

"That's a lot of money."

"It sounds like it, but the odds are impossible. It's a

sucker bet."

"So it's sort of like a lottery."

"That's right."

She made a face, as though this all seemed ridiculous to her. "Still, I don't understand why something so harmless would be anything you would want to expend your valuable time and energy on."

"A lot of people have the idea that the numbers racket is harmless. Maybe it is. I do know that nickel-and-dime bets aren't as common these days as quarter ones, and dollar ones aren't unusual. And most bettors bet daily, or anyway six days a week. That means real money in times like these. I've got crime figures from New York that show over a hundred million dollars gets gambled away every year in that city on numbers alone. A city the size of Cleveland is going to be playing in the same ballpark. How would you like to be the mother of seven, and your husband plays his entire relief check on the numbers?"

"No, thank you."

"And the mob into whose pocket this money goes is using it to finance labor union infiltration, loan-shark syndicates, and expansion of organized crime activity of every stripe . . . prostitution, narcotics, you name it."

"I never thought of it that way."

He grunted. "But the real problem with the policy racket is that it encourages cops to go on the pad."

"The pad?"

He gestured with his wineglass. "The pad's a police-okayed list of spots, of locations, where a policy writer can operate. It might be a grocery store, it might be a luncheonette, a bank of elevators in an office building, or a newsstand on any street corner."

"And these 'spots' can get a police 'okay'? How?"

"It starts with the cop on the beat. Precinct detectives get a taste. So do lieutenants, sergeants, and especially the captain. It makes crooks out of cops, and it lends itself to the forming of a structure, a, network of crooked cops, within a police department."

Hence, Ness thought, the need for an "outside chief" to coordinate all the corruption. But this he didn't mention to Gwen. He and Wild hoped to make the concept public once the "outside chief" himself had been nabbed.

"I really shouldn't be boring you with this," Ness said. He wondered what it was about the girl that made him open up so. He had rarely talked so openly to Evie about his work. Not since the days when Evie was his secretary back in Chicago, anyway.

But Gwen, as worldly as she apparently was, was naïve about cop concerns, for a cop's daughter, Cooper had obviously sheltered her from it all.

"I don't even know how you can find time to do all this police work," Gwen said, starting in on the antipasto that the waiter had delivered during their discussion of the numbers racket. "Just your speaking engagements alone take up enough of your time."

That was true. In the past two weeks, he'd shared his "experiences as a G-man" in addresses to the Advertising Club, the Auto Club, Cleveland College, and the Boy Scouts of America—Wild had a laugh on that one.

"It comes with the territory," he shrugged. "The mayor wants me visible. We're trying to pry a big budget out of a largely unsympathetic city council."

"So you have to be a star."

"If that's what talking to the Boy Scouts of America makes you." He nibbled at the antipasto plate. "How are the other girls in the office treating you?"

"Very nicely. I'm surprised that they are, since I'm a young upstart put suddenly in charge of things."

"I've had some experience in that line, myself."

"Didn't your former secretary resent being shuffled out?"

"Betsy? No. She didn't like the pace of my office. She's working in the City Hall Library now. Much more restful."

"Eliot, maybe I shouldn't say anything ..."

"What?"

She was looking past him. "There's a man at a table in the corner. He's been watching us. Or at least I think he has."

Ness turned and looked. A small man in his late thirties dressed in a gray suit and blue tie sat with a blonde even more lovely than Gwen, at least superficially so. They were being serenaded by the violinist waiter—"Come Back to Sorrento." The blonde was big and buxom, wearing a lot of make-up and a tight, dark blue gown. She was perhaps eighteen years old. The small man was balding and had a bulbous nose and squinty eyes and a pleasant smile. He put his fork down to smile at Ness and lift his hand in a gentle wave. Then he returned to his spaghetti.

Ness, who had not waved back, turned and looked at the food which the waiter was putting before them. Gwen was looking at him with concern.

"What's wrong?" she asked.

"Nothing."

"Who is that guy?"

"It's not important."

"Don't go tight-lipped on me now, boss. My curiosity's killing me."

"It's Mo Horvitz."

"Who?"

"He's a gangster."

"Really?"

"Really." Ness couldn't stop the frown. He shook his head. "He's the one they should call 'untouchable.' Come on. Forget it. Let's eat."

Later, as they were finishing their meal, the violinist waiter finally came around to their table, but not to play the fiddle. He wasn't fiddling around at all, actually.

"This is from Mr. Horvitz," the violinist said softly, handing Ness a note.

Ness took it but did not tip the man; that was Horvitz's job. The note read, "A few moments of your time. In the parking lot. M.H." Ness nodded to the violinist, who departed. He wadded up the note and tossed it in a small glass ashtray.

"Have some spumoni," Ness told Gwen, smiling tightly and rising. "And wait for me here."

She reached out to him. "Eliot ..."

"Have some spumoni," he repeated.

As he got his topcoat and left the restaurant, he noted that the gaudy young blonde was still at the table. She was smoking. She looked bored. He wanted to feel sorry for the child, but couldn't quite.

The parking lot, behind the three-story building, was small and secluded.

There was no lighting at all, and the night was typically overcast and cold.

Ness glanced around, looking for Horvitz, and heard the honk of a horn.

It led him to a black Lincoln, parked, its motor going. Behind the wheel sat a pockmarked thug in a chauffeur's uniform. The back door swung open and Horvitz's nasal voice called out, "Please join me, Mr. Ness."

Ness slid in beside the dapper little man. It was warm in the car. Horvitz had apparently instructed his chauffeur to keep the motor running while he and his bimbo ate.

Horvitz offered a slim, diamond-heavy hand. Ness thought about it-then, what the hell, shook it.

Horvitz had a pleasant smile. It wasn't particularly sincere, but it was pleasant. He sat with his arms folded, his head back, the gesture of a small man who wants to look down at you.

"Some of my business associates," he said, "are concerned about your little hobby."

"My little hobby?"

"These raids. The gambling joints. And today, the policy bank. Really. They're annoying. Like bee stings."

"Then you and your business associates better buy some heavy clothes. Because you're going to get stung again. And again."

"You're certainly a determined young man."

"Did you follow me to Antonio's? Or did the manager call you, or what?"

The smile widened momentarily. "Does it matter? Perhaps the hand of fate brought us together."

"What do you want, Horvitz? I don't like to talk to gangsters unless it's in a courtroom or a jailhouse."

Horvitz, without unfolding his arms, gently patted the air with one jeweled hand. "Take it easy, Mr. Ness. We heard about Chicago. We know where Al Capone is these days. We take you seriously."

"That's wise."

"We know you have a job to do. My people can help you do it."

"Help me?"

"Sure. We can point you toward some of our competitors. We can keep some of what we do outside the city limits—the larger casinos, say—even outside the county, if you insist. And more and more of our business interests are legitimate now. I know that frustrates you, but I would think a member of a Republican administration would appreciate good old-fashioned American free enterprise."

"I do, unless you define free enterprise as stealing."

Horvitz shook his head gently no. "I'm interested only in business, Mr. Ness. But you need to be reasonable. There will always be some gambling in a city like Cleveland, and the numbers? You're not going to get popular taking that away from people."

"Who says I want to be popular?"

Horvitz laughed. "Please. I just ate. Don't make me bust a gut. You're an ambitious man. I like that. We can make you look good. You can make some flashy arrests, no problem. We might even be able to arrange to make the local court system more sympathetic to some of those arrests. You might actually get a conviction now and then that didn't result in a suspended sentence."

"Imagine that."

"You might even find certain members of the city council more disposed toward passing your budget next month."

"Do tell."

"Mind-boggling, isn't it? But anything is possible in a world where reasonable men, men of business, cooperate."

"No kidding."

"Will you cooperate, Mr. Ness?"

"No."

"Fifty thousand dollars a year and all the headlines you can fit in your scrapbook. Think about it."

"I have. Good night, and go to hell."

Ness opened the door and began climbing out. Behind him, Horvitz said, "I can give you your crooked cops."

Ness paused, then pulled the door shut. He looked at the little mole-like man.

"Well," Horvitz smiled, "not all of them. We need

some friends on the force, after all. Isn't that what this conversation is all about?"

"This isn't a conversation, Mo. It's a bribe. And if I had a better witness than your 'chauffeur' here, you'd be in cuffs. Keep talking, and I'll cuff you another way."

"I'll give you a special fish, Mr. Ness. A great big blue fish."

"What are you talking about?"

"I'm talking about the name of the high-ranking cop who controls every bent bull on the department."

The 'outside chief.'

"Why in hell would you want to give me that name?"

Horvitz shrugged. "Maybe he's getting too big for his britches. Maybe it's just time for a change."

"Then why don't you just give me the name, no strings?"

"Are you interested in my offer?"

Ness grabbed two fistfuls of Horvitz's gray suit lapels and pulled the little man within an inch of his face and stared into frightened rodent eyes.

"I'm interested in the name," Ness said.

Then he felt something in his neck.

Something cold, something metallic, something very much like the nose of a revolver.

Ness let loose of Horvitz and shoved him, easily, back to the other side of the car. The revolver withdrew from Ness' neck.

Ness withdrew from the car.

Horvitz leaned out the rear door. He'd regained his composure but he was a little ragged around the edges.

"I never took you for stupid before, Ness."

"You're not going to take me for anything," Ness said as he walked away, talking back over his shoulder toward the Lincoln. "I'll let your blonde know she can come down and join you now. It must be past her bedtime, anyway."

CHAPTER 17

Ness, in a gray sweatshirt and black gym trunks, dove for the birdie, slicing with his racket, knocking the projectile back over the net so that it dropped gently at the feet of the similarly dressed Mayor Burton. Burton winced in good-natured defeat and said, "That's all, folks," and the four men, Burton paired with John Flynt, and Ness with automobile manufacturer Alexander Wynston, one of his slush-fund angels, left the court, breathing heavily, and picked up their towels and wiped off the sweat, except for Ness, who was the youngest and didn't sweat much anyway, Burton and Ness met before lunch several times a week here at Dewey Mitchell's Health Club in the Standard Building, for workouts that included badminton, hand-ball, or jujitsu. Ness was giving His Honor lessons in the latter. By mutual consent they left all discussions of budgets and ticking clocks outside the building, except that today, Burton had broken the rule.

In the locker room, as they'd gotten dressed for their game, Burton asked Ness if he was any closer to finding the 'outside chief.' Ness had admitted he wasn't.

And Burton had said, "We need him, Eliot. Or we need something just as big. It's a matter of weeks now. And the way the factions in the council are squabbling, the rocky way the budget hearings are going, it doesn't look good."

Other than that, today, Wednesday, had been no different than any other workout at the club—except for the presence of the stocky figure who stood waiting in the doorway between the badminton court and the weight-lifting room, virtually barring the way. He was an absurd, potbellied figure in an unseasonal straw hat and a brown topcoat open over a brown suit, with a black bow tie and a red rose in his lapel. He was smoking a cigar and looked as out of place in this health club as a nun in a beer hall, and had a similar holier-than-thou demeanor.

"Oh, Christ," Burton muttered under his breath, behind his towel as he rubbed his face. "Vehovic."

The man, whom Ness recognized as Anton Vehovic, Thirty-second Ward councilman, stepped aside and let Flynt and Wynston by. But he blocked the way for Ness and the mayor.

"Councilman," Burton said, his patience strained, "I have a luncheon date."

Vehovic, a round-faced man in his mid-forties, with a wisp of gray in his coal-color hair, blue eyes alert behind wire-framed glasses, folded his arms and smiled.

"I heard you guys hung around here together sometimes," he said.

"That's right," Burton said. "Could you excuse us?"

"You could stand some excusin'. You guys talk real big about cleanin' things up. And that's what it is: just talk. Or was I dreaming you vetoed my slot-machine ordinance?"

Burton sighed. "I've told you more than once, Councilman, that my veto was reluctant, that I agree with you

on principle. But my law director advised me that your
ordinance wouldn't hold up in the courts. Get some legal
advice and try again."

Vehovic snorted. "You got an excuse for everything.
What's your excuse for all them vice resorts running high,
wide, and handsome all over town?"

"That sounds like a subject you should discuss with my
safety director," Burton said, smiling politely. "Why don't
you handle this, Eliot?"

And having passed the buck, towel slung around his
neck, His Honor moved on into the weight-lifting room
and headed for the showers.

Ness knew Burton considered Vehovic a crank. And
the councilman was a bit of a roughneck. He was a union
man, a machinist at the New York Central Railroad shops in
Collinwood, where even now he was an organizer, and had
a reputation as an outspoken, square-shooting but eccentric
champion of his people. He was also a man of direct action,
a regular blue-collar hell-on-wheels. Not long ago, weary
of waiting for the city road crew to fill some ruts in his district, the councilman—whose hobby was bicycling—rented
a truck, bought a load of cinders, and filled the potholes
himself, billing the city for the damage. The city paid up.

Ness rather admired the rough-as-a-cob hunky's zeal,
but he understood why a polished pol like Burton would
not. Vehovic was constantly on his feet in city council
meetings making resolutions and proclamations and in-
troducing ordinances in less-than-King's-English. On at
least one occasion he showed up, straight from work, in
his scruffy machinist's overalls.

Sometimes, when not in an oratorical mood, he would
sleep and snore. And now and then, not having had time to
eat supper between work and the evening session, he sat in

his councilman's chair eating from a can of sardines, the fishy fragrance wafting across the staid council chambers.

"You been pulling some raids, I see," Vehovic said, smelling something fishy himself, arms still folded over a husky chest, incongruous straw boater tilted atop the large round head. "But the big one wasn't inside the city limits. Wouldn't be afraid of steppin' on Fink's toes, would ya?"

Vehovic regularly feuded with the powerful Fink, councilman for the downtown district. Nominally a Democrat, Vehovic was, in practice, an Independent. And an independent Independent at that.

Ness didn't know what Vehovic was getting at, and said so.

"You gonna pretend you don't know that Fink's brother Tommy, his racetracks ain't enough for him, runs gambling joints all over the city, wide open? My ward included?"

"I've heard that rumor. We've raided a few of Tommy Fink's reputed joints and come up empty."

"Well, sure you have. Everybody at City Hall is either on the take or dead from the neck up. Why you think I cornered you and His Honor here at this sweatbox 'stead of there?"

Ness put the towel around his neck and smiled pleasantly. "I'm not on the take. Why don't you lead me to one of those 'wide-open' places?"

"Sure, only by the time we get there, they'll be puttin' on a church social in the joint."

"Why don't you give me a try."

Vehovic thought about that. He said, "You got that guy Savage working for ya, don't ya?"

"Yes I do."

Vehovic frowned. "He's down on the unions."

"I'm keeping an eye on him."

"You better not be down on the unions, or you'll have an enemy in me."

"I don't think we're going to be enemies, Councilman."

"He tossed me in the jug, once't."

"Pardon?"

"Your pal Savage. Tossed me in the jug, once't."

"Did you deserve it?"

"Hell, no! I was just tearing down this fence that was keeping the residents of my ward from usin' White City Beach."

"Wasn't that fence the property of Bratenahl Village?"

He lifted the thumb and fingers of one hand to his nose as if something stank, and it wasn't sardines. "Everybody agreed that fence oughta come down. He's a wise-guy, that Savage."

"Oh?"

"Yeah, he stood there watching me tear down the fence, and when I asked him why he hadn't arrested me yet, said, 'I figure you need to work off some of that extra weight, Tony.'"

Ness stifled a laugh and said, "Look. Why don't you meet me at my office in an hour?"

Vehovic checked his pocket watch. "Yeah, why in hell don't I? I took a half a day off anyways. Bein' the president of the local union has its advantages."

"I bet it does."

He pointed a stubby finger at Ness. "Just you and me. Nobody else. Including that fella Flynt of yours."

"Fine."

Vehovic nodded and trundled off like a small tank.

Ness shook his head and went to the showers. Later he joined the natty John Flynt for lunch at the Bronze Room in the Cleveland Hotel.

"Vehovic's a nut," Flynt said, matter-of-factly, dipping a spoon into French onion soup. The remark seemed strange, coming from this proper lawyer, with his tiny waxed mustache and formal bearing. He looked like a British colonel out of a Kipling story about India.

"He's his own man," Ness said. "I don't think he's crazy. He didn't go to Harvard, but he's not stupid, either."

Flynt pursed his lips in a frown. The mustache twitched. "He's a pest. Why's he such a social reformer? You know as well as anyone that he was in the speakeasy business."

"He wasn't. His father was, as I understand. That was before I came to Cleveland, long before."

"Well, he was vocally against Prohibition."

"You seem to be having a martini with lunch yourself."

Flynt bristled. "I just don't think he's sincere. I figure he's against vice in his ward because he wants to move one bunch of crooks out and another group in. His bootlegger cronies from the old days."

"Do you have anything to back that up? Or is that opinion, or instinct, or what?"

"It's an informed opinion. Let's let it go at that. But I'll tell you this: lining up with him in his feud with Councilman Fink would cause us nothing but grief."

"Why's that?"

"I know you don't like to talk politics ..."

"Particularly not when I'm eating. But go ahead."

"Must I remind you that Fink carries more weight than any other single councilman? That he's a Republican, and our Independent mayor needs to have the regular party types on his side? Fink was a Davis man in the primaries, you know, but he got out the vote in his ward for Burton in the final election."

"You're thinking of the budget hearings."

"And the upcoming vote. Fink is helping decide your fate right now. And he'll carry a lot of weight with the voters in his ward if a bond issue has to get itself floated, to get your budget met. Do you really want to cause him trouble and embarrassment right now by going after his brother's interests?"

Ness smiled. "And when *should* I go after his brother?"

"If I were in your shoes, never. There are enough crooks to go around in Cleveland. Why not pursue some who don't have brothers on the city council?"

"Has Vehovic ever talked to you about this?"

Flynt shrugged. "Several times. He came around to see you, and I deflected him."

"Deflected him?"

"That's part of my job, isn't it? To keep you from getting your time wasted by the lunatic fringe?"

Flynt was a more than competent assistant, but there were times when Ness would have liked to be well and truly rid of him; this was one of those times. But the mayor had made it clear that Flynt was necessary political baggage.

Nonetheless, Ness' voice was tight with barely concealed anger as he said, "I don't think any member of the city council, particularly one requesting that I crack down on vice, qualifies as a part of the lunatic fringe."

"Perhaps I misjudged. But I called it as I saw it."

After lunch Ness sent Flynt on an errand to Cullitan's office in the Criminal Courts Building, and when he met with Vehovic at City Hall, the safety director and the Thirty-second Ward councilman were alone.

They sat at the conference table in Ness' office.

"I hear some good things about you," Vehovic admitted, with apparent reluctance. "This cemetery racket that the grand jury's looking into, they say you broke that wide open."

"I didn't have much to do with that. A reporter friend of mine did most of the work."

Ness did have some people on the case, looking into the possible death-by-arson of the two old men in the Joanna Home. Two McGrath Agency investigators Heller had chosen were showing the drawing of the phony G-man around, but so far had had no luck. Ness was beginning to think the son of a bitch had bolted town by now, but he still had hopes of collaring him. He'd convinced Wild not to air the arson suspicions or publish the drawing, but as the grand jury investigation drew to a close in the weeks ahead, all that would come out.

In the meantime, the bulldog face in the cartoonist's sketch haunted Ness.

Some distant memory was stirring, but only stirring.

"That was my people," Vehovic said, with some passion. "Not just in my ward—those bums hit my ward, too, you know—but I mean Slavs, like me. Poor ignorant immigrants that believe in this country and got fleeced for it. If you helped break that racket open, my hat's off to you."

His hat *was* off actually; the straw boater sat on the table between them, next to an ashtray where the councilman's latest foul-smelling cigar smoldered.

"The city should set an example," Vehovic continued, shaking a fist, letting Ness know that all compliments had ended. "If you aren't ready to do it, I'll do it myself. I'll take a baseball bat and show you how to really raid a bookie joint."

"You have any particular bookie joint in mind?"

"Sure. The biggest one in town."

Publicity. Ness could smell it. This wasn't as good as nabbing the 'outside chief,' but it would carry some weight. Yes it would....

Vehovic was saying, "The joint's on the top floor of the Paradise Hotel on West Twenty-fifth. There's a greasy-spoon saloon downstairs called the Club Cafe."

"That isn't even in your ward."

"I'm interested in cleaning up the whole goddamn town! Aren't you? Besides, that's Tommy Fink's place. Not his only one, but the biggest."

"Give me the exact address."

"Two-oh-seven-seven West Twenty-fifth."

Ness wrote that down. "That's in the Eighth Precinct."

"Yeah, but them cops is no good over there."

"Have you tried them?"

"Lineham told me not to stick my nose in his business."

"Captain Lineham? The precinct commander?"

"That's him. His kids work summers for Tommy Fink at one of his racetracks."

"Are you sure of that?"

"You're supposed to be a detective. Look into it."

"I will. Give me a couple of days on this. A week at most."

"You really gonna do something?"

"Yes."

"Then maybe we can hit some places in my ward?"

"Sure."

"And I can come along?"

Ness nodded. "But leave your baseball bat at home, okay?"

"It's a deal."

Vehovic stood and offered his hand, which Ness shook.

"You know," the stocky councilman said, "ninety percent of the police force is honest and would clean themself up if they wasn't under the thumbs of some old-timers who had to pay for their appointments and want to get their money back. The honest fellas get shoved in some shit job if they don't do what the crooked ones say."

"You're probably right."

"No probably. I am right. Ever ask yourself why the only councilman makin' waves is crazy ol' Tony? Why aren't these other councilmen getting out and saying there's vice in their wards?"

"What are you saying?"

He shrugged elaborately. "They're grafters. Not all of 'em. But sitting right there on the council with me is grafters. I turned down four grand from a Chicago slot-machine salesman to lay off the slots. He said the other councilmen are getting theirs and I should get some, too. I told him to go fuck himself and I put my ordinance through. It passed, too, till your friend the mayor nixed it."

Could the mayor have vetoed Vehovic's bill simply to placate some crooked councilmen whose votes were needed to pass the budget? Ness dismissed the thought as quickly as it came, saying to himself as much as to Vehovic, "Burton's no crook."

"I know, I know. He's just another fancy-pants, that's all. He's like all mayors—he attends his banquets, never misses a chicken. He says hello to me at least. That's more than that weasel Davis ever did."

Ness, feeling a bit like he'd been run over by a friendly truck, showed the councilman to the door. He said, "Thank you for coming to me with this."

About to go out, Vehovic paused and looked at Ness curiously, as if he were a species of animal he'd never seen before. "Are you for real? I'll be damned if I don't think you're maybe for real."

"Give me a week and see. You need a lift anywhere? I can call up a car for you."

"No. I pedaled over from Collinwood, and I'll pedal back."

"Pedaled?"

"Yeah, I go everywheres on my bicycle. I don't get my goddamn exercise at no health club."

"But it's winter."

"Ain't you the Sherlock Holmes to figure that out," Vehovic said, and he put his boater on, tipped it to Ness and went out.

Ness buzzed for Gwen, who came in, steno pad in hand. She was wearing another knit pullover, a light blue one with a dark blue skirt, and looked very pretty, even with her hair up and her glasses on.

"Put the pad down," Ness said, "and pick up the phone."

"Why?"

"I want you to call the Eighth Precinct and report a bookie joint."

She shrugged and lifted the phone receiver. "Okay," she said.

Ness gave her the phone number and the address.

As she dialed, he said, "You're the wife of a W.P.A. worker who lost all his money in the place."

"Got ya," she said, and waited as the phone rang.

The safety director's standing orders to all precincts, well-publicized in the papers, were that such tips should immediately be acted upon.

Then she was talking to a desk sergeant, and she told him what Ness had said to say, putting the proper outrage in her voice.

She listened for a moment, then went on, "If you say so. But if you don't raid that joint immediately, I'm going straight to the safety director's office!"

She listened again, momentarily, and said, "Fine. Do that. I pay taxes!"

And she hung up.

"How'd I do?" she asked.

He put a hand on her shoulder; the sweater felt warm, the wool tickling his palm. "Swell. You ever think about going into acting?"

"Not since my high school's production of *Hamlet*. You think they'll raid the place?"

"They'll raid it. Whether it'll still be operating when they get there, that is the question."

"I got a hunch it won't be operating."

"I got a hunch you're right. But why do you say that, Ophelia?"

She sighed. "Well, when I told the desk cop that my husband lost all his money at this place on West Twenty-fifth, he said, 'Oh—you must mean that bookie joint just down the street.' "

She smiled and shrugged and went back into the outer office.

Then Ness used the phone and left word at the Hollenden for Nate Heller to check in with him. He had a special job for his private-detective friend.

When, soon after, Flynt got back with some papers from Cullitan's office, Ness didn't mention Vehovic, or the raid that should now be under way in the Eighth Precinct.

CHAPTER 18

On the following Tuesday, mid-afternoon, Ness, looking like a successful young banker in his gray vested suit with black and white tie, sat at the counter of Clark's Restaurant on East Ninth, drinking black coffee and waiting for Nate Heller, who was ten minutes late.

Ness was reflecting on Friday's raid by the men of the Eighth Precinct on the bookie joint at West Twenty-fifth Street, a raid which had proved just as fruitless as the one the previous Wednesday.

He had again instructed Gwen to call the desk at the Eighth Precinct, posing as the W.P.A. worker's wife whose husband was gambling away his meager paycheck, threatening to go straight to the safety director's office if the joint wasn't shuttered "this very minute."

As had been the case with Wednesday's raid, however, it had taken a little over an hour for the boys from the Eighth Precinct to hit the bookie joint "just down the street," by which time all gambling operations had—gee, what do you know?—ceased.

The difference tonight was that a handful of Ness' undercover men were on the scene as the raid was about to get under way. One of them was a McGrath Agency man, recommended by Heller. The others were actually Cleveland cops.

Ness had picked five of twenty-one rookie patrolmen he'd recently sworn in, and sent them to the West Twenty-fifth Street joint to play the ponies at the city's expense. They had witnessed the raid, or, more importantly, what had gone before: warning lights had flashed and the patrons were given an opportunity to exit, while the gambling equipment was quickly stored away.

The manager had told the patrons that they could wait downstairs in the cafe, if they liked; it shouldn't take more than an hour to get the place up and running again, once the cops had stopped by, seen the empty room, and headed back to the precinct house. And, according to the undercover men, it hadn't. The place was soon in full swing again.

This had been reported to Ness by one of his rookies, whose frustration and disgust made Ness feel very good.

Heller arrived at the restaurant sixteen minutes late. He hung his topcoat next to Ness' on the metal tree just inside the door, then sat on a stool to Ness' right, took off his hat, and put it on the counter. His thick reddish-brown hair needed cutting. He said, "Sorry I'm late. I just can't get the hang of these goddamn Cleveland streets."

Ness grunted. "I know what you mean."

The counter waitress, a slim, rather plain girl whose make-up made her nearly pretty, smoothed her apron and tried out her smile on Heller; he gave her one back, briefly, absently, not noting her look of disappointment as she filled him a cup of coffee.

Heller was still bitching about the Cleveland streets. "It's like navigating the spokes of a big, busted wheel. Every time I turn around, I'm facing one of those flatiron type buildings."

"I'm not used to it either. Probably never will be. What didn't you want to tell me over the phone?"

"Hey, when you spend your time listening in on other people's phone conversations, you're careful about what you say on the line yourself."

Heller had been tapping the Eighth Precinct's phones since last Wednesday.

"Understood," said Ness. "We already know the warning call to the bookie joint came direct from the desk sergeant. That's incriminating enough, isn't it?"

Heller shook his head, smiling. "Nope. I got better. Today I heard Tommy Fink himself chewing out somebody's ass."

The councilman's brother didn't like getting raided, apparently.

"Whose ass would that be?"

"None other than Captain Timothy Lineham. The precinct commander."

"Do tell," Ness said, angry but pleased, pounding a fist on the counter. His coffee cup jumped and spilled a bit.

Heller seemed faintly amused. "Fink was extremely pissed off about these raids, two comin' so close together. 'What am I payin' good money for?' he says. He said if Lineham couldn't do his job, maybe somebody else would be commanding the Eighth before long; he was 'takin' his beef to Lineham's boss. Who would that be? This 'outside chief' you been talking about?"

"Probably. No name mentioned there, I suppose?"

"No, that was pretty vague. Still, it was some conversation. Too bad you can't use this stuff in court."

"We'll hang Lineham by his balls with this, admissible evidence or not."

Heller put a hand on Ness' shoulder. "Don't let it get you down. A little honest graft never hurt anybody."

"Then why did you quit the force back in Chicago?"

"A weak moment. By the way, I poked around that West Side neighborhood over the weekend, like you asked. From what I hear, that West Twenty-fifth Street joint— which everybody seems to refer to as Tommy Fink's' —has been running almost continuously for at least ten years."

Ness laughed humorlessly. "Why not? Lineham's been commanding the Eighth that whole time. He's been a cop for twenty-six years."

"He must be a wealthy man by now."

Ness looked at his watch. "Do you have to check back with your operatives?"

"No, not for a while. They're big boys."

"Then go take a load off your feet at the Hollenden. I'll call you sometime in the next hour or two."

"What's up?"

"I'm going to raid that joint myself, and I want to take a few trusted men with me. You're one of them."

"Trusted? Me? Gee, I haven't been so excited since I ran across a Melvin Purvis badge in my Post Toasties."

"Why don't you bring that badge along? It's worth at least as much as the Cleveland variety. And your gun."

"Bullets too?"

"Why not? Live a little."

Ness reached for the check, but Heller stopped him.

"Let me," he said. "I'm on an expense account."

Ness laughed shortly, shook his head, and headed for the pay phone on the back wall. He rang Chief Matowitz at the Central Police Station and filled him in about Lineham.

"What do you suggest we do about the bastard?" Matowitz said.

"Call him up right now. Tell him to get over to your office straight away.

Don't tell him why."

"Then what?"

"Have a resignation written and ready for him to sign."

"We'll need a lawyer to do that."

"You're a lawyer."

There was a pause, as if that fact had slipped Matowitz's mind.

Then he said, "I'll get right on it. Are you coming over for this?"

"I wouldn't miss it."

Ness phoned the *Plain Dealer* and happened to catch Sam Wild in. He filled him in and Wild promised to stay at his desk till Ness phoned back.

Then Ness walked quickly through the white-tiled restaurant, (Heller was having another cup of coffee and chatting with the waitress, apparently trying to decide whether she was pretty or plain,) and stopped to pluck his topcoat and fedora off the metal tree. He went out the door onto the cold Cleveland street and turned left toward City Hall, where his city sedan waited in the parking lot.

When he arrived at Matowitz's first-floor office at the Central Police Station, he found the chief once again at the birdcage in the corner, feeding his parakeet bread crumbs.

"You're going to fatten that bird up," Ness said, shutting the door, "till it's just a round yellow ball with legs."

"I know," Matowitz admitted, with an embarrassed little smile. The blue eyes behind the wire frames showed worry. "When I get nervous, either I eat, or the bird eats. Better him than me."

"Any sign of Lineham?"

"No. But I told him to come right over. It should be any minute." Matowitz smoothed his blue uniform and straightened his lighter-blue hat. Then he moved to his desk, which was filled with paperwork, neatly arranged, and in the midst of it all was the resignation. Matowitz handed it to Ness, who read it.

"Simple, to the point, and very legal," Ness said admiringly, handing it back.

Matowitz laughed nervously, pressing the sheet of paper flat on his desk before him, like a placemat. "Sometimes I wonder why I bothered taking the bar. What does the law have to do with a job like mine?"

"Too bad you aren't a judge," Ness said, pacing. Wishing Lineham would show.

"We could use somebody on the bench," Matowitz said, nodding, "who'd give out something besides suspended sentences and slap-on-the-wrist fines."

Ness agreed, then stopped pacing and found himself a chair. He figured he better sit down or he'd start feeding the parakeet himself.

Matowitz, a Slovak after all, was inquiring about the status of the cemetery investigation when the pebbled glass of the office door shook. It wasn't an earthquake; somebody was on the other side, knocking.

"I don't think that's my secretary," Matowitz said to Ness, lifting his eyebrows. Then in a booming voice he said, "Come in, Captain."

The door flew open in a show of confidence and defiance that was undercut entirely when Lineham stumbled in. He was a big man, and his blue topcoat was open to reveal his rumpled uniform, his loose tie, and several buttons open over a protruding belly, revealing the red of longjohns.

His cap was in his hand, and he held it as if he were about to throw it. He was nearly bald, with white hair at his temples and thick black eyebrows over sleepy, beady black eyes. His nose was vein-shot, his lips petulant, and only the firm jaw reminded you that this fleshy face had once been roughly handsome.

Ness stood.

Lineham stumbled forward. He reeked of alcohol. It shimmered off him, like heat over asphalt.

Ness said, "Lineham, you smell like a goddamn brewery."

"Are you sayin' I'm drunk?" Lineham said. His voice was a pleasing baritone, his enunciation exaggeratedly precise.

"I'm saying you're drunk. I'm also saying you're suspended from duty."

He waved his arms. "Let's get a doctor in here. Let's go to some hospital and see if I'm drunk or not. I can't be drunk. It ain't even dark."

"It's been dark all winter, Captain. Have you been drunk that long?"

Lineham shambled past Ness and stood before Matowitz's desk, where he tossed his hat. "What do you say, Chief? I've known you for a long time . . . twenty-six years. Twenty-six years on the force together."

Matowitz, his expression grave, pushed the resignation on the desk toward Lineham.

Lineham leaned his hands on the desk and read the sheet without picking it up.

Then he moved away from the desk, and almost lost his balance in the process. "Make up your minds, gennle-men," he said, his enunciation finally slipping away from him. "Am I suspended, or fired?"

"No one's firing you," Ness said. "You're suspended for intoxication on duty. Meanwhile, charges against you will be drawn up."

"Charges? What on?"

"Ask Tommy Fink," Ness said.

Lineham's face turned pale and even more slack. "You

ain't gonna put no charges together."

"I hear your sons work summers at Bainbridge—Tommy Fink's dog track."

Lineham stumbled around; he nearly knocked the birdcage over. He was ranting, raving. "It's unfair, it ain't just, to question my conduct as a police officer 'cause three of my kids happen to work at a dog track."

"You can have your day in court, if you want."

"They got the jobs themselves, they're helping pay their way through school!"

"Commendable."

"I ain't resigning."

"That's up to you. Your pension's a hundred and forty dollars a month. Think it over."

"You little pipsqueak."

Ness put his hand out. "Your badge and your gun."

Lineham managed to form his rubber lips into a sneer, and, with some difficulty, he managed to unpin his badge from his shirt and hand it to Ness.

"Cap, too," Ness said.

Lineham swallowed and took his cap from Matowitz's desk and unpinned the badge and handed it to Ness.

"Gun," Ness said.

Lineham unholstered his revolver, looking at Ness as though considering using it on him. But he handed it, butt first, to the safety director.

"Thank you," Ness said. "Now go home—in a cab."

Lineham glared at Matowitz. "I expected better of you," he said.

"Look who's talking," Matowitz said.

Ness pointed at Lineham. "Don't go back to your precinct. Stay away from there, or you'll get hauled down here and tossed in the lock-up upstairs."

Lineham tried to give Ness a look to kill, but it was really kind of pitiful.

He shuffled out, moving side to side as much as forward. He didn't slam the door. He didn't even shut it. Ness did.

Matowitz sighed heavily, rising from his desk. He looked at the flowers lining his frosty windowsill. He touched them, gently, as if he were petting animals.

"We were on mounted patrol together," he said.

Ness said, "He's a bent cop."

"I know." Matowitz turned to Ness. "You know, bad eggs like Lineham weren't always bad. They didn't make the system. They just woke up and found themselves in it. Sink or swim. They swam."

"They're about to sink," Ness said, and turned to go.

"Where are you off to?" Matowitz said.

"To show the West Side what a raid is all about," Ness said. He smiled and nodded at Matowitz, who smiled sadly back, shaking his head, patting a nearby flower. Then Ness went up to the Detective Bureau to round up some men he could trust. There had to be a few of those in this goddamn building.

CHAPTER 19

Tommy Fink's joint, as the neighborhood called it, was in the Paradise Hotel, a three-story brick building on the corner of West Twenty-fifth and Lorain Avenue. Rows of tall, arched windows dated the building to the late 1800s. The second-floor windows were for the most part dim, but those on the upper floor glowed yellow, their shades drawn. The lower floor, its windows made of glass blocks, was the Club Cafe, a name written in red neon over the front entry. Painted in white on the side of the building, and conveniently illuminated by a street lamp, were the words RESTAURANT and MEALS. The name of the hotel was written higher up, toward the top of the third floor, the word PARADISE in very large letters—a promise this building wasn't likely to keep. The Paradise was a small hotel—albeit not of the Rodgers and Hart variety—rather a men-only semi-residential hotel just a notch or two up from a flophouse. Its extra rooms went to farmers and truckers who stayed overnight whenever they did business at the nearby West Side Produce Market. The hotel was in the midst of a successful if vaguely run-down commercial strip.

Autos lined West Twenty-fifth, a major thoroughfare, and the side streets too. Factories were nearby. That, and the produce market, made this a swell place for a bookie joint.

It was a cold but uncommonly clear night. Ness found a parking place in front of a pawn shop a block down from the hotel, and climbed out into the chill air. The second raiding car cruised by, found a spot half a block down and pulled in. Heller stepped out from the driver's side of the second car, another city sedan. With him was Detective Captain Savage. They joined up with Ness and his rider, Captain Cooper, in front of the pawn shop.

"Thanks for letting me come to the party," Savage said, digging his hands in his topcoat pockets. He was shorter than the tall, heavyset Cooper, but he was formidable just the same, a pale, beefy dick of about forty-five, with one of those pleasant faces that can turn into a frightening parody of itself when its owner is angered or just plain feeling mean.

"I know this doesn't have a hell of a lot to do with the Vandal Squad," Ness admitted, as the four men huddled under a pool of streetlamp light. "But I had to ask people I can trust. And you're one of the few, Jack."

"Funny thing," Savage said. "I was in this place just a few weeks ago."

Savage had been investigating a series of stink bombings of cafes that had refused gamblers permission to install slots and dice games.

"I know," Ness said, nodding. "I remember. That's another reason I invited you. You can fill us in on the layout."

Savage did so, quickly. The Club Cafe was a typical workingman's bar, with a long counter along the left wall for stand-up drinks and lunches, a wall of booths at the right, and tables in between. The back wall had double doors into the kitchen, a chalkboard menu, and a Paradise

Hotel sign, with rates and an arrow that pointed to a closed doorway at the right.

"That," Ness said, "is the stairway to the third floor. But if they've seen us coming, it'll be locked, my undercover boys say."

"That means the cafe employees work for Tommy Fink, too," Savage said.

"He owns the building," Ness shrugged.

Cooper, his round face flushed with cold, asked, "Is there an alley exit?"

"Yeah," Heller said, who'd been told as much by the McGrath operative.

"I'll cover that, if you like."

"There's probably a hundred patrons up there," Ness said, "and only four of us. Can you handle that exit alone?"

"Sure," Heller said, patting under his left arm. "I'll have a gun and they won't."

"You hope," Savage said.

They walked down the street toward the corner building. Cars and trucks were going by, but the night was cold enough to keep the sidewalks nearly empty. Heller headed around the building to cut into the alley, while the others went into the cafe.

Savage walked up to the bar, where a little Irish bartender was serving beers to a couple of truck drivers, and told the man, "Put your hands on the counter. This is a raid, and I'm in no mood for a warning buzzer."

"Too late," Ness said, pulling a heavyset guy out of a booth just inside the door, grabbing him by the upper arm, tossing him on the floor like an empty beer bottle.

"What the hell," the guy said. He looked up from the floor with a scowl, fists ready, tiny pig eyes narrowing, wondering who the hell Ness was.

By way of explanation, Ness tapped the gold badge on his topcoat lapel.

The guy's eyes went wide, or as wide as they could. He was a man whose ugly face had been made uglier by punching, an ex-pug in his late thirties, wearing a cap, a plaid shirt, and faded brown slacks.

"I saw you hit the buzzer," Ness told the pug. "And you're sitting by the only window in the place you can see out of. You're the lookout. You're under arrest."

The lookout squinted his eyes in something like thought. He got up slowly, brushing dirt off himself; the Club Cafe wasn't spotless, nor was this guy's record, most likely.

Then he shoved Ness with both hands, and Ness went back against a table, bumping it hard, where a couple of factory workers were eating; one of them said, "Hey!"

And the lookout was out the door.

"Let him go," Ness said, as Cooper leaned out the front door, gun in hand.

"Let's get upstairs before Heller gets trampled out the back way."

A skinny, weathered woman who'd been a waitress longer than Ness had been alive was pouring coffee for a customer at one of the tables near the door that led upstairs, unimpressed by the presence of the police. Ness asked her if she'd unlock the door. She sat down mutely at the table, joining the startled customer. Ness shrugged and walked over and kicked the door in.

With Ness in the lead they went up the two flights of stairs three at a time, guns in hand, whisking by the second-floor landing, and soon were on another landing, facing a second locked door, which Ness also splintered.

"Do they pay you by the door?" Savage asked with a grin.

"That's an idea," Ness said, and as he led them into the

bookie joint.

The room was large; it had once been the hotel's ball-room, taking up nearly the entire upper floor. Red warning lights, high up on the walls, were still flashing to signal the raid. Ness' estimation of the number of patrons—men and a few women, a mixed bag running from workers to high-hats—seemed low. There were at least a hundred customers on hand. The flashing lights had kept them from going down the front stairs, and they were mobbed about the rear exit, jammed there, panicking, shouting. Heller, apparently, was blocking the way.

Ness shouted out: "If you're not an employee, you won't be arrested! Stay where you are!"

That settled them down. They started to mill about, but stayed over by the rear exit.

The high-ceilinged room had the usual wall of payoff windows and huge blackboard where racing results were posted, but there was also a scattering of blackjack tables. Against the racing-results wall were seven men, employ-ees apparently, wearing white shirts and black pants, their hands against the bottom of the blackboard. Ness' five fresh-faced rookies, dressed in business suits, were holding revolvers on the seven.

The McGrath detective, Mike McCune, who at twen-ty-six was older than the rookies by some distance, ap-proached Ness with a pleased grin.

"Sorry to spoil your fun," McCune said, gun in hand, "but once those lights started flashin', we figured we ough-ta shut this place down."

"Nice job of it, too," Ness said, holstering his revolver under his left arm.

He took off his topcoat and slung it over a chair at a blackjack table. "Let's get to work," he said.

Ness sat the seven employees down at two adjacent black-jack tables. One of them, a horse-faced, one-armed man of about forty, said he was Nick Selby, the manager. Savage seemed to know Selby, whispering to Ness that this was "One-Arm Nick, the famous blackjack dealer." Famous in Cleveland, maybe; Chicago boy Ness had never heard of him.

At any rate, he put Savage in charge of getting Selby's statement, and had two rookies stand watch on the other six, instructing the eager beavers to put their guns away. He put the other three rookies in charge of taking the names and addresses of the patrons, and then releasing them.

The rookies had frisked the employees already and found no weapons, but in the pockets of the three cashiers were envelopes of money with the stamp of Tommy Fink's Bainbridge Race Track.

Heller came up the back stairs and joined them, taking in the big bookie joint and shaking his head.

"I can't believe I helped shut this down," Heller said.

"Why?" Ness asked.

"I like to make a bet now and then myself."

"So do I," Ness said.

"Then what's the idea?"

"Any police department that lets gambling operate openly is a corrupt department."

"Yeah," Heller said. "So?"

Ness smiled and said, "Go downstairs and get yourself a drink. Put it on your expense account."

Heller put a hand on Ness' shoulder. "This means a lot to me. I guess I'm really one of the 'untouchables,' now, huh?"

"Don't touch me," Ness said, plucking off Heller's hand with a mock nasty look, making the private detective laugh. Then Heller went down for a drink while Ness began going over the premises methodically.

Cooper accompanied Ness to the office behind the payoff windows. On the floor, splayed open face-down where the cashiers had discarded them when the warning lights started flashing, were the ledger books in which bets were recorded. A scattering of cash, also dropped by the fleeing cashiers, littered the floor with green, together with curls of adding-machine paper—each window had its own machine. A big safe in the office stood open, containing several hundred in cash, but, more importantly, revealing books and various other papers stacked within. Ness began thumbing through a volume.

"These are very complete records," he said. "Daily business summary sheets. Lord, they're making a killing here. Daily totals of receipts range from five to ten grand."

Cooper whistled softly.

Ness ran his finger down a ledger page. "Here's a typical day. Overhead is minimal, to say the least. They're paying ten bucks a day for the wire service, ten more for racing forms and scratch sheets, nine for rent . . . get this: 'D.P., seventeen dollars.' "

"What do you make of that?" Cooper asked.

" 'Daily payoff,' " Ness said.

"Or 'department of police,' " Cooper offered.

"Either way," Ness shrugged. He knelt and traced a finger across the spines of the books within the safe. "Damn. These things go back to '29. Ha. I'd say there's a good chance we've got Tommy Fink, councilman's brother or not."

"How so? The judges won't back you up on this. We're looking at the same old suspended sentences and nothin' fines."

Ness stood. "Doesn't matter. There's enough here to call in the tax boys."

"I get it," Cooper said, smiling. "You're talking income tax evasion, not gambling."

"It worked in Chicago," Ness said, and went out in the other room, where Savage approached him and spoke *sotto voce*.

"They copped to it, all of 'em but One-Arm Nick: recording bets, running the wire service, dealing blackjack. We got a good bust here."

"What about this One-Arm character?"

"He's protecting Tommy Fink."

Ness walked over and smiled and sat down next to the one-armed man.

"We know for a fact Fink owns this building."

"I heard that myself," Nick said. He was smoking a cigarette, trying to look calm. He wasn't.

"So you admit you work for him."

"I don't work for anybody. I run this place."

"So you just rent the room from Fink then."

"Naw. I rent it from somebody else."

"Who?"

He shrugged. "Funny. I never caught his name."

"Funny," Ness said, and stood, calling to the rookies. "Get a Black Maria and haul them to the jug. The Ninth Precinct, not the Eighth. We'll get a stenographer and get down their stories." He looked at Fink's men. "You can all have a restful night in jail till you get your fines and suspended sentences tomorrow."

The men at the two tables grinned at each other.

Ness put a hand on the back of Nick's chair and said, "Of course, your evening's not going to be so restful, Nick."

"Yeah? Why not?"

"I'm going to have some nice bright lights set up, and then I'm sending somebody out to look for your arm."

"My arm? What . . . ?"

Ness smiled pleasantly and said, "I've never conducted an interrogation at the Ninth Precinct before. They may not have any rubber hoses handy. We may need something to beat you over the head with."

Nick didn't like the sound of that.

It took several hours to cart out the gambling equipment and the stacks of records, which the rookies loaded into paddy wagons from the Central Station. Spectators gathered, perhaps a hundred of them, braving the cold to witness this unheard-of event: a successful gambling raid in Cleveland.

Heller was sitting in the Club Cafe drinking coffee, not rum, when Ness came down to leave for the precinct house.

"How much cash was up there?" Heller asked.

"A couple grand," Ness said, "more or less. Today's receipts."

"Healthy little operation."

"It isn't feeling so good now."

Heller stood, yawned. "For a guy who likes excitement, Eliot, you seem determined to turn the world into a dull damn place."

"That kid we saw in the ditch," Ness said, moving out into the chill evening, Heller following, "isn't in the world at all, anymore. Dull or exciting."

"Well, I get your point, and this town sure could use some cleaning up. Just don't overdo it. Need me anymore tonight? Any of your cop pals need rides home?"

"No, Nate, on either count. Thanks for your help."

"You coming home tonight? Or are you heading out to the boathouse again?"

"The boathouse. You'll have the apartment to yourself tonight."

"Not necessarily," Heller said, smiling a little, tipping his hat, pushing through the throng of spectators and heading for his car.

Under bright lights at the Ninth, One-Arm Nick Selby

didn't change his story. Ness, who didn't use either a rubber hose or a dismembered limb during questioning, took satisfaction in simply ruining Nick's evening, and complicating his life. He wanted Nick to give serious consideration to a new line of work, or at least a change of scenery. And he wanted to send a message to the Mayfield Road mob, and to gamblers like Fink, and to Fink's councilman brother, as well.

It was almost midnight when Ness left the Ninth Precinct house, and nearly one A.M. when he reached suburban Lakewood. He pulled into the private drive, checking in with the guard in the little booth, before heading down the winding drive to the nest of cottages and boathouses, one of which was now a hideaway of sorts for him.

The boathouse, on Clifton Lagoon in the ritziest part of Lakewood, was a fringe benefit compliments of Mayor Burton's friend Alexander Wynston.

Legally, the safety director had to maintain a residence in Cleveland; he had to have a listing in the city directory, so the Lake Avenue apartment had to stay, death-threat phone calls and all.

But Ness wanted a place where he could get away, where he could spend some time alone or with a lady friend, like Gwen Howell, without having to worry about the prying eyes of neighbors. Even with the papers on his side, gossip could get around and do damage.

So Burton had arranged this additional residence for him, the third counting the Bay Village house where Evie was, but he hadn't set foot out there since they moved. Ness had been staying here most evenings for several weeks now, leaving his apartment to Heller.

For a relatively small building, the boathouse looked massive, its design—like a castle, with two stories of gray stone topped by a squat tower—setting it apart from the more traditional frame structures of the surrounding cottages. Its yard was walled off with more gray stone, and there was even a moat of sorts, frozen over now.

Ness didn't feel much like a king, however, even if a queen of a woman waited within, probably long since asleep. He felt like a very tired cop. He parked the car in front of his castle, behind Gwen's little Chevy coupe, and paused to look at the front yard, which was Lake Erie. The lake was just across the drive, or anyway the lagoon that became the lake was—an endless stretch of gray-blue in the moonlight.

He wondered whether tonight had been a triumph or a disaster. The papers would love the story and the mayor would get the best Ness publicity yet.

But Tommy Fink's brother on the city council would hardly be happy.

Somehow he couldn't make himself care. He had done his job. What the hell else could they ask of him? He was a tired cop who'd done his job.

Then he let go of the thoughts and wandered into the boathouse without turning on any lights. He hung his topcoat in the hall and drifted into the living room which took up half the lower floor; its pale yellow stucco walls were trimmed with dark wood, and occasional wildlife paintings and prints gave the place a male ambiance. He tossed his jacket on a chair and loosened his tie and dropped himself into a soft brown sofa in front of the fireplace, wishing it were going. He thought, for a moment, about sitting in front of the fireplace with Evie, back in Bay Village.

"It's not too late," a female voice said.

For a moment he thought it was Evie. But of course it was Gwen. She was in a sheer blue nightgown. Even in the dim light, he could see the lovely shape of her, the generous breasts, the supple muscles of her stomach, the blonde triangle, the sleek legs. Evie would never have worn such a gown. Evie was no prude, but neither was she forward. Gwen was a modern, anything-but-modest woman. He liked this quality in her, but was nonetheless a little thrown by it. He wondered if he'd ever get used to it.

"Too late?" he asked.

She settled in next to him. "For a fire. We could still build a fire."

"Let's just go to bed."

"Did you have anything to eat? I could fix you something."

"Let's just go to bed."

"And sleep?"

"We can negotiate that."

"I don't know why I'm even speaking to you."

"Oh?"

"You said you'd be home early tonight. I didn't know you meant early in the one-in-the-morning sense."

Ness winced. "I'm so tired I forgot to apologize."

"You also forgot to call."

"I know. I know. I'm a heel."

"You just get caught up in your work. Don't apologize for it. I admire that in you."

"You do now. It'll wear thin eventually."

"Think so? Did you have a good day?"

"Not bad. Not bad at all. Your father was in on it. We finally hit that place you made the calls to in the Eighth Precinct."

"Really?"

Briefly he told her about the raid.

"It makes me think all this trouble is worth it," he said.

"How's that?"

"Well, when I see old-time cops like your father and Savage pitching in with those rookies, busting the biggest bookie joint in town, suddenly I stop feeling like I'm chipping away at an iceberg with an ice pick. Suddenly I start feeling like maybe this job can really be done. If the clock doesn't stop ticking first."

"Clock?"

"Never mind. Never mind ..."

"I have faith in you, Eliot. I know you can do anything you put your mind to."

"Do you? Do you, really?"

"Sure. I'll show you."

"Hmmm?"

"Upstairs," she said, and took him by the hand.

CHAPTER 20

It struck Ness as especially ironic that Cuyahoga, the river from which the county took its name, took as its name an Indian word for "crooked." The Indians surely had nothing metaphorical in mind for the river, which snaked crazily through the industrial valley Cleveland residents called the Flats.

Steel mills, factories and warehouses sprawled throughout this bottomland area; loading machinery lurked like prehistoric beasts turned to framework iron, lording it over a flat prospering wasteland of decaying docks, iron-ore hills, industrial debris, and railroad tracks. Flames licked the gray sky and clouds of smoke mingled with it, a study in progress and its price. The skeletal steel structures of the various bridges spanning the valley cast shadows upon the land, like those of the Depression itself, which had cut into but hardly halted the activity of the industrial Flats. During the day, the Flats had a solemn, scarred beauty, the makings of a prize-winning black-and-white photograph. But to Ness, day or night, the Flats remained a mystery. To a Chicago boy, raised in a city where the lakefront was sacred, where lakefront parks and recreation and clean beaches thronged with people at play, not at work, this oily, yellow river that flowed out of Lake Erie, winding through a landscape dominated by machines, was a puzzle.

Something in the back of his mind nibbled at him, reminded him, that the men helping him, the angels lining his slush fund, were the same ones who helped turn this valley into a pockmarked, profitable hellhole.

At night, to Ness, the Flats was an otherworldly place, a world of darkness cut only by an occasional streetlamp or the muted glow of a run-down waterfront bar and the blush on the cheeks of the low-hanging clouds, projected there by the open-hearth furnaces of steel mills. Looking toward the Cleveland skyline, all that could be made out was the lighthouse that was Terminal Tower. You could, Ness reflected, wander into the Flats at night and never come out. It was the perfect place to be set up for a rubout.

Which was much on his mind this Thursday night, because Ness, angling on foot down a steep cinder road into the Flats, was here to meet somebody.

A Cleveland cop who'd insisted on his coming alone.

He left the city sedan half a block away and now stood by the mesh fence which separated him from a vast graveyard of taxi cabs. These cabs were here for storage and repair, the Depression having cut down the demand on the streets. Several streetlamps made this location slightly less dark—slightly—than most others in the Flats. Looming nearby, a vast, black abstract shape against the strangely rosy sky, was the massive Detroit-Superior High Level Bridge, the major east-west span across the valley, a double-decked structure of steel and reinforced concrete with a lower deck for streetcars, their occasional screech cutting the night like fingernails on God's blackboard.

He checked his watch. He was right on time—ten

o'clock. He kept his right hand in his topcoat pocket, on his revolver. He kept his back to the wire fence, hoping if anyone were waiting for him here, with something other than a meeting in mind, that they weren't parked inside the lot with the taxi cabs. A streetcar screeched again, sparks of electricity flicking through the darkness, reminding him of the El back in Chicago. Only this was one hell of an El.

Several more minutes passed. Ness seldom felt nervous; tonight he did. He chewed his left thumbnail. He tugged at the brim of his hat. It was cold down here, by the river, colder than anywhere else in the city. And darker.

Another screech of a streetcar split the night, but when it faded, Ness could hear the sound of footsteps on the cinder pathway.

The man was young, almost a boy, baby-faced, pale, in a brown topcoat and brown hat. Both his hands were in his pockets. Ness kept his right hand in his.

The stranger withdrew one hand from his overcoat pocket; the hand was empty. He used it to remove his hat. His hair was dark brown and slicked back. He seemed nervous. His breath was smoking, as if his insides were on fire.

"Thanks for meeting me here, Mr. Ness."

"You're Curry?"

"Yes, sir, I am."

"When I found the note under my windshield wiper," Ness said, keeping his hand and gun in his pocket, "I didn't know whether to believe it."

Curry shook his head side to side, lifted his shoulders, put them down. "I didn't know what else to do. I knew I shouldn't call you. You never know who's listening."

"You're right on that score."

"I didn't think I should come to your office. I didn't know what to do. So I left that note on your car."

"We've never met. How do I know you're Curry?"

"You have a gun in your hand, don't you, sir? In that coat pocket, I mean."

"If you're not Curry, you'll find out soon enough."

Curry—if he was Curry—swallowed, and smiled nervously. "Let me just open my coat."

He held it open, like a pervert in the park showing a woman his prize possession. But Curry's prize possession was a police officer's uniform.

"You can close your coat," Ness said. "That uniform doesn't necessarily make you a cop, and, even if it did, a lot of cops in Cleveland would like to see me dead."

"Can I get out my wallet and show you my i.d.?"

"Slowly."

He reached into his topcoat pocket and withdrew a wallet, flipping it open and handing it to Ness. His police i.d. card and photo were there. This was Curry, all right.

"You're the man Captain Cooper selected to go undercover," Ness said.

Curry sighed, and smiled, in relief. "I was afraid maybe the captain hadn't given you my name."

"He did. I insisted that he do so. You were a detective?"

He nodded. "Youngest one on the force. I was working traffic—I pulled some people out of a burning car and got promoted."

"You didn't buy your promotion."

"No, sir. My family doesn't have that kind of money."

"And you allowed yourself to be put back down to uniform for this undercover assignment."

"Yes, sir."

"Which was?"

"Well, you know that, sir."

"The question is, do you?"

Curry nodded in understanding. His teeth were chattering, possibly from the cold, possibly not. "Captain Cooper sent me to the Fourteenth Precinct. He said that it, and the Fifteenth, were thought to be trouble spots."

Ness nodded. "Gambling and prostitution running wide open. Right."

"Right. I was supposed to keep an eye out for things like that. Also, I was supposed to keep an eye out for any other officers taking, well, graft."

"Anything else?"

He shrugged. "The captain said you suspected a network of crooked cops working together. If I had the chance to get in on that, I should do it."

"Infiltrate, you mean."

"Exactly."

"And?"

He sighed heavily and scuffed the cinders with his right shoe. "That's the problem. It's the cleanest precinct I ever saw. I haven't seen anybody so much as accept an apple from a fruit peddler."

"You've seen nothing at all suspicious?"

"I didn't say that, I said I haven't seen any graft. But there's this bookie joint called the Black Swan Club."

Ness grunted.

"You've heard of it?" Curry said.

"Yes. From Councilman Vehovic. You've heard of him?"

Curry smiled. "The nut with the bicycle and the boater?"

"That's him. Tell me about the Black Swan Club."

The kid seemed more at ease now; he glanced toward the sea of cabs through the Crosshatch of fence in the shadow of the bridge. "Well, we've had a couple calls to raid it. And we *have* raided it. It's on Ivanhoe Road, behind this little beer parlor. Anyway, there's never been any evidence of gambling. Just some guys sitting around drinking beer. But I stopped in off duty once, and it was hoppin'. I got out of there quick, though."

"Why?"

"I saw somebody I knew."

"Who?"

"You're not going to believe me."

"Try me."

Curry sighed. "I saw the captain."

"Of the Fourteenth Precinct, you mean?"

"No."

Streetcar screech; sparks in the night.

"Cooper," the young cop said. "Captain Cooper."

It should have felt like a body blow, but as the boy had been talking, the inevitable had slowly dawned on Ness.

"No surprise, really," Ness said, trying to keep the disappointment out of his voice.

"Sir?"

"No one but Cooper and myself knew what your assignment was. Only Cooper or I could have spread the word at the Fourteenth to keep the lid on, where you were concerned."

"They only let me see what they wanted me to see."

"Oh, yes."

"That's why I came to you. I obviously couldn't go to Captain Cooper. And I think the precinct captain's in on it, too."

"Why?"

"He's been too nice to me. Real fatherly. Really going out of his way to make sure I was 'fitting in.' "

"So?"

"When did you ever hear of a precinct captain behaving like that?"

"Never," Ness admitted.

"I had to come to you."

"I'm glad you did."

"I'm afraid, Mr. Ness. If Captain Cooper knew I was talking to you—if he's followed me or anything—I could be in big trouble."

"You could be dead. A lot's at stake, here."

"What should I do?"

"Stay on the job. Let me give you a number no one has."

Ness took a notebook out of his inside coat pocket and scribbled the boathouse number.

"Use a pay phone," Ness said. "Call late at night."

"Will anyone else be there?"

That was a point.

"If a woman answers," Ness said, "don't give your name. If I'm not there, just say you'll call back later."

Curry nodded.

"You need a lift to your car?" Ness asked.

"No. It's not far. I'll walk. Thanks, Mr. Ness."

Curry extended his hand and Ness shook it.

"Thank you, Detective Curry."

"I'm still a detective, then?"

"Unless one of us gets killed in the very near future," Ness said, "yes, you are."

Curry rolled his eyes, grinned quickly, and walked off into the darkness, footsteps stirring up cinders.

Ness stood there and soon felt a hand on his shoulder.

He whipped his revolver out of his pocket and whirled.

"Easy!" Wild said. "Did you forget I was here?"

Ness sighed heavily, put his gun back in his topcoat pocket and said, "I didn't think you'd come up on me so soon after he left."

"I wasn't ten feet away."

"Did you hear it?"

"Every word. It was worth riding on the floor in the

back seat of that goddamn Ford of yours."

"Of the city's. You want to give me that gun back?"

Wild patted his own topcoat pocket. "I don't think so. I'll keep this little baby till we're out of the Flats, at least."

"You can't use any of what you heard. Not yet."

"I know that. Anyway, to me, it's good news."

"Why?"

"You remember asking what was eating me, earlier tonight?"

"I have a vague recollection."

Wild gave a wag of his head and said, "I'll tell you in the car. Let's get out of this place. Gives me the goddamn creeps, down here."

They walked to the car. Wild, about to open the door, one foot on the running board, said, "Okay if I ride in the front seat this time?"

"Do I really have a choice?" Ness said, getting behind the wheel as Wild climbed in.

Then the reporter reached out and touched Ness' arm, stopped him from turning the key. "Maybe we better talk now. Here."

Ness smiled on one side of his face. "Think your revelations will be so startling as to make me run into a lamp post?"

"No. But just sit here a minute. Let me tell you."

"Okay."

"I was looking for a way to get into this with you, especially since it's kind of ... well, it's kind of thin, I got to admit it's kind of thin. But after what that undercover guy said, it's put some weight on. And I guess you've already had the safe dropped on you. It ain't gonna hurt if I let the piano down, now."

"What the hell are you talking about?"

"It's the cemetery racket."

"What about it?"

"I been working hand-in-hand with Cullitan and his eager-beaver young lawyers, you know. I got access to just about everything they're looking at."

"Right."

"They been going over the books of the various cemetery companies, so they can track down who the cemeteries laid off their lots to cheap for obvious resale. That way Cullitan hopes to track down who's behind the sales organizations that've been bilking these old immigrants."

"You want to tell me something I don't know now?"

Wild ignored that. "The sales organizations themselves have folded up. Cullitan figures some of the salesmen and officials have taken a run-out powder, figures some others are just lyin' low until the grand jury either shits or gets off the pot."

Ness nodded. "Right. It hasn't even been shown that what the salesmen did was illegal yet. All of the buyers signed contracts for what they were buying, after all. So?"

"So I was going through the books and found one of the major real estate holders is one S.J. Corepo."

"What kind of name is that?"

"A phony-as-hell name, I'd say."

"Any Corepos in the phone book?"

"Nope. Not a one. You want to hear what I think?"

"That's what I'm waiting for."

"Don't laugh. I think it's an anagram."

Ness didn't laugh; instead, he thought for a second, and said, flatly,

"Cooper."

Wild shrugged. "Cooper."

Ness sighed, and said, "Pretty common name to bother disguising," knowing he was reaching for straws.

"Cooper's initials are J.S.," Wild said, holding his palm

out like he was showing his winning hand. "S. J. Corepo. It's all there, brother."

"How much has 'Corepo' invested in cemetery lots?"

"Over one hundred grand."

"Christ, that's more than Cooper's made in his career."

"The guy must really know how to watch the nickels and dimes, know what I mean?"

Ness pounded the side of the steering wheel with a fist. "Shit."

Not far away, a streetcar on the bridge screeched. It was like a cry of pain.

Wild gestured with both hands, apologetic. "I been wanting to run this past you, but I couldn't quite get it out. Then I heard what Curry said, and ..."

"It would explain some things." Ness pushed his hat back on his head, eyes narrowing.

"Such as?"

"Such as why Mo Horvitz was willing to give me the name of the 'outside chief,' if I'd play along."

Wild bent his head, as if not believing what he'd heard. "You're saying Cooper's the 'outside chief?"

"It makes sense. I was figuring the top man was one of two precinct captains ..."

"From the Fourteenth or Fifteenth, right."

"But a Detective Bureau guy like Cooper floats from precinct to precinct. He can make the rounds easier. And my promoting him to bureau chief put him in an even better spot to do that." Ness laughed without humor. "As you once pointed out, he's 'popular with the men.' "

"What does that have to do with Horvitz offering to give up the name of the 'outside chief?'"

"Plenty. What's been the most surprising thing about this cemetery scam?"

"That the marks would bite in the first place."

"No, in times like these, that's no surprise. What's surprising is that the Mayfield Road mob hasn't turned up in it. They're nowhere to be seen."

Wild nodded slowly. "And they always have a piece of the action in this burg. Look at their policy-racket takeover."

"Exactly. And in every neighborhood where the cemetery scam's been run, cops have vouched for the 'G-men' or the "bank presidents' or 'real estate men' who've come around."

"What are you saying? That this whole scam is cops?"

"Damn near. I'd guess that Cooper's the major investor— 'Corepo' is probably only one of the phony names he owns land under. And you can bet Corepo and the rest of Cooper's names have well-stuffed bank accounts in town and out. And other cops have money in the racket, that seems a safe bet. Safer than investing in cemetery lots, anyway. The salesmen and the sales organization officials who ran the scam were most likely con artists from the outside. Whether the cops invited them in, or they came in and linked up with the cops, who can say. What's the difference, really?"

"Then where does the Mayfield mob come in?"

"That's just the point: no place. And you can bet they tried. But 'Chief' Cooper told them to take a hike. He's that powerful now."

Wild nodded, not slowly. "Powerful enough for Mo Horvitz to want to depose."

"I think the 'department within the department' has gotten so powerful, under Cooper, that it's become virtually a rival mob. The cops are running their own rackets now. This cemetery scam may be only one of many."

"Christ." Wild swallowed thickly. "I think you may be right."

Ness shrugged. "It's mostly supposition."

"I bet we can find the facts to turn supposition into a jail sentence for Captain Cooper." Wild clapped his hands. "I can smell the headlines! Am I glad I teamed up with you!"

Ness started the car. He made a U-turn and headed up out of the Flats.

"We'll start with Cullitan," Ness said. "We'll have his boys dig into Captain Cooper's finances. We'll find out how a guy making thirty-five hundred a year can afford to sink a hundred grand into cemetery lots."

"Think of what that hundred grand got turned into, when the lots got signed over to those marks at inflated value."

Ness guided the Ford onto Huron.

"It's within your grasp, Eliot."

"What is?"

"The big bust, the big collar that'll give you your safety department budget. You may be able to pull this thing off yet."

Ness said nothing. Neither did Wild for a while.

Then the reporter said, "I'm sorry."

"Sorry?"

"About it turning out to be Cooper. About Gwen, really."

Ness said nothing. Behind them the Flats slipped into darkness, as the underbelly of the clouds glowed a peculiar faded red. Like blood, but diluted.

CHAPTER 21

It took only a week for Cullitan and his young staff of lawyers to do the financial research, but it was the longest week of Ness' life. Patience was not his long suit, and waiting for that other shoe to drop, where Cooper was concerned, drove Ness quietly crazy.

He tried to tell himself that Gwen should not be held accountable for the possible sins of her father. He tried to convince himself that she had entered his life, his confidence, by chance. He nearly made himself believe it, too.

They spent much of the weekend together, as they had the last several, and Saturday had been fine. They'd gone to the Hollenden Hotel where the newly redecorated Vogue Room was a futuristic dream world of coral and blue, silk wallpaper, and stainless steel, and they'd danced to Benny Goodman's orchestra, which played a bittersweet arrangement of "Pennies from Heaven" and an intoxicating "The Way You Look Tonight." And when they wound up back at the boathouse, he'd had enough romantic build-up—and enough to drink—to believe in her, to believe in what they'd been sharing these past weeks.

Sunday had been tougher. He'd taken her to a movie, "Born to Dance," at the Hippodrome. She loved musicals. He didn't like any kind of movie, really, and his boredom led to daydreaming which led to sober reflection about the beautiful daughter of Captain Cooper, the lovely divorcee sitting next to him, eating popcorn as she stared at the silver screen, enthralled by Eleanor Powell who was dancing and singing "her jinx away," if the lyrics of her song were to be believed. He desperately wanted out of the theater suddenly; the matinee audience, a packed house, seemed like a mob that might turn on him any moment. Silly thought. He chewed his thumbnail.

Gwen had cooked a meal for him after the show. She'd done this a few times, perhaps to show him she could. She waited on him, wearing her red silk Chinese lounging pajamas. She catered to his simple meat-and-potatoes tastes, which he appreciated. And she seemed to be a good cook, good enough to suit him, anyway.

But it made him sad, somehow. The time he was spending with her here at the boathouse was too much like the time he used to spend with Evie at the Bay Village house. Gwen's brash modern-girl outlook was something that didn't show up much during these quiet evenings. Sitting in front of the fire together; playing two-handed rummy; taking turns stroking the fur of the cat who'd shown up at the back door last week. It was all so familiar. *I've been here before,* he thought. Why was he moving out of one life into another one, when the new one so resembled the old?

Any man, getting romantically involved for the first time after his marriage had gone on the rocks, was bound to have such feelings. This Ness knew. He also knew, as they sat in front of the fireplace, the moment fast approaching when they would head upstairs and tumble into bed, that the strain of the situation could not withstand the pressure of what he suspected about her father. Suspicions which, of course, extended to her motives for getting involved with him.

None of which he could discuss with her.

"I'm going to sleep down here on the couch tonight," he said.

Cuddled up in a ball next to him, she looked at him and smiled the crinkly smile. "Sure."

"I mean it, Gwen."

Her smile faded and her face became a blank, pretty mask that she hid behind, studying him. The soft flickering light from the fireplace made her look especially lovely. Without make-up, she seemed younger than her age.

She had a very fresh-scrubbed and Midwestern farm-girl look at odds with her practiced air of big-city sophistication.

"You do mean it," she said, after a while.

"Yes."

She stared at the fire. The stray gray cat was curled up in front of it, sleeping. "Why, Eliot?"

"I think we're moving too fast. I don't think I'm ready for us to be where we've gotten to."

"Am I that bad a cook?"

Laughing in spite of himself, he slipped his arm around her, his affection for her genuine. "Not at all. You can make gravy with the best of 'em. It's just, I'm not ready to set up housekeeping yet."

She pulled away from him. It wasn't a gesture of anger—of hurt, perhaps, but not anger. She sat there hugging her legs, staring into the fire.

"Have you finally gotten afraid of the publicity?" she asked. Softly. "Have we been too bold? The hotel rooms—spending so many nights together here?"

He sighed. "That's not it."

Now she looked at him, her eyes moist, her lips trembling. Just a little. Just a little. She wouldn't crack, this girl.

She said, with the slightest tremor in her voice, "You're keeping something from me, Eliot. I haven't known you long, but I know you well. What are you keeping from me?"

"Nothing."

"Don't lie to me. Don't you lie to me."

"Baby, I ..."

"Don't call me 'baby.' Don't tell me we're through and then still call me 'baby.' "

"I didn't say we were through. I just said we were moving too fast."

"What is it? What's come between us?"

"Please don't ask again."

"It's Evie, isn't it?"

"What?"

She was nodding to herself. "It's Evie. She wants you back. That's it, isn't it? She's had second thoughts and wants you back."

"Yes," Ness lied. "You're right."

She sat Indian-style now, her arms folded across her generous bosom. Her expression was firm, her tone ironic. "And you feel you've invested too many years in the marriage not to give it another go. Give it a fair trial."

"That's it exactly."

She sat there peering into the fire, its warmth soothing. Outside the wind was howling, but it seemed far away. Her anger seemed to fade. Without looking at him, she reached out a hand and put it on his arm.

She said, "I guess I can't blame you. And I don't blame her for wanting you back."

He didn't know what to say to that. Evie, in the few phone conversations they'd had, had shown no sign whatsoever of wanting him back.

She stood. She smoothed her Chinese pajamas with both palms and smiled bravely. "Better change my clothes."

"Why?"

"I'm not staying the night, Eliot. I have my own car. I think I should just go."

"You don't have to."

"I think it would be easier on both of us, don't you?"

He said nothing at first, then nodded.

"I still plan to be in for work tomorrow morning," she said.

"I plan for you to be. You do a fine job for me there."

"Boy," she said, with a one-sided smile as crooked as the Cuyahoga, "knowing that makes me feel just swell."

And she'd gone, and this morning at work, she'd been pleasant and businesslike and no one would ever have guessed anything was wrong between the two of them. But then they'd always kept their romance out of the office—even when they were alone in his private office, nary a knowing glance, let alone a kiss, was ever exchanged—and so it was business as usual.

And the first order of business had been to go over to Cullitan's first-floor office at the Criminal Court Building, where the other shoe finally dropped, but good.

Behind the wire-framed glasses, Cullitan's eyes were bloodshot. He'd been putting in even longer hours than usual, and Cullitan was perhaps the one local government official who put in longer hours than Ness. The big man sat at his big desk in his Spartan office and gestured to the ledger books and other papers stacked there.

"We've had good cooperation from the banks," he told Ness, "and even the cemetery companies. Of course, everybody's playing dumb where the racket's concerned, and the officers at the banks as well as those at the cemeteries are eager to show us what good citizens they are."

Ness, standing across the desk from the smiling but weary prosecutor, nodding toward the paperwork said, "What do we know now about Captain Cooper's financial circumstances?"

Cullitan gestured. "You better find a chair, unless you just prefer falling on the floor."

Ness sat.

"Under a variety of names, including Corepo," said Cullitan, referring to a small notebook, "Captain Cooper has sums totaling over a hundred and ten thousand dollars on deposit in four banks."

Ness was glad he was sitting down. He whistled slowly. "That's in addition to the hundred grand in cemetery real estate?"

"Yes. And we probably haven't tracked down all his phony names. And we believe—we know—he's filtered other money into the accounts of various relatives. His son, who owns several restaurants, for example."

Ness sighed. "How much has he earned as a cop?"

Cullitan checked his notes again. "Sixty-eight thousand since he came on in 1906. His present salary is thirty-one hundred a year. Before the Depression, he was up to thirty-five and then when salaries were reduced in '33, he was down to twenty-six fifty."

"Any other outside business interests?"

"Just his son's restaurants."

"Any money in the family? His, or on his late wife's side?"

"No."

Ness lifted his eyebrows, put them down. "Then he's dirty. Real dirty "

"Can you help us prove that?"

"I'll have my best man on it."

"Who?"

"Me."

Cullitan's smile seemed damn near cherubic. "You'll have to leave your desk for a while—won't *that* be rough on you."

"I take no joy in this. I thought Cooper was a good cop. I trusted him."

Cullitan nodded, the smile gone. "It does make you wonder," he said.

"How did you turn all this up so fast? Even with the banks and cemeteries cooperating, this is damn quick."

"We had some luck. Cooper has a brother-in-law, name of Emil Kobern, a housepainter by profession, who doesn't appreciate his in-law getting him in bad with the law. When we got a line on Cooper's son being a repository for some of his old man's money, we started checking other relatives."

Ness had to ask. "What about his daughter?"

"Nothing there, except alimony money from her ex-husband. But we found that Kobern had forty-four thousand dollars in the Pyramid Savings and Loan Company, only when we questioned him, he said he'd never set foot in the place. He told us Cooper asked him permission to use his name, so that if anything bad ever happened to him, Cooper that is, in the line of duty, his brother-in-law would have immediate access to some money to help the family out."

"That's a hot one."

"Well, the brother-in-law went along with it, and much to his irritation he occasionally found himself having to go to the bank to withdraw money for Cooper's friends and business associates. For better than a year, at one point, he even took monthly payments from somebody, for Cooper, and deposited them in the account."

"Is Kobern willing to testify?"

"Yes. He's very put out with Cooper for involving him in this."

"Any chance he'll tell Cooper you questioned him?"

"I doubt it. Unless he was performing for us when he gave his statement. I think the lid's still on, where this investigation's concerned."

"Somebody at one of the banks might let it slip. Or the cemetery company."

"Perhaps. But I get the feeling Cooper may not be as popular with his business associates as he is with certain of the boys in blue. In fact, a lot of people will be happy if the heat for the cemetery racket shifts to Cooper."

"The investigation can progress even if Cooper knows," said Ness. "But it would be nice to keep him in the dark a while."

"Yes, it would."

"Well, thanks, Frank," Ness said, rising. "Thanks for your hard, fast work."

Cullitan shook hands with Ness and said, "This thing ought to be right down your alley, an old Prohibition agent like you."

"Why's that?"

Cullitan shrugged. "Cooper was amassing his fortune during Prohibition—1921 to 1931, the very time when he was operating as the supposed protector of the law in precincts like the Fourteenth and Fifteenth. Where, in reality, booze was flowing freely, thanks to paid-off police."

Ness snapped his fingers. "That may be the way to build our case."

"What do you mean?"

"The bootleggers! They're who Cooper was squeezing protection money out of."

Cullitan's smile was a thin line. "You know the old saying: bootleggers never squeal."

"That was never really true, and it sure as hell isn't true since Prohibition became not-so-ancient history. I think some former bootleggers might like to get back at the cops they paid protection to. When I was working with the Alcohol Tax Unit, busting stills and playing 'revenooer,' we used to always hear the bootleggers bitching about how they never really made a decent buck in the speakeasy days. That police payoffs had bled 'em dry."

Cullitan smiled, thinking, nodding. "Bribery charges. That's what we'll get him on. Bribes paid to influence him with respect to his official duties as a police captain in the enforcement of laws of the State of Ohio."

Ness smiled, nodded, and finished the sentence, "Particularly relating to the possession, manufacture, and sale of intoxicating liquors."

"Can't quite get being a Prohibition agent out of your system," Cullitan said, "can you?"

"It worked in Chicago," Ness said, and he hoofed it over to the Standard Building.

He found Agent Hedges at the same old stand, a corner desk in the cramped room shared by five Alcohol Tax Unit agents. The other men were out in the field, but Hedges was taking care of the paperwork that was choking his desk, and manning the phone.

"Slumming?" Hedges asked Ness, with a smile that didn't hide his dislike. "It's a little early to be going to the health club to play footsie with the mayor."

Ness pulled a chair over and sat on it backwards. "You really like not having me for a boss, don't you, Bob?"

Hedges grunted and shook his head no. "Actually, the guy that took over is even worse than you were."

"Gee, that's hard to picture."

"This place is going to hell in a hand basket," Hedges said, glancing with wide eyes around the claustrophobic office. "Hundreds of joints are selling hooch. Rotgut and raisin jack and white mule. And we're not doing anything about it."

Ness made a sympathetic clicking sound.

"At least you're knocking some places over," Hedges said. "I gotta hand you that much."

"I'm working on it. I need a favor."

"From me?"

"From you. You were in this office a good many years before I was."

"I outlast all my bosses. It's my favorite trait."

"I need a list of known bootleggers who operated in Cleveland from '21 through '31. Can you put that together for me?"

"I could. But why should I?"

"Hedges, you don't like me, and I'm not nuts about you, or anyway I'm not nuts about your style. But we've got one thing in common: we aren't bent."

"That I agree with."

"Then help me. Do me that list. I'm trying to put some bent cops in jail."

Hedges thought, just for a moment. Then said, "Sure. Why not. It'll take me a day to do it, I'd say. And it'd help if you'd tell my boss you requested it, so I can get away with taking the time out."

"That's no problem. Could you give me a head start, though?"

"How's that?"

"Can you think of anybody in particular in those days who was especially resentful about paying police protection?"

Hedges laughed briefly. "We heard that sad song from just about every bootlegger in town."

"Then give me the name and address of a real prize whiner. Especially somebody who might've operated in the Fourteenth or Fifteenth Precinct. Somebody who really felt he was bled white."

"I can think of one. Joe Brody. Brodzinsky. He used to run a joint at East Sixty-fifth and Fleet."

"What's he doing now?"

"He's got a saloon in Garfield Heights. He told me he moved out there to get away from the Cleveland cops."

"You think he'd talk? Think he'd name names?"

Hedges shrugged. "You never know till you ask," and he returned to his work.

And Ness set out to do his.

CHAPTER 22

Brody's Bar and Grill was on Broadway, near Garfield Park, just south of Cleveland in the blue-collar suburb of Garfield Heights. The interior of the unpretentious square yellow building resembled a restaurant more than a bar, being less dimly lit than most, with plenty of tables, and booths lining three walls. Behind the bar, which took up only half of one wall, was the kitchen, somewhat visible through a short-order window, but nobody was cooking back there, because nobody was eating out here. It was after two in the afternoon, and the place wasn't very busy. Some truckers and a couple of grounds keepers from nearby Calvary Cemetery were drinking bottled beer at the bar. At the far end of the bar, by the wall, a young guy in white, probably an orderly from the state hospital close by, was playing a countertop pinball machine. An empty stool separated him from a uniform cop, city not suburban, who quickly headed for a corner booth as Ness came in, Sam Wild close on his heels.

Ness slid onto an empty stool and Wild sat at a table nearby. Behind the bar was a thin dark man of about forty in a bartender's apron. He'd been talking to one of the truckers but now he fell silent. His face was blade narrow and his nose blade sharp. So were his dark eyes, as he studied the man in the tan topcoat and brown fedora.

Ness took off his hat and smiled blandly at the bartender. "Beer," he said.

"Any special brand?"

Ness shrugged. "You're the doctor."

Speaking of which, the hospital orderly down the bar hit the jackpot on the pinball. "Hot damn!" he said. He hopped off his stool, ran over and squeezed between Ness and the trucker, and showed the bartender two handfuls of slugs. He was pale, about twenty, with acne on his neck, and he was grinning like an idiot.

"Pay up, Joe!"

The bartender smiled without much enthusiasm and said, "Lay 'em on the counter. We'll count 'em."

Ness smiled at the hospital orderly. "Going to trade those in for real money?"

"You bet!" the orderly said. The teeth in the idiotic grin were bucked.

"That's against the law in this county, you know," Ness said.

"Yeah, sure," the orderly said, smirking, waving Ness off.

The bartender was breaking a roll of nickels on the counter. He frowned at Ness and said, "Don't give my customers a hard time, bud."

"I could arrest you both," Ness said, neutrally.

The bartender filled the orderly's palm with real nickels, and smirked.

"You're a cop? You don't look like a cop."

"What do I look like?"

"Teacher. No. Banker, I'd say. You got the clothes for it."

Ness turned to Wild and said, "Sam, find a phone and call Central Headquarters for me, will you? Have them send somebody over to take that machine out."

"Who are you?" the bartender asked, suspiciously.

"My name's Ness."

One of the truckers leaned forward to have a look at this, and snorted a laugh. "Oh, yeah? And I suppose you're the safety director, too."

"That's right," Ness said.

The bartender cocked his head back and looked at Ness through slitted eyes.

The trucker wasn't through. "Listen, pal, go peddle that bullshit somewheres else. It just so happens the director's a personal friend of mine."

"I see," Ness said. He raised his voice. "Well, if you don't believe me, ask the cop who's been hiding in that back booth since we came in. His drink's still at the bar."

At which the patrolman quickly slipped out of the booth, pulling his cap down over his lowered head. He moved quickly around the room, between the booths and the edge of the tables, and out the door.

Wild was laughing quietly at his table.

Ness turned to him. "You want a beer? Or are you working?"

"Yes to both," Wild said.

"You heard him," Ness said to the bartender, who got two bottles of Pabst.

The hospital orderly was standing there with a handful of nickels, his mouth hanging open like a yawning window.

"That's damn nice of you," Ness said.

The orderly thought for a moment, then said, "What is?"

Ness nodded at the cupped palm and its nickels and said, "Buying our beers."

The orderly shut his mouth, frowned in childlike disappointment, then slammed the nickels on the counter; he returned to his stool, where he sat drinking a beer and looking at, but not playing, the little pinball.

Ness said to the bartender, "Got a minute?"

"You gonna pull my machine?"

"That depends on if you've got a minute."

"I got a minute," he said. "If you'll give me one first, that is. To see if anybody's thirsty, and then I'll join you at a booth."

Ness nodded, and he and Wild moved to the booth the patrolman had been nervously warming. They sat on the same side, leaving the other side for the bartender, who joined them shortly.

"You're Ness," he said, then pointed at Wild. "But who's this?"

"He's Sam Wild."

"That name sounds familiar."

"He's a reporter."

"*Plain Dealer,*" Wild said.

"I don't need any publicity."

"You won't get any," Ness said. "Not unless you want it. He's taking some notes for me, but he's operating on the understanding that he can't use anything in print unless this gets to the grand jury."

The bartender reared back. "Grand jury! What the hell is this?"

"It's about Captain Cooper, Mr. Brody. You are Joe Brody, aren't you?"

The bartender's hand rubbed the slightly blue chin of the blade-like face.

"I'm Brody," he said. "Brodzinsky, I was born under. Captain Cooper, huh? His little show finally about to close, is it?"

"Possibly. If a few people are willing to talk to me."

Brody laughed deep in his throat, his eyes widening. "Don't tell me I'm the first."

"Not quite. The first I've interviewed personally."

"Why should I tell you anything? I'm out of that business. Didn't you read about Repeal in the papers? I'm legit, now."

"Relatively speaking."

"Don't go breakin' my balls over a lousy pinball machine, Mr. Ness. I'll haul it off the counter and put it in your fuckin' back seat, if you want."

"I was thinking more along the lines of this place of yours, which I assume you own."

"I own it."

"And bought with the proceeds of your bootlegging activities, no doubt."

"Ha! I sure did, and it ain't the Vogue Room at the Hollenden Hotel, either, is it? There weren't very many of us who got rich bootlegging, not in this town."

"Because the cost of protection was so high?"

Brody winced at the memory. "Paying fines if we got busted, or payoffs if we didn't wanna be. Either way, we were screwed."

"You want to talk about it?"

"Tell your reporter friend to get lost."

"I can do that, but I promise you he's not going to use any of this, unless you decide to go to the grand jury with it as a witness."

"Why in hell would I want to do that?"

"Because the cops in this town kept you from making the kind of dough you otherwise could've, in those years. Years that should have been gravy years for a guy like Joe Brody."

Brody said nothing. He sat there thinking, brooding.

"If you'd been in Chicago back then instead of Cleveland," Ness said, "you'd be living today in some fancy suburb or on the Gold Coast. Most of those guys made out pretty well."

"I hear Capone didn't do so good."

"He did fine. He just forgot to pay his taxes."

"I paid my taxes."

"Did I say otherwise?"

Brody sneered. "But you could make a phone call . . ."

Ness shook his head no. "I'm not here to blackmail you. Maybe you did pay taxes on the dough that went into this little joint, maybe you didn't. That's not my job or my concern."

Brody's sneer disappeared but his suspicions remained. "What *is*?"

"Captain Cooper. I hear he's a crook. I want to find out if that's so. If you didn't pay him tribute, well, I want to know that, too. I'm not looking to hang anybody, or whitewash anybody, either."

Brody's eyes narrowed to slits again. "You mean you want the truth? That's what you're after?"

"That's right."

"Ain't you the damnedest cop. What's in it for me?"

"Satisfaction."

"Revenge, you mean."

"Call it that. If Cooper bilked you back then, why not say so now? You're no longer working in criminal circles. Like you said, you're legit. You don't have to worry about payoffs to crooked cops. What good can they do you? Hell, you're not even in Cleveland proper."

"They could still cause me trouble. Some of them bastards are pretty vicious."

"You'll be protected. Besides, while they're on trial they're going to be trying to paint themselves lily-white. And after the trial, they'll be in jail."

"If they go to jail."

"With your help, that's where they'll go. And you know what a good time a crooked cop has when he goes to stir."

Brody smiled; the smile was like a cut.

"I'm part of a new regime," Ness reminded him. "Mayor Davis isn't in office anymore."

"You're the new broom," Brody said, wryly.

"Help me sweep clean."

"You interest me," he said. "Let me think a second. Let me go see if my customers are thirsty. Let me make a phone call."

Brody rose and went to the bar.

Wild said, "He's going to talk."

"Maybe. Depends on the call he makes."

"What call do you think he's making?"

"I think he's calling somebody connected."

"Connected? As in, the Mayfield Road mob?"

"Yeah."

"Why in hell?"

"To get permission to talk. To see if protection would be coming from their quarters, as well."

Wild began to nod. "If so," he said, "that would seem to indicate that the 'department within the department' has become a virtual rival mob, as you've theorized."

"Yes, it would," Ness said.

They sat and drank their beers. A few minutes later Brody came over with two more bottles of beer and a friendly expression.

He slid in across from them and said, "I'll play."

Ness and Wild exchanged glances.

"You understand I'm gathering background information for an investigation?" Ness asked. "Later I'll ask you to make a formal statement to Mr. Cullitan's office."

"Fine. No problem."

Ness smiled without pleasure. "It would seem I have allies in strange places."

"Mr. Ness," Brody said, "a man has got to get in bed with the damnedest people sometimes to make a go of it in this world."

"Agreed. Tell me about how you first got in bed with Captain Cooper."

Brody told his tale. He had run a speak at East Six-ty-fifth and Fleet in the early days of Prohibition, but had expanded into the wholesale distribution business, selling alcohol and bonded stuff in large quantities, fifty to a hundred gallons at a crack, to some fifty speaks. He lived in and worked out of the Sixth Precinct, which was where Cooper was stationed at the time as precinct captain.

"It started the day I did the bastard a favor," Brody said, referring to an afternoon in December 1924. "It was raining. I was in my car and I spotted him standing on a street corner. Gave him a lift to the precinct. On the way he said, 'Gee, I sure appreciate this.' I said, 'Think nothin' of it, Cap.' And he said, 'I could avoid putting you out like this if I had my own little car.' "

At first Brody thought Cooper was kidding, just making idle chatter; but

"Cap" repeated his desire for a "little car" several times, and finally Brody had told him, "I'll talk to the boys, and see what I can do."

Brody and several of his partners in the wholesale boot-leg business put together twenty-five hundred dollars for a new Hudson, which they delivered to Cooper, calling it, "A little present from the boys." A year later, Cooper nudged the boys into another little present—a new Auburn. The ashtrays in the Hudson were apparently full.

"It wasn't too long after that," Brody said, "that he hand-ed me a list of names and addresses. About fifteen speaks. He had me hit 'em up for fifty bucks each, a month."

"Did you get a cut?" Ness asked.

"No. It was just a favor I was expected to pay the Cap,

in return for not going to jail."

"Did anybody refuse to pay?"

"Sure."

"What happened to them?"

"They went to jail."

"How much a month did you collect for him?"

"Little over a grand. This was back in '26, '27."

"How much did you collect, total?"

"Twenty-five grand, easy."

"Why did you stop collecting for him?"

"He turned that over to some people working for him, and started hitting me up for dough."

"People working for him? Who?"

"Who do you think? Cops."

Ness paused for a moment. His mouth felt dry. He drank some beer and said, "You've been very helpful."

"Cooper's greedy. He wasn't satisfied with what he had coming to him. He wanted the other guy's share, too."

"I'll be satisfied," Ness said, "to see Cooper get what's coming to him. Do you think you know of others who might be willing to talk out against Cooper? Former associates of yours, perhaps?"

Brody suddenly got cautious again, eyes narrowing. "I can think of a couple ..."

"There's safety in numbers. If I can take a crowd of you former bootleggers to the grand jury, there will be less chance of reprisals from Cooper's cops."

Brody tapped his fingers on the table. "Let me go see if my customers are thirsty. Let me make another phone call."

He got up and went to the bar.

"What do you think?" Wild asked.

"I think Cooper's a corrupt son of a bitch, and I think we're going to nail him."

"So you think Brody's going to come back here and give us some names?"

"Yup," Ness said.

And in fifteen minutes, Brody did.

Ness and Wild drove directly to a modern two-story brick home in upper middle-class Cleveland Heights, overlooking Cleveland and Murray Hill. It was a gently rolling, somewhat wooded residential area, reeking nicely of money. Not wealth, exactly, but plenty of money.

Abe Greenburger had plenty of money. Unlike Joe Brody, he had stayed in the wholesale liquor business after Repeal. Ness had heard rumors that Greenburger had ties with the Mayfield Road mob, ties which may have explained why he'd prospered to such a degree. Like Brody, he chose to live in a suburb, beyond the reach of Captain Cooper's 'department-within-the-department.'

Greenburger, a small dark bald man, was dressed in an expensive suit. He had only an hour for Ness and Wild before a business meeting "downtown."

A handsome, serious-looking man of about fifty, he ushered them into a study dominated by dark wood and leather-bound books, pulling up a swivel chair from behind his desk for himself while his two guests sank into a soft brown leather couch.

"My experiences collecting money were much the same as my friend Joe Brody's," Greenburger said. "But I only did so for about a year, collecting perhaps nine thousand dollars. The captain fired me, in a sense. Because I used bad judgment."

"How's that?" Ness asked.

"I delivered a satchel of cash to his home. He was furious about the intrusion."

"Where was the usual drop?"

"In his office at the precinct house. On his desk. Did Joe tell you about the clambakes?"

"Why, no."

Greenburger smiled, his teeth very white in his tan face. "That was an extra gouge the captain devised. He would have his cops sell tickets to the things, above and beyond the regular payoff."

"Tickets to the clambakes, you mean?"

"Yes. They'd rent a hall or use some speakeasy, some-place with a big back yard for standing around steaming and eating the clams, and there'd be gambling, chuck-a-luck mostly, and liquor, cheap liquor, for sale. And two big empty beer barrels, into which the guests, bootleggers mostly, were to toss money."

"How much would that amount to?"

"I counted the proceeds on one occasion, when Captain Cooper was too drunk to do so himself. It came to slightly over three thousand dollars. Can I offer you gentlemen something to drink?"

The third interviewee of the afternoon did not offer Ness and Wild anything to drink. Lou Shapiro had been out of the beer business a long time. And his surroundings did not resemble those of his former associate Greenburger, nor those of Brody, for that matter.

Shapiro was the only one of the three former Cooper collectors still in Cooper territory—the Fourteenth Precinct, to be exact. He was unemployed, living in the basement of a transient workingman's rooming house, in an apartment, a "crib," that was a converted coal bin. The stark unpainted rough wooden walls, the bare mattress on a steel frame, the hooks on the wall that held his patched clothes, seemed bitter reminders to Shapiro of what had been denied him.

"They took it damn near fast as I could make it."

Shapiro had the same basic build as Greenburger. Unlike Greenburger, however, Shapiro had a full head of curly hair, the only possession of his that Greenburger might envy. A skinny unshaven rat of a man, he sat on a tattered, at-one-time overstuffed chair that he'd scavenged. His hands were in his coverall pockets. It was cold in the former coal bin.

"I paid the bum twenty-five grand over five years. I was running a little beer parlor that should've been a gold mine. To try and get on his good side, I gave him the names of some places and offered to collect for him."

"Did you?"

"Yeah, two hundred to two-fifty a month. This was in '27 and '28. Then the cops took over collections. And the monthly rate went up, even for me, who used to collect for him. As long as we paid off, they didn't raid us. But the first month you missed a payment, or said you didn't have the dough, you got hit. If you tried to operate without paying off, they'd frame you with a phony raid, if they couldn't catch you for real. Then they'd offer to fix the case, if you kicked in."

"Do you know anything about these so-called 'clambakes'?"

"Clambakes, picnics, benefits. Every few weeks some cops would come in and, in addition to the regular bite, would shove five of these tickets in your mitt at five bucks apiece. I went to one of these shindigs once, since I bought the tickets anyway, hoping to get something out of it. There were so many police there I was sure they must've imported 'em from Chicago or someplace. The party lasted all day and into the night. There was a lot of booze that the cops got free from us and then turned around and sold to us at fifty cents a shot. That was rubbing it in, don't you think? I didn't stay till the thing was over because the cops were getting drunker and drunker and fights began breaking out. I didn't like the looks of it and that's the last one I ever went to."

"But you kept buying tickets."

"Sure. Once I complained when they tried to peddle me tickets for a 'benefit' that took place the night before. A cop grabbed me by the throat and said, 'What the hell difference does it make? You never go to them, anyway!' I bought the tickets."

The scruffy little man raised a fist and shook it at a small basement window, railing against his lot in life.

"I worked my butt to the bone for years and look what I got to show for it! And that bastard Cooper's within spitting distance of me, raking it in."

"What do you mean?" Ness asked.

"Just down here on Ivanhoe Road—bookie joint, the dough just rollin' in. The Black Swan Club. That's his place."

"His place?"

"Sure. He owns it."

CHAPTER 23

The sun was in the sky. It was definitely in the sky, playing hard-to-get with some clouds that were white. Not gray. White. It was the first Saturday in March and, while not exactly balmy, it was not exactly cold, either.

Spring had not yet sprung, but it was clearly lurking, waiting to make its move.

Ness wasn't waiting. On Monday the city council would be voting on his safety department budget. He'd made a lot of headlines in his two months or so in office, but he'd made some enemies too, including a certain Councilman Fink. So the odds of his getting his budget passed, at this point, were even, at best. He aimed to improve those odds this fine Saturday afternoon.

He had asked Councilman Vehovic, Captain Savage, Sam Wild, and Detective Curry to meet him in his office at two P.M. City Hall was pretty well shut down by that time Saturday, the safety director's office included.

The secretaries, including Gwen, had gone home, as had Ness' assistant, Flynt. As the men arrived, Ness made introductions where necessary, and with no more explanation than, "It's a nice afternoon for a ride, boys," herded them downstairs and into the parking lot and into his Ford. It was a little crowded and, on this spring like day, a little warm for men still wearing their winter topcoats.

"Okay," Wild said from the back seat where he was squeezed in between Curry and Savage. "It's a nice afternoon for a ride. A swell afternoon for a ride. The question is, where are we riding to?"

"I'm very careful," Ness said, "about what I say to reporters."

"Come on—spill."

"We're taking in one of the hottest spots in town, gentlemen. The Black Swan. Fill them in, Councilman."

The round face under the straw hat beamed. "If I'd a known that was what we was up to, today, I'd a brung my baseball bat."

"That's one reason I didn't tell you," Ness smiled. "Would you mind filling them in?"

"Dee-lighted, Mister Director," he said, and did.

Wild, who knew all of this and more, said, "Is it all right if I add a little something to that, 'Mister Director'?"

"Go ahead."

Wild turned to Savage and said, "Captain Cooper owns the joint."

"Cooper!" Savage said.

Vehovic's smile was gone. "You can't mean it. I've known Captain Cooper for years. Cap's the original hail-fellow-well-met!"

"He's met a few too many people," Ness said, "too well. I've talked to twenty-some former bootleggers in the last week who paid him thousands upon thousands in protection money before Repeal."

"Cooper," Savage was saying, nodding. "It makes a lousy sort of sense. Nobody else on the department gets around like that guy does. Or has more buddies in blue."

"Because of his buddies," Ness said, "I've limited this raid to just the few of us. And I don't dare call backup from the local precinct."

"No, you don't," Curry said, his expression grave.

The others fell silent. They just rode. Nice day for it.

Before long they were turning off St. Clair onto Ivanhoe Road. Sun or no sun, there was still snow on the ground and the trees were gray and skeletal.

On the left hand side of the road was a factory and several warehouses. On the right were various small businesses, spaced well apart, and visible behind them, the back ends of working-men's boarding houses, from the next street over. Lou Shapiro's coal-bin crib was over there somewhere.

A weathered old two-story frame building, good-size but not massive, housed the Ivanhoe Cafe. The upper floor appeared to be residential, but the first floor was a restaurant, its windows decorated with frilly curtains. In front of the building were two gas pumps and painted on the left side of the building, in bold letters, ZIP GAS!, and below that, FILL'ER UP QUICK!

On the other side of the building, near the roof, was the word BLACK, in white letters on black, with a white arrow that angled down and turned black as it cut through the word SWAN, in black letters on white. The arrow pointed to a second, smaller building that had been added on. A wooden latticework fence with a gateless opening led into a big shed-like structure, which housed the Black Swan Club.

Ness pulled the sedan up to the gas pumps, got out, stretched, and yawned.

The gas-pump jockey was a kid in overalls and a cap with earmuff flaps, and Ness directed him to fill the tank.

"Okay if I use the restroom?" he asked.

The kid nodded and pointed toward the restaurant.

Ness ambled inside. It was a fairly nice little place, a big yellow room with one wall of booths, cloth-covered tables, and a counter with short-order service. A young couple was having a late lunch at a side booth, and a few workingmen were sitting at the counter having coffee. At a table by the front windows was a heavyset guy with cauliflower ears. He wore a plaid shirt and no steam came from the cup of coffee before him.

"Got the time?" Ness asked him.

The guy checked his watch, and Ness grabbed that wrist and flipped him onto the floor with a thump.

"What the hell!" the guy yelled.

Ness grinned down at him. "I guess I got a better eye for faces than you do. The last time I saw you, you were working lookout at Tommy Fink's. I guess there's always a job opening for a specialist, even in hard times."

Ness pointed a finger, gently, toward a pretty, plump middle-aged woman behind the counter. "If there's another buzzer back there, please don't press it. I hate arresting women."

The guy on the floor was scrambling to his feet, looking toward the door.

Ness kicked him in the ass and he bumped his head hard against the door and flopped on his belly. A moment later the door opened and hit the ex-pug on the head again, and Savage came in.

"Sorry," Savage said, more to Ness than the unconscious lookout.

Ness was yanking the buzzer out of the wall, ripping it out from along the lower window frame. "Head on back there," he told Savage. "Put Curry in back, in case there's a rear door. I don't think they've been warned, but you never know."

Savage nodded and went out.

Ness dragged the heavy, slumbering lookout over to a steam radiator and dug in his pocket for one of a half dozen pairs of handcuffs he'd brought for the occasion. He cuffed the guy to the radiator, turned to the handful of customers, and said, "Pardon the intrusion," and went outside.

Ness walked through the latticework entryway and joined Savage, Wild, and Vehovic near the door, which was shut and locked. The muffled sound of a loudspeaker came from behind it, filtering through its speakeasy slot, but Ness was not in the mood to give anybody the password.

He raised his foot and let fly. With a satisfying splintering crunch, the door flew open and out rushed the cranked-up sound of a horse race being called out, which was immediately interrupted by Ness' shout: "Police raid! Somebody shut that damn thing off."

Somebody did, and an abrupt silence filled the room.

More than fifty people were packed into the large, unadorned space. Many of them were seated in folding chairs arranged in irregular rows, where they'd been listening to the loudspeaker which hung on one wall, over a large racing' blackboard. Along the wall at left were the betting and payout windows, three of them, with three surprised male faces behind the wire mesh, and at right a bar, its heavyset bartender looking at the raiders as if they were an apparition.

Nothing about the layout was fancy—makeshift was the word. The floor was gritty cement, with torn betting slips scattered like confetti. Empty beer bottles decorated floor and tables randomly. Along the periphery were blackjack tables lit by low-hanging, conical-shaded lamps. The dealers still had their decks of cards in hand, as Ness swung into the room, gun in hand.

The group was largely male, workers from the neighborhood enjoying the mom-and-pop bookie joint. In their white shirts with sleeves rolled up, seated on wooden folding chairs, the group could've been gathered for a revival meeting. There were a few women, in their twenties. They looked scared, whereas most of the men just looked embarrassed.

Ness put the gun away and told the dumbfounded group not to worry. "No one but employees will be arrested," he assured them. "I'd like to ask you to relax, because we're going to be taking statements from all of you. We need to establish that you made, or saw bets made here this afternoon, that you played, or saw blackjack played here."

Savage was rounding up the three cashiers from behind the makeshift betting counter. He sat them down at one of the blackjack tables, just as a door at the left, connecting this building with the restaurant, flew open almost as if Ness had kicked it.

A bear of a man in a white shirt and tie but no coat lumbered in, red-faced and angry. He had sleepy sky-blue eyes and a cupid mouth and a double chin. His eyebrows were upside-down V's and his brown hair was rather long and combed slickly back.

He said to Savage, "What the hell is this?"

"Ask that fella over there," Savage said, smiling faintly, pointing to Ness.

The bearlike man swaggered over and placed himself in front of Ness, saying, "What the fuck's the idea?"

"I take it you're in charge. What's your name?"

The cupid mouth formed a little sneer. "Dick Cooper is my name, and you're goddamn right I'm in charge. My old man's head of the detectives in this burg. Just who the fuck do you think you are?"

"Eliot Ness."

The bear blanched. He swallowed, looking hard at Ness, squinting. "You look different in the papers."

"I guess you never saw me in color before."

The sleepy eyes tried to open wide. He stumbled back and bumped into a blackjack table. He fumbled for a chair, pulled it up, and sat heavily.

He looked at Ness oddly, like he was having trouble focusing his eyes.

"Don't you, uh ... go with my sister?"

"I used to," Ness said.

Dick Cooper thought about that, as he sat at the table leaning on his elbow, his hand covering his lower face like a mask. Ness went to the bar and used the phone. He called the Central Police Station and ordered up a paddy wagon and some patrolmen to help take the statements of the detained patrons.

"I'll question you myself," Ness said to Cooper, looming over the heavyset young man who sulked at a blackjack table.

"I want to make a telephone call."

"Go ahead," Ness said, and nodded back toward the bar.

"I want to make it in my room."

"Where's that?"

"There's apartments over the restaurant. One of them's mine."

"Are you denying you run this place? You said you were in charge."

The cupid lips smiled nervously. "I meant, I own the building. I don't know nothin' about this activity here."

"I see."

"I rent the place to a guy named Nick for sixty bucks a month."

"You've never been back here before?"

"Can I make that phone call?"

"In your room?"

"Yeah."

"Mind if I come along?"

"I guess not."

"Good," Ness said, and took Cooper by his fleshy arm and guided him across the room to the connecting door. Ness had, after all, made this raid without notification to the local precinct and without obtaining a search warrant. His excuse for doing neither of those things was that he was merely responding in person to Councilman Vehovic's charges that the Black Swan and other clubs were running wide open in the Fourteenth Precinct. Young Cooper's invitation to look at his apartment was nice to have, in lieu of a search warrant.

Cooper led him through a narrow hall to the stairway. Ness followed the man up. At the top, Cooper said, "You gonna search this whole building?"

"I expect," Ness said, who hadn't been planning any such thing.

Cooper gave Ness a blank, sleepy-eyed look and nodded once and turned to the right and knocked on a door.

"If it's your room," Ness said, getting suspicious, "why are you knocking?"

"I gotta check in with a friend of mine."

"Just use the phone in your room, okay?"

The door Cooper had knocked upon cracked open, however, and a slice of unshaven face peered out.

"What is it?" The voice that went with the unshaven bulldog face was a pleasant baritone, despite the irritation it conveyed. Something about the face tugged at Ness' memory . . .

"I don't think we can get together tonight," Cooper said. "Huh?"

The *suspect sketch,* Ness thought. This guy definitely resembled the cemetery scam-artist Wild's cartoonist had sketched, but some other bell was ringing, too . . .

"The Swan got raided and I'm gonna be tied up," Cooper was saying. "The cops are here havin' a look around."

"Okay," the guy said, and shut the door.

Cooper smiled at Ness and pointed to the door opposite. "Sorry. I'll just go use the phone, okay?"

Ness brushed the big man aside and knocked on the door. No answer.

He glared back at Cooper, who shrugged. He quickly pulled the fat young man to the railing of the stairs and handcuffed him there. Then he yanked his revolver from his shoulder harness and stood before the closed door, yelling: "Open up! Police!"

As if in response, a gunshot cracked the air.

Ness reflexively ducked to one side, but if a gun had been fired at the door, the shooter had missed: no bullet holes splintered the wood.

Then he remembered—Curry was still out back.

Maybe the shot was fired out a window at Curry.

Ness kicked the door open and dove inside. From the cold wood floor, he looked up and aimed his gun, but all he saw was an open window.

He got up and rushed over and leaned out. The man had jumped over to the roof of the addition to the building, and was now edging along the slant of the roof, belly down, .38 in his right hand, having made the leap, obviously, because the smaller Black Swan building might be easier to climb or jump down from.

Ness yelled out the window. "Curry! Are you all right?"

Curry's voice came from below. "I'm okay!"

Ness looked down. He could see Curry splayed against the side of the Black Swan, around the corner from where the guy was doing his rooftop tango.

And the guy with the bulldog face was looking back at Ness, and squinting.

"I don't believe it!" Joe Fusca said, almost shouting. "I

FOUR

MAY 26, 1936

CHAPTER 24

As the jurors filed in, Ness checked his watch. The five men and seven women had reached their decision in one hour and twenty-three minutes, one of the fastest verdicts Ness could remember in a major criminal trial in Cleveland.

He was glad it was over. He didn't much like sitting in courtrooms, despite the fact that his job often called for it. At the moment, a courtroom only served to remind him that his wife was in the process of divorcing him. But perhaps the outcome of today's proceedings would be more pleasing.

Captain Cooper sat quietly at the defense table with his attorneys. The big bald man in the rumpled brown suit looked massive. His attorneys had apparently instructed him not to slump. The trial had taken nine days, during which Cooper had sat erect, but stolidly, his face betraying' no emotion whatsoever except an occasional faint appreciative smile when his character witnesses—eleven police officers, a former police captain, and Councilman Fink—took the stand.

Cooper's counsel had depended on the cops' testimony holding more sway with the jury than Cullitan's nine bootleggers. But, it seemed to Ness, the detailed and convincing tales of the latter made the vaguer testimony of the former seem thin indeed. So did the defense attorneys' efforts to show that an "underworld plot" against an honest cop had brought Cooper here.

The Cap, as the bootleggers often referred to him, did not take the stand in his own defense.

The only confrontation Ness had had with Cooper was the same Saturday afternoon that the Black Swan had been raided. Ness had gone back to his office, called Cooper there, and informed him he was on suspension.

"Your badge and gun," Ness had said, seated at the conference table.

The big man had stood there and complied, slowly, his round face no longer jovial, the gun clunking on the table.

"I don't have to tell you what happened this afternoon," Ness said. "You've talked to your son by now no doubt."

Cooper said nothing. His face was blank, though his eyes seemed rheumy.

"This department," Ness said, "is just going to have to get along with one chief from now on. Yes, I know you're the so-called 'outside chief.' But before too very long, believe me, you'll be inside." He nodded to the door.

"That's all."

Cooper cleared his throat, then spoke, tentatively: "You're definitely filing charges?"

"That's right."

"Suppose I was willing to retire?"

"No."

Cooper smiled, but with a trace of scorn. "You can't give me the break you'd give anybody else, can you? You need the publicity I'll bring you. To get your budget passed, Monday."

"Yes."

Cooper's faintly sneering expression remained. "I see."

"But I'd bust you just as hard even if that weren't the case."

Cooper's face went blank. "I—I see."

The man turned slowly and trudged toward the door, where he paused and looked back at Ness and said, "Being a cop is a hard job, Mr. Ness. Maybe if you weren't so goddamn young, you'd know that. There's a lot of suicides in this trade. There's a lot of long hours and misery. There's also a lot of wrong people with too much money. I just wanted the right people to get some of it. I just wanted them to be able to take care of their families. I'm not ashamed. I just made sure I treated my boys right."

"What would you know about it?"

Cooper narrowed his eyes, confused. "Know about what?"

"Being a cop."

And Ness looked down at the paperwork before him—Cooper's suspension—and heard the door click shut.

As for Gwen, there'd been no confrontation at all. She hadn't shown up for work on Monday. On Tuesday Ness received a businesslike written request from her to be transferred elsewhere in City Hall. He saw no reason not to, and passed the request along to Personnel with his approval.

He had seen her in the City Hall halls, from time to time, but she had looked right through him, stonier than the marble under her feet. She looked thinner, but as pretty as ever, despite the glasses and pinned-back hair that marked her office style.

He'd gone back to the apartment, when Heller headed back for Chicago, because the boathouse was too full of her. For right now, anyway.

There had been minor cuts, but his budget for the police and fire departments had passed, even though it required a tax hike. Even Councilman Fink hadn't dared vote against it, what with the press Ness had gotten. And Fink had gotten the vote out in his district to help float the necessary bond issue.

In the weeks, months, since the Black Swan hit, Ness had again been away from his desk, working as his own chief investigator. He'd been down gloomy alleyways and in grimy basement apartments and in fancy suburban homes. He had personally interviewed sixty-six witnesses who said they'd paid money to policemen for protection.

No police witnesses had come forth yet. The city's corrupt cops, with the usual code of silence, were locked into shielding each other. But, their leader gone, their network smashed, all that remained for Ness was to root them out one by one. Which he had set about to do.

He had completed an eighty-six-page report, which he'd delivered two weeks ago to the county prosecutor's office. He figured Cullitan and his boys would have at least twenty cases to prosecute, among them two precinct captains (of the Fourteenth and Fifteenth), a deputy inspector, two lieutenants, and a sergeant. He expected these cases would flush out other bad cops, sending them scurrying into early retirement.

But he'd made one mistake. After he handed over the graft report to Cullitan, he took a week's vacation at a lodge in the woods on the lake, courtesy of one of his slush-fund angels. And during that week, he left his assistant, John Flynt, in charge.

Since Heller's phone taps hadn't come up with anything against Flynt, and since Flynt had been minding the store effectively while Ness was away conducting field investigations, the young safety director had thought he could get away with leaving the department in Flynt's hands. In that week, however, Flynt leapt like a hungry dog on the job's patronage opportunities and began appointing fire wardens left and right, with the apparent guidance of councilmen like Fink, and without seeking the approval of, or even informing, Chief Grainger.

What had really torn it, though, were Flynt's efforts in Cooper's favor. The acting safety director had immediately put through the paperwork on Cooper's retirement.

Ness, who'd been without a phone during his vacation, immediately put the brakes on the retirement upon his return, and called Flynt into his office.

Flynt stood like a man waiting for the firing squad to have at him, and proud of it.

Ness took aim. "What in the hell was the idea of putting Cooper's retirement through? You're well aware I turned him down."

"I believe you're wasting the taxpayers' money. I object to Cooper being brought to trial."

"On what grounds, for God's sake?"

"On the grounds that the evidence is such that he won't be convicted, and this office will be embarrassed."

"I see. You figure any jury is bound to take a cop's word over that of bootleggers."

"Yes, I do."

"Well, I tell you what, Mr. Flynt. I realize gambling in this city is more or less illegal, but as two gentlemen of the old school, what say we have a little wager?"

"A wager?"

"If Cooper is found guilty, you'll resign."

Flynt's smile under the twitchy little mustache was smug. "And if he's found innocent, you will resign?"

"No," Ness said, smiling blandly. "You just won't have to."

Flynt lifted an eyebrow. "And if I don't care to wager?"

"Then I'll fire you right now. I'd like to see you go to the Civil Service Commission for help, after all the shit you've given them."

Flynt swallowed dryly. "I accept the wager."

"We needn't shake on it. I promise that if the outcome of the trial is such that you must resign, I won't embarrass you in front of the press. You've contributed to the department's efficiency and morale. I'll say so publicly."

"Then why do you want my resignation?"

"We just don't think alike, Mr. Flynt. You're too damn political."

Flynt smiled. "And you're not? The next weekend you spend at some industrialist's lodge, or some quiet evening at Alexander Wynston's boathouse, why don't you ponder your *own* political debts?"

And John Flynt had left, in a fleeting moment of victory.

Fleeting, because now, as Ness sat in the courtroom of the Criminal Court Building, the foreman of the jury was pronouncing John S. Cooper guilty on seven counts of bribery.

The courtroom sat in stunned silence, briefly, then a murmuring moved like a tide across the gallery, until the judge had to bang his gavel to stem it.

Judge Day announced he would sentence Cooper on Saturday. Each of the counts of bribery carried a penitentiary term of one to ten years. Ness figured some of them would be served concurrently, however; he estimated this particular judge, an honest one, would hit Cooper with a good twenty years.

As the packed courtroom slowly emptied, Ness went forward to shake hands and trade smiles with Cullitan and his assistant McAndrew.

"That little tome you dropped on my desk," Cullitan said, referring to the graft report, "is going to keep me looking at the inside of this courtroom for a long, long time. Thanks for a fine piece of work, Eliot."

"Thanks for putting Cooper away. He has a little place in history, now—the first cop in Cleveland ever to be tried on bribery charges."

"Hardly the last," McAndrew said.

"That's right," Ness said. "I think, with your help, gentlemen, we're going to have a police department in Cleveland again."

He thanked the prosecutor, whose hand he shook a second time, and moved up the aisle, feeling good, smiling, but his smile froze as he saw the attractive woman in the simple blue dress with a white collar, her blonde hair brushing her shoulders. She had lingered, keeping her seat, and only now stood, moving out into the aisle to block his way.

"Thank you, Eliot," Gwen said, through her pretty teeth. "Thanks for nothing."

"Is that what we had? Nothing?"

"Nothing. We had nothing."

"I'd like to think we had something. I'd like to think you were more to me than just your father's daughter."

Her upper lip curled. Her dark blue eyes were hard and cold and wet.

"How would you like our little affair to go public? I don't think even your newspaper pals could resist gossip this juicy—the safety director's dalliance with the daughter of the convicted crooked cop. It has a sweet ring, doesn't it?"

"It's a little late for blackmail, isn't it?"

"It's never too late for revenge."

"Revenge isn't my style, Gwen. Only time will tell if it's yours."

He walked around her and away from her, on up the aisle, his smile gone. Sam Wild was waiting for him in the hall outside.

"I see the captain's daughter waited to have a word with

you," Wild said.

"If you'd wanted a juicy story, you could've hung around and eavesdropped."

They walked.

"Can you still see," Wild asked, "after having your eyes scratched out?"

"I don't blame her for being bitter."

"Don't give me that! After what she did to you—"

"What did she do to me?"

"Well. That's between you and her, I guess."

"Right."

Their footsteps echoed.

"Don't you figure her father put her up to getting next to you?"

"I don't honestly know."

"Don't you care, Eliot?"

"I care. But I don't know. And Gwen's one mystery I'm not about to investigate any further."

The sun was shining on the skyline of Cleveland this May afternoon in 1936, as Eliot Ness and Sam Wild walked to Mickey's, a hole-in-the-wall bar on Short Vincent Avenue. The safety director drank straight Scotch, and the reporter drank bourbon. By the time a wobbly Wild escorted a quite drunk director of public safety to a room in the Hollenden to sleep it off, darkness had once again fallen.

Acknowledgements:
A Tip of the Fedora

I could not have written this novel without the support arid advice of my friend George Hagenauer. George accompanied me on a research trip to Cleveland where we visited the sites of the action in this novel, from the Clifton Lagoon boathouse to the old Central Police Station (where we got an impromptu tour of the mostly out-of-use facility, from a friendly Cleveland cop). Also in Cleveland we conducted research at the Western Reserve Historical Society, where the Ness papers are kept, and at the City Hall municipal reference library and the Cleveland Public Library. We encountered friendly, helpful people at all of these well-run facilities.

As a child I was a faithful fan of the *Untouchables* TV show, and I suppose my interest in true crime stems from knowing that the classic Robert Stack television series had a basis in fact. However, with the exception of the early episodes (primarily the two-part pilot, "The Scarface Mob"), the series had little to do with the real adventures of Eliot Ness. In writing my historical novel *True Detective*

(1983), I included Ness as a character primarily because I had always wanted an excuse to dig in and find out the real scoop on the man.

I expected to be disappointed, because many—most—modern crime historians dismiss Ness; I had been led to believe Eliot Ness the gangbuster was largely a myth. Even as distinguished a figure as Hank Messick, whose *Silent Syndicate* (1967) is the only book-length study to date of the powerful Cleveland Syndicate, tends to shrug Ness off. I believe this tendency grows out of a sour-grapes attitude found among many of Ness' contemporaries in both the law enforcement and criminal communities.

They resented the attention their better-known peer received, and in

interviews with crime historians have unfairly and in-accurately debunked Ness. This post-TV backlash extends to John Kobler, who in his fine biography *Capone* (1971) downplays the role of Ness and his

"Untouchables." This term really did appear again and again in newspaper headlines (and not just in Chicago), primarily after the conviction of Capone. That news coverage singled out Ness, who was responsible for the only non-tax-related grand jury indictment against Capone, covering five thousand separate Volstead Act indictments.

Eliot Ness and the Untouchables were not, as revisionist historians would have you believe, an invention of the television age; Ness really did gain world-wide acclaim as "the man who got Capone." I have seen thousands of newspaper articles that prove it—in the personal (and very thick) scrapbooks of Ness himself.

The problem with dealing with Ness, post-Capone, in Cleveland, is not a lack of material. Particularly in his first several years as safety director, Ness was so active that his "adventures" defy the necessarily tidy shape of a novel. For that reason I have compressed time and used composite characters, on the one hand. On the other, I have largely ignored certain of his activities (sometimes mentioning them in passing), particularly labor racketeering' problems and the ongoing "Mad Butcher of Kingsbury Run"

torso slayings. Some of this material may find its way into a later book or books about Ness.

It should be noted that only a handful of the characters in this book are given their real names—Ness, of course, Mayor Harold Burton, Frank Cullitan and Chief George Matowitz are among these. Most of the others have been given names similar to their real ones, sometimes a variant spelling, off by a letter or two; this is my shorthand way of saying that I feel their use as characters, while based in fact, has wandered well into fiction.

Other characters are composites, such as "Mo Horvitz," who represents a number of Cleveland syndicate members; and the two cemetery-scam victims. Also, the Ness investigation into corrupt cops was lengthy and complex and, in order to cover it properly here, elements of the Michael Harwood, Louis J. Cadek and Ernest Molnar cases were combined into the Cooper case. Gwen Cooper Howell is a fictional character; however, a bitter courtroom confrontation did occur between Ness and Captain Louis J.

Cadek's daughter. Joe Fusca is a fictional character, based largely upon newspaper accounts of various cemetery-lot scam artists; his family history is based upon that of a real con-man clan. A few characters here are wholly fictional, although they too had real-life counterparts—Sam Wild, for example, represents the many reporter friends of Ness, particularly Ralph Kelly of the *Plain Dealer* and Clayton Fritchey of the *Press*. Fritchey, who did the work on the cemetery-lot racket attributed here to the fictional Wild, was assigned by his editor to cover Ness fulltime, and became a virtual investigator for the safety director. And Ness did make use of private detectives like Nathan Heller and the McGrath Agency ops.

Numerous books, magazine articles, and especially newspaper accounts of the day have been consulted in researching *The Dark City*. Several books deserve singling out. Hank Messick's previously mentioned *The Silent Syndicate* provided a helpful overview, as well as some specifics on the Harvard Club raid and other events.

Another basic tool, and the only previous book on Ness in Cleveland, is *Four Against the Mob* (1961) by Oscar Fraley, the co-author of *The Untouchables*; this is a rather compressed, somewhat fictionalized account (most names have been changed, dates altered, etc.) which deals not at all with Ness' personal life, but portrays well his achievements as public safety director.

Of help in getting a fix on police procedural matters was Eliot Ness' own 1938 reorganization plan for the Cleveland police department. Such obscure documents as this, as well as various pamphlets, maps, and tear sheets, were dug out by diligent Cleveland Public Library personnel, in particular Karen Martinez of the City Hall branch and Joe Novak of the main branch.

Three books by Cleveland journalists proved invaluable. *Cleveland: The Best Kept Secret* by George E. Condon (1967) has an excellent chapter on Ness, delving somewhat into the man himself; and it provided considerable local color. So did *Cleveland: Confused City on a Seesaw* by Philip W.

Porter (1976), which digs into the politics of the city and also has some insightful Ness material. Both Condon and Porter were *Plain Dealer* reporters. Peter Jeddick's

Cleveland: Where the East Coast Meets the Midwest (1980), a collection of *Cleveland Magazine* articles, includes a lengthy chapter which is the best biographical piece on Ness I have seen, an excel-lent, fact-filled character study which I drew heavily upon.

An unpublished article written for the Cleveland His-torical Society in 1983, "Eliot Ness: A Man of a Different Era" by Anthony J. Coyne and Nancy L. Hubbert, was also useful. A number of unpublished scholarly studies on ethnic groups in Cleveland were also of help. So was *The Ohio Guide* (1940), the Federal Writers' Project volume (in which Ness is mentioned rather prominently).

A major source of insight into Ness was an unpublished, twenty-two-page article on his Capone days written by Ness himself, and used by his ghost Fraley as background for the book *The Untouchables*. Ness wrote very well; meaning no disrespect to Mr. Fraley, I feel it is unfortunate that Ness did not write his book unassisted, as his own voice was distinct and flavorful.

A few other books deserve specific mention, including: *Cleveland: Prodigy of the Western Reserve* (1979), George C. Condon; *Crime in America* (1951), Estes Kefauver; *Cleveland, the Making of a City* (1959), William Ganson Rose; *The Years Were Good* (1956), Louis B. Seltzer; *The Encyclopedia of American Crime* (1982), Carl Sifakis; *Cleveland's Changing Skyline* (1984), Jim Toman and Dan Cook; *The Terminal Tower Complex* (1980), Jim Toman and Dan Cook; *Organized Crime in America* (1962), Gus Ty-ler; *U.S.A. Confidential* (1952), Jack Lait and Lee Mortimer.

A special tip of the hat to the Hastings family of Cleve-land, for impromptu tours, background info, and hospitality.

I would like to thank my editor, Coleen O'Shea, for giv-ing me the opportunity to write this book and, once written, suggesting ways to improve it; my agent Dominick Abel, about whom you read in this book's dedication (and whose idea it was to provide Ness with "a ticking clock"); and my wife, Barbara Collins, for her love, help, and support during this difficult project.

A Look At: Butcher's Dozen: An Eliot Ness Mystery

Award-winning author Max Allan Collins has skillfully woven fact and fiction to create a unique mystery series based on the life and exploits of one of America's most memorable heroes, Eliot Ness.

The former Untouchable teams up with a rookie cop, a headline-hungry reporter, and a beautiful woman in order to catch a crazed killer whose butchery has Cleveland in terror.

"The Eliot Ness series is a non-stop roller-coaster ride, not for the faint of heart. Jump on and enjoy."

About the Author

Max Allan Collins was named a Grand Master in 2017 by the Mystery Writers of America. He is a three-time winner of the Private Eye Writers of America "Shamus" award, receiving the PWA "Eye" for Life Achievement (2006) and their "Hammer" award for making a major contribution to the private eye genre with the Nathan Heller saga (2012).

His innovative Quarry novels were adapted as a 2016 TV series by Cinemax. His other suspense series include Eliot Ness, Krista Larson, Reeder and Rogers, and the "Disaster" novels. He has completed twelve "Mike Hammer" novels begun by the late Mickey Spillane; his audio novel, Mike Hammer: The Little Death with Stacy Keach, won a 2011 Audie.

For five years, he was sole licensing writer for TV's CSI: Crime Scene Investigation (and its spin-offs), writing best-selling novels, graphic novels, and video games. His tie-in books have appeared on the USA TODAY and New York Times bestseller lists, including Saving Private Ryan, Air Force One, and American Gangster.

Collins has written and directed four features and two documentaries, including the Lifetime movie "Mommy" (1996) and "Mike Hammer's Mickey Spillane" (1998); he scripted "The Expert," a 1995 HBO World Premiere and "The Last Lullaby" (2009) from his novel The Last Quarry. His Edgar-nominated play "Eliot Ness: An Untouchable Life" (2004) became a PBS special, and he has co-authored two non-fiction books on Ness, Scarface and the Untouchable (2018) and Eliot Ness and the Mad Butcher (2020).

Manufactured by Amazon.ca
Bolton, ON

36987276R00173